D1563206

EXPERIMENTAL ANIMALS

EXPERIMENTAL ANIMALS

ANIMALS

(A Reality Fiction)

THALIA FIELD

SOLID OBJECTS

NEW YORK

Many thanks to the estate of Rebecca Gershenson.

Design by Jennifer Heuer

Printed in the United States of America

Cloth
ISBN-10: 0-9862355-2-0
ISBN-13: 978-0-9862355-2-8

Paper
ISBN-10: 0-9862355-3-9
ISBN-13: 978-0-9862355-3-5

Library of Congress Control Number: 2016948123

SOLID OBJECTS
P.O. Box 296
New York, NY 10113

"1. Pose a human physiological case;

2. Put in its midst three forces;

3. Lead the characters by logic of their particular being to the denouement;

4. Logic and deduction."

—Émile Zola

§

"The growing good of the world is partly dependent on unhistoric acts; and that things are not so ill with you and me as they might have been is half owing to the number who lived faithfully a hidden life, and rest in unvisited tombs."

—George Eliot, *Middlemarch*

§

"Each of us is more a portrait of a collectivity than of himself."

—The Goncourts

CONTENTS

1.

MARRIAGE |CURARE

Paris, February 17, 1878:

"Claude Bernard is dead!
   How to express all that this name signifies? Genius incarnate of experimental medicine? Creator of general physiology and the experimental method? Author of discoveries that have delivered the secrets of life's mechanisms? Claude Bernard, in a word, is physiology personified; he is physiology itself."

—*Medical Tribune*

§

Did you hear him say that to understand a watch isn't to watch it but to break it?

Claude Bernard: "We give the name 'observer' to the man who applies methods of investigation to the study of phenomena which he does not vary and which he therefore gathers as nature offers them. We give the name of 'experimenter' to the man who applies methods of investigation so as to make natural phenomena vary, or so as to alter them with some purpose or other, and to make them present themselves in circumstances or conditions in which nature does not show them."

Slicing along the spine of an uncomprehending dog, Claude holds the writhing animal in place, announcing: "Thus we open our book!" A hundred faces balance toward the stage; toward the scientist engrossed in his lesson.

§

To know the husband's character, don't they say look at the *wife's* face? Hundreds of faces, come take your look—at this wife stuck in a torrid purgatory, gossips hungry for evidence of my every deed. Why? Because one person's deed is another's torment, and that goes for dogs too. "Shush, Fanny," the grimacers grumble, "why are you always so hot to tell doers from done-tos, or split deeds from each other?" Well, my husband Claude had his deeds, and I had mine, but it's only my eye into which history jabs its finger. A dog is not a book, and neither, by the way, is a wife: our pages sit blank—dogs' and wives'—our lives neither exactly forgotten, nor remembered. And don't tell me how lucky for the historians that my husband unrumpled a few of my old letters and lists during a cleaning. A face knows when it's been made up, and this wife stands smeared with a villainous countenance—and our daughters too. So tell me, who wouldn't parcel out confessions, given half a chance? Listen close. No flies get caught on a burning pot—and she goes safely to trial whose Father is a judge.

§

Anatole de Monzie, from *The Abusive Widows*, "The Case of Claude Bernard":

"On April 16, 1878, the city council of Villefranche-sur-Saône planned to erect a commemorative statue where Claude Bernard was born, until the mayor refused to celebrate someone who'd been a Senator under the Empire—and worse, had separated from his wife. So Claude Bernard was refused a statue.

Republican orthodoxy, like all orthodoxy, can't resist a chance to segregate the cemetery. Think of Claude's mother, dead of shame that her son had left her daughter-in-law—yet none could ignore, in the life of Claude Bernard, what his wife was—an honest woman, surely, but in the pejorative sense that Leon Bloy meant by it: 'the eternal *bourgeoise* who refuses hospitality to the baby Jesus and throws the mystic rose to the north wind.' Madame Claude Bernard never forgave her husband his poverty and lack of pretense, and she never admitted the glorious successes with which he repaid the dowry she cried over with every passing year. Also, Madame Claude Bernard, born Fanny Martin, raised and trained her two daughters against the scientist who was forced to hide his labors in a humid cave.

I repeat these details in the certainty that documents to support them will come to light. Until then, the oral tradition attests to my version, which Émile Zola had wanted to translate into fiction. Zola's mistake—his partisan error—was to represent the enemy-spouse as a bigot fighting the freedoms of modern science. Religion was not the issue for Madame Bernard, whose greed and stupidity provided the relevant disappointments. Science only inspired hostility from her inasmuch as it symbolized the target of her evil curses: her husband. No being was more continuously a victim of ferocious paranoia. This executioner-woman eventually had widow's rights, and she used them pretending to defend the legacy of the man she tortured."

Tortured? That's a mighty big word, given all the deeds and done-to's around here. Just goes to show how rumors do become true. Napoleon was rumored, for instance, to say: "History is nothing but a book of lies, written by the winners." He, of all people, knew that battlefields tell as many tales as the dead who litter them.

§

Consider a young and very alive Claude Bernard—a rudimentary protagonist—with humble origins in a stable behind the manor of the chevalier Lombard de Quincieux. Humble origins and miserable odds (i.e., lazy or unclever, Claude failed his 1831 baccalauréat), and then fortune: that his father weaseled him an apprenticeship at a Lyon pharmacy, where he would make potions for the veterinary school, and blend opium and spikenard, myrrh and wine, for the catch-all people's cure of *theriaque*. Throw in a dastardly foreshadow (his father borrows heavily to buy Claude out of military service), and that's the drunkard's match to get this situation going.

My dear Anna Kingsford, you and I also had humble origins and miserable odds, but as women we could only watch from the chorus. Power may excite fear, but only action, crusty old Aristotle warned, centers the drama. Action leads to suffering, and suffering to character. Characters then move together toward catastrophe, which may be the culmination, but it's in the *peripety* that the chaser becomes the chased—the object the agent, and the agent the object. At the beginning, you and I offstage barely knew the roles we'd play in the hero's story, though you could say "our fate was man" and it wouldn't be wrong. Didn't we avoid the twists of fate as long as possible: me tending my father, laying up treasures, and you with your guinea pig and talents? It's hard to believe the bounty of trouble we organized in such a brief time, despite the onslaught of deeds, doers, and done-to's deployed against us. It just goes to show that as sparks do fly upward, every person is born equally into an argument.

While working at the pharmacy, Claude Bernard stages an amateur vaudeville so popular it gains him an introduction to the Parisian literary critic, Saint-Marc Girardin. In the new July Monarchy, oil lamps are becoming gas, and the Funambules have the master Duburau as their Pierrot. Quitting his job to put the final flourish on his great tragedy, *Arthur de Bretagne*, Claude fancies a future in literary Paris: his five-acter on the boards, and he, a lamp of French culture. In the play, Richard the Lionheart's nephew, sole hope of France, falls for lovely Fanny des Roches, but is captured and tortured until a merciful guard helps him:

Arthur: *What more can I do?*

Guard: *Make a longer, more eternal plea; dare the light to leave you your life...Or I'll burn out your eyes with a hot iron!*

Arthur: *I'm shaking.*

Guard: *Without your soul's eyes, what good are your body's?*

Arthur: *Death! Give me death!*

Guard: *Renounce your pride.*

Arthur: *I ask only for death.*

Guard: *You are more cruel than your torturers, unnatural heart!*

Finally, the tormenter relents:

Guard: *What would my good little wife say to see me covered in such blood! And my sweet children, would they not be afraid of me...I'm going to hide you in the tower, I'll say you've died...*

Arthur: *God gives me hope, for he gives me a friend. Show me the way!*

Oh, stop! Theater is for fools. If you're going to sit in shadow and believe what you're told, why not go to Church? Alone in Paris, awaiting his rendezvous, Claude subsists in an attic room. A nub of flame is helpless to fight the cold. A few weeks later, Girardin breaks the bad news: "You may love the theater, but it will not love you."

"Try another career," the professor counsels, "You've been a pharmacist, be a doctor." *Fanny*, Arthur de Bretagne's made-up love, is also coincidentally what I'm called. But wait—each fire must be built correctly or it won't burn completely; the littlest branches are crucial, their order and how they support the larger pieces. The air must circulate, the atmosphere must breathe, the flue must be open. My dear Anna Kingsford, you will have your fire just as I have mine, just as Claude has his. "Why, Fanny, is yours so hot?" Well, bit players like us ladies sometimes steal the show, and when fire spreads, if there is abundant old and dry material, it will not stop, nor rest, but grow to devour everything that once caused or contained it. The last line of *Arthur de Bretagne*: "Justice is the best revenge."

§

Bunked in maid's quarters, scrounging the dining halls, tucked in to a reading room for a few moments of Balzac—as Girardin counseled, Claude-the-medical-student struggles to succeed. Yet how unbearable he finds the complaints of patients on their gurneys, slumped blind and stunned to the walls; how tedious the endless discussions of therapies and cures.

Luckily for him, one ambitious medical professor, Francois Magendie, long ago accused his colleagues of unscientific methods, cursing their hospitals as "superstitious ante-chambers to the true sanctum—the laboratory." A short walk from the Hotel Dieu, across the river to the windowless basements of the Latin Quarter, he led a gang of rebellious students: "I compare myself to a scavenger; with my hook in my hand and my pack on my back I go about the domain of science, picking up what I can find." A break between alley and gate slams sun on a stray dog feeding on a bone, distracted. In stairwells, cellars—wherever he could secure a spot—Magendie offered private courses in vivisection.

Claude fails the doctor's practical exam, and finishes last among his peers on the other tests. Professor Rayer quietly suggests that he try Magendie's experimental course, now set up outside the medical establishment at Collège de France. Stepping forward, live cat held against the table, Claude wins a glance of Magendie's praise for his dexterity and showmanship, the ability of his fingers to peel through wet and palpitating muscle, leaving tendon, nerve, and blood vessel intact. Unlike medicine, which relies on returning people to health, and unlike anatomy's lackadaisical sprawl, Magendie's *physiology* stakes a duel directly with death— the thrill of following a nerve or pulse as far as it will go in a gasping, surgically disassembled body. Scalpel, cautery, syringe, perforator, stylet, tenaculum—Magendie borrows his tools from the operating room, and keeps bodies breathing with crude bellows. Hospitals are useless, he scoffs, because medicine without vivisection is "like trying to tell what happens inside a house by watching what goes in by the door and out by the chimney."

§

I don't know about your England, but as a child in Paris, I hated the clanging carts and odd jobs of night, the array of groans mysteriously linking cannon fire and men. Noise penetrates the body, shaking it awake because ears haven't lids to close, though we can often choose deafness. My father said an excess of hearing is a medical disorder, a disease of the mind. He was a real doctor, providing relief so people could resume their lives. To maintain the flock, Church fathers insisted, "Fanny, no reading!" but I stole glances of every page that crossed my sight. I tried not to read the *sensational* novels: wives driven mad, poisoned and murdered, murderous themselves perhaps, revenging odious husbands. I tried not to read every book in my father's library, the bookstalls, the kiosks. At the end of the day, was there visible evidence on my face of what I'd read? Or was it as if my Paris gained a twin, and there I was, a young girl emerging from piety…

All these years later, in this vast cemetery, only the cats repay me with their languor and late-night love-fights. You of all people know what it's like to hear "fanatic" yelled at you, but I didn't write down the insults each time because writing wasn't my way. The cats scatter when feet crunch a leaf, but I am not who tourists seek in this famous graveyard; I bask only in *reflected celebrity.* Paris at night filled me with such dread, I myself eventually became as terrifying and bitter as smoke people pass through as quickly as they can.

§

Every afternoon in Magendie's demonstration theater, Claude carefully slices skin and muscles of the rabbits and dogs that must be introduced onstage without distracting from speaker or scene. Any mistake, any excess bleeding or shrieking, and Magendie kicks Claude to the street. Claude and a friend decide to start their own physiology laboratory on the rue St Jacques, but the lousy fees don't cover animals or rent, and Claude sulks back to the wooden stage at Collège de France. His thirty-second birthday passes, leaving only discouragement. His chemist friend, Pelouze, proposes a plan: he's mixed nostrums for a prosperous Dr Henri Martin on the right bank, and knows his daughter, who at my equally ripe age, would suggest a decent dowry. More specifically: marrying me would bring 60,000 francs, two-thirds of it in cash, the rest in yearly installments, and an income of 5,000 francs a year over nine years—all of which Claude would control, as is the custom and law since the Napoleonic Code of 1804 reduced women to the status of minors.

It's said Zeus gave his twins arrows: to Artemis soft and painless moonbeams that kill without suffering, and to Apollo striking rays as hard as the sun's. Apollo, aloof and remote, shoots arrows of plague into our cities. Arrows of love, on the other hand, were supposed to be shot by the minor character Cupid, mostly to set plots in motion, and were sometimes thought to be aimed at the liver, from some ancient notion of *foie*, faith, blood. So there's my brother at the Church Saint Gervais, serving as my witness for the hasty marriage. Witnesses for Claude: Pelouze, Magendie, and Magendie's wife—yes, the wife the old man lives off, so sour she barely looks at me, too aware, perhaps, of the farce unfolding. With my trousseau, a few of Claude's furnishings, his books, clothes, and my cash, we stuff every corner of our apartment at 5, rue Pont-de-Lodi, close to the medical school and away from my familiar Faubourg Saint Denis. In this neighborhood, tenements divide until rooms are shared by shifts of families, carts clatter through filth, and the foul slop of the Seine routinely floods. "Fanny, didn't you reach tenderly toward this husband, even once?" Cupid, as the bastard son of Venus and Mars, shoots arrows tipped sometimes with gold, sometimes with lead. The crowd stares expectantly at the wife's face.

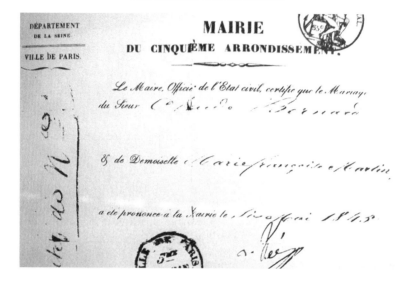

A tiny *bishon*, a wedding gift from my brother, affords Claude the chance to lecture us how a puppy's personality is retained until death; how a playful dog will wag at you until her last breath. What is pain for, he muses, if not to show who we are? An elevated heart-rate to speed blood to the muscles? Learning not to visit a painful thing twice? I stare, I'm sure, blank of face and understanding. Claude: "One always starts with observation. Then induces." On the kitchen table, Claude leaves his Red Notebook, in which he jots his laboratory notes and other musings. Maybe he thinks I'm going to be impressed? I certainly read a lot of things. It is later called by his disciples, his "philosophical thesaurus."

CLAUDE'S RED NOTEBOOK:

I have noticed that dogs in which I had exposed the lumbar spinal roots for recurrent sensitivity produced very large quantities of fetid gas. I later noticed, while performing the autopsy, that the cecum was distended by gas, and that the intestinal glands of Peyer were considerably hypertrophied.

Did this relate to the stimulation of the lumbar spinal nerves? Can it be that these glands have a role in the production of gases?

Try to put lead salts in the intestine and see if hydrogen sulfide develops in quantity.

Galvanize and stimulate the nerves to increase this formation of gas, and collect it on the outside if possible.

Instead of sleeping, my new husband spends his nights out of doors, procuring animals for his next day at work: a basket of rabbits, a glass receiver of frogs, two pigeons, an owl, a dog, several tortoises, two cats. I never considered, but all of a sudden I notice, how Paris adores and despises its animals. In every home at least one pet, and courtyards are lousy with cows and hens, shit on stairs and stones. Paris loves animals more than it hates shit-covered stairs, and women would rather walk their dogs than their children. Not to mention shit is good business—sold to tanners by stooped ladies fighting with spoons over the biggest droppings. Meanwhile, the fanciest dog market at Saint-Germain-des-Prés jacks up prices, and ladies strut up and down Pont Neuf with their fluffy prizes. Regulating this surge in pets, a new law requires dogs to be muzzled, and a tax is announced—from one to ten francs depending on the breed. Now people just toss their animals in the river. So the first pound opens, rue de Pontoise, in the shadow of Notre Dame. Dogs are stuffed behind bars, then hanged or struck on the head. "Well bred, good looking" dogs are stored eight days, then sold back to the stalls, while "mongrels, or those without collars or breed," live without food or water for three days, and are given to people like Claude who show up to take them. As with humans, "class is determined by breeding and partly by occupation."

Night after night Claude departs into the streets, returning covered in filth, reporting how the city crawls with animals like meat with flies.

Frustrated with Magendie, and this time flush with my money, Claude opens his own 'demonstration theater' in a cellar at 13, rue Sugar, where to the public, and to me impatiently when I inquire, he trumpets: "This is science as it will become!" Sometimes he 'starts' an animal at a friend's on rue Dauphine, and then leads the audience to rue Sugar to finish the lesson. To curious ladies and gentlemen, as well as to artists and other students, Claude performs these physiology experiments, even if they are only staged facts. One popular 'experiment' is on the fifth pair of nerves (the ones for the face) stimulated by mechanical and electrical means. Claude might say: "The scientific principle of vivisection is easy to grasp. It is always a question of separating or altering parts of the living machine, so as to study them and thus to decide how they function and for what." The audience in his basement sees live rabbits and dogs undergoing this puppet show. A second act might be to damage the brain of a pigeon or cat so it turns only around and around, no longer able to walk straight; more of a comedy, on days that need brightening. Claude laughingly calls himself "the physiologist in the theater."

CLAUDE'S RED NOTEBOOK:

Cut off the ear in newborn rabbits; extirpate it. Then have them reproduce and again extirpate the same ear in order to see if it can finally be caused to disappear (theory of multiple germs).

For writing up the results of their 'medical experiments', Magendie invents a three-paragraph form: hypothesis, action, conclusion. These paragraphs never mention failures or repetitions, and Claude borrows this shorthand, too, for in his scrawled notes one often forgets there's any animal involved: *The lung did such, the vagus nerve such.* "Why think," Magendie shouts from the stage, "when you can experiment? Exhaust experiment, and then think. When I experiment I have only eyes and ears; I have no brain." Claude also learns the primacy of the choice of experimental animal, which is, he later writes, even more important than tool technique: "The precision of the dog and not that of the instrument."

§

If Pelouze hoped this hasty marriage would provide Claude comfort, he forgets that if the devil can't catch you outright, he tricks you into joining him. Besotted with anti-clerical fulminations, no one around these slums seems to respect even basic virtues. In the stove, a chunk of wood deprived of air smokes in an outpouring as though grieving, until a breeze rushes reprieve and the proud log stands to ten times its height, clutching everything once beyond reach. One chooses of one's will to separate and turn from God. You might say this is the source of error: I was promised a good doctor from the medical school and Claude's course is anathema, his practice concerned neither with people nor with health. I knew Pelouze as my father's soft-spoken and gentle colleague, but soon came to doubt the trap he so charmingly laid.

Balzac, from *Physiology of Marriage*:
> "14. Physically, a man is a man for a longer time than a woman is a woman.
>
> 15. Morally, a man is more often a man, and for a longer time, than a woman is a woman.
>
> 16. Morals are the hypocrisy of a nation; and hypocrisy is an art that has been brought almost to a state of perfection.
>
> 26. Never begin marriage by rape.

27. Marriage is a science.

28. A man cannot marry before he has studied anatomy and has dissected at the least one woman.

53. A married woman is a slave who must be enthroned.

56. The moment during which a husband and wife may understand one another is as short as a flash of lightning, and it never returns.

60. The more one criticizes, the less one loves.

62. In marriage the bed is everything."

For while I try fussing and caring for the home (the coverlets, silver and dishes), puttering in the pantry and armoires, I can't help asking: what is care? Is it simply where you put your attention? Is it a feeling of fellowship, or can you care about unknown things? If I say I care about you, is it because I acknowledge that we share something in common? What is pain for, I also wonder: it speaks in a thousand inarticulate ways, yet seeks a conversation.

Our first baby boy, Louis, lives only three months, and I don't have to tell you that nothing can repair time's garments from the rending of a death—not pregnancy, birth, motherhood—these do nothing but patch over—and I should know because a year later, a healthier baby is born, our first daughter, Jeanne-Henriette (we call her Tony). Claude only returns later from work, with fresh clots of blood on his shoes, skipping dinner with nothing to say to my queries except to repeat what he tells everyone entering the laboratory: "Leave your imagination in the coat-room."

Fire starts so stubbornly, it frustrates all efforts and makes me red in the face, the logs still fresh, petulant, defiant. David said to Nathan, "I have

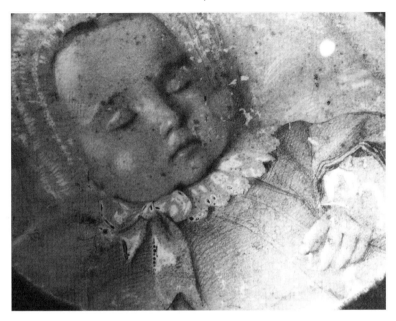

sinned against the Lord." And Nathan said to David, "The Lord also has put away your sin; you shall not die. Nevertheless, because by this deed you have utterly scorned the Lord, the child that is born to you shall die." I pace and worry as Paris fills with revolutionary dreamers, their fantasies ignited by imagined ancestral *sans-coulottes* raging from political 'banquets' to proclaim the Second Republic in a violent all-out class war. Where they're too tightly touching, no path for air is left between logs, and the thickest wood smokes aggressively without giving up. But as fire wears on, even the largest pieces collapse, glowing quietly under a cloak of ash, or wasting from the blackening crust that finally implodes at the slightest poke. Tonight General Cavaignac's army moves against the workers; thousands savagely killed and left to rot, tens of thousands arrested. The Goncourts: "Then Soulie told us that during the revolution, a man walking across the Pont des Arts saw a blind man's cur bite its blind man, whereas he rushed off to sell his government stock, saying, 'The end of the world has come!'" Sudden voting rights sweep peasants in to outnumber Parisian radicals, and Louis Bonaparte, nephew of Napoleon, and a longtime exile, wins the election for his great talent of being practically unknown. They're calling him 'president' of this new Republic.

Claude: "Animals fight for love and for shelter; men fight for everything."

Let's just say I think more about animals this past year than in all years combined: howls and barks echoing down the narrow streets, and the animals Claude lodges in the kitchen—bleeding or half-conscious—crawling with high-pitched yells into the corners, or lying in a tight ball licking their fur. The rest of Paris seems preoccupied—with revolutions, with international affairs—the French people taking it on themselves to flock and petition on behalf of the world, an agitation that at Church we are told mostly to ignore, though broadsides and pamphlets are shoved relentlessly. Victor Schoelcher, an outspoken French abolitionist, publishes *History of Slavery in the Last Two Years*. Gustave de Beaumont travels through America with Alexis de Tocqueville, and his novelization, *Marie, or Slavery in the United States*, circulates through France, just like the eleven editions of *Uncle Tom's Cabin*. Harriet Beecher Stowe: "It is a comfort to hope, as so many of the world's sorrows and wrongs have, from age to age, been lived down, that a time will come when sketches similar to these shall be valuable only as memorials of what has long ceased to be." To support her novel's basis in truth, Stowe publishes a companion "Key" of first-person accounts of slavery, and other documentation. *A Key to Uncle Tom's Cabin* is equally a best-seller, spinning off plays, comics, and endless commentary, including Flaubert's, who officially declares it all trite and sentimental.

Next it's John Brown's name hovering over every dinner table in Paris; his conversion to the anti-slavery crusade, and how the "sobbing of the slaves in his ear" became too much to bear, so that with his sons he seeded rebellions, until caught and jailed and judged to hang. "I pity the poor in bondage that have none to help them;" he writes from jail, "that is why I am here; not to gratify any personal animosity, revenge, or vindictive spirit. It is my sympathy with the oppressed and the wronged that are as good as you, and as precious in the sight of God."

Victor Hugo to the Editor of the *London News*:

"...When we reflect on what Brown, the liberator, the champion of Christ, has striven to effect, and when we remember that he is about to die, slaughtered by the American Republic, that crime assumes an importance co-extensive with that of the nation which commits it—and when we say to ourselves that this nation is one of the glories of the human race; that, like France, like England, like Germany, she is one of the great agents of civilization; that she sometimes even leaves Europe in the rear by the sublime audacity of some of her progressive movements; that she is the Queen of an entire world, and that her brow is irradiated with a glorious halo of freedom, we declare our conviction that John Brown will not die; for we recoil horror-struck from the idea of so great a crime committed by so great a people..."

JOHN BROWN.

§

Seeing so many dead bodies, it takes effort to believe one is not dying. Shaking can be caused by illness or merely exhaustion, but the signs of cholera are unmistakable: bruises and stiffened limbs, the horrible diarrhea. There is an unbridgeable chasm between the healthy and the sick, seen in the guilty way the healthy enjoy a day's simple efforts, the freedom of merely persisting. Meanwhile, it seems only symbols truly speak right now: white flag, monarchists; tricolor, republicans; black flag, anarchists; red flag, the international workers' movement. Claude tells me, "Morals do not forbid making experiments on one's neighbors or on one's self." As if to an unclever child, he explains that physiologists travel through live bodies because pain is physiology's helpful guide. But not to worry (he shakes his head at my stunned expression), he warns his students against demonstrating on a monkey or ape: "…his hands, his gestures, his painful looks, always cause a certain hesitancy to torture it." But I know that when the animals make anguished noises, the experimenters hold them harder, and that Magendie outright laughs in order to reassure the audience that pain is normal. Later in bed, I'm afraid to move as the last bells ring, and the horrific agonies of a dog just outside the door—Claude's brought home an animal in worse shape than usual—I fear what I'll find if I go. I can't bear it a moment more, but nor can I move. I just want the animal to die and be gone—but the howls reverberate until some neighbors call, Police!—Police!

CLAUDE'S RED NOTEBOOK:

To decide the question of whether the pneumogastric produces movements in the larynx, it is absolutely necessary to have exposure. It is necessary to remove the cerebellum, avoiding the sinus, then, the larynx being exposed by the ordinary procedure, it is necessary to cut the vagi, and respiration will be seen to stop immediately. On cutting the spinal accessories the voice will be seen to stop while breathing nevertheless continues.

Claude proudly reports he's discovered the trick of cutting dogs' vocal cords at the beginning, saving himself a lot of trouble. Albert Leffingwell later confirms: "Bernard was the first to succeed in following the spinal accessory nerve back to the jugular foramen, seizing it with forceps and drawing it out by the roots." If the aim is silence, or to make the world shut up around him, I have no doubt Claude would build his laboratory behind ten-foot walls, never to be disturbed again. When he's out at night, I squint at his black or blue handwriting. The words practically dare me to read on, even as I wish I couldn't read them. Baudelaire, "The imagination is the most scientific of the faculties."

Into our home: more filth, more arguments, more mutilated animals, and a new little baby, Marie-Louise-Alphonsine, we call her Marie-Claude. *I will repay, saith the Lord.* Who was it said that every great tragedy takes place in 24 hours—and in one room, if possible? Claude: "Our existence doesn't take place in air any more than a fish lives in water or a worm in the sand. The atmosphere, the water, the earth are certainly environments where animals move, but the cosmic environment doesn't contact or immediately affect the elements of our daily lives. The truth is that we live in our blood, in our internal environment." Thus the *milieu intérieur*, which Claude boasts he's 'discovered.'

§

By the third year of his term, facing an unsure election, Louis-Napoleon proclaims he'd prefer to be called 'president' forever, if it's all the same to everyone. Well actually, forget the Republic, call him *Emperor* Napoleon III, and violently silence his critics. "The Empire is Peace," he decrees. A *coup d'état* moves from within—a disease rather than a blow—a small matter like a killing illness spreading rot to those members of its body least likely to resist. Victor Hugo, who already thought little of Louis-Napoleon as president ("that man lies as other men breathe"), is one of the first to be exiled, for calling the new Emperor a traitor.

By now I have more than sufficient proof of what's going on thanks to my dowry: a husband arriving home, frogs and rabbits in his pockets from the quai de la Megisserie, not to amuse little Tony, but to pin to boards and flay alive. "O but Fanny, isn't money by definition always someone else's money?" Well, isn't that just like Proudhon's people, to turn an idea around until it disappears. Claude's Red Notebook: "There are two factors in intelligence: an observer and an active agent, and an excretory agent of some sort. Example: the formation of ideas that develop spontaneously (dreams). One is a spectator." I return time and again to this notebook for help in accessing the man, but am left with half-cooked nonsense:

CLAUDE'S RED NOTEBOOK:

I am not a materialist.
I am not a vitalist, either.
The vitalists affirm, materialists affirm the opposite.
Myself, I say, I affirm nothing. I know nothing.

§

It seems Pelouze handed Claude not just a wife, but also poison-tipped arrows from South America. *Oorali, wurari, curare* comes from lianas trees, the bark boiled to a tar. Claude collects the jars, and explorers' stories—beginning with Sir Walter Raleigh—and the arrows of hardwood tipped with reeds and fastened with waxed cotton. Into a hole, a poisoned piece of wood is placed.

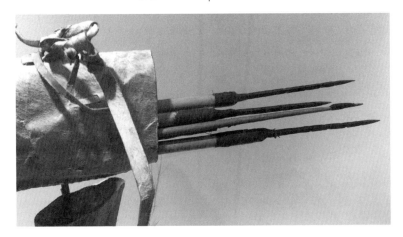

CLAUDE'S RED NOTEBOOK:

When the brain of a frog is removed, it becomes much more difficult to poison with curare. Why?

After hundreds of experiments in which animals become paralyzed and yet continue to live, Claude realizes that this poison acts neither on the brain, nor the motor nerves, but on their connection. "With curare, no agony, life seems extinguished, but"—Claude pretends astonishment—"this is not to be! Appearances deceive! This death, which seems so free of pain, is actually accompanied by sufferings more atrocious than the imagination can invent. The victim is not deprived of sensation or intelligence, but only of the means of expressing these through movement."

Maybe these apple-like fruits were what poisoned the insubordinate Eve, her jaw slackening without a scream. "Curare offers the chance to enter this living machine, this theater of detrimental actions that we will define for you, and explain." The heart still beating; the blood still turns red in the air. Of course the animal feels every poke and jolt without a way to cry. Claude: "What morality says we can't do to those like us, science authorizes us to do to the animals."

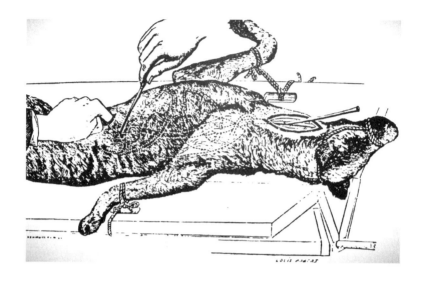

As too often happens at night in my room, dread freezes my body, then the bed, apartment, the streets as I picture them, the wider city, the countryside, the heavens—everything is stranded and still—until a raspy whine pulls me to a rabbit in a box in the kitchen. She is cut practically in half, and relaxes into death when touched on the head. *What kind of greeting is this?* I think, holding her paw.

CLAUDE'S RED NOTEBOOK:

Rabbits lose their sugar when they are varnished. Would it be the same if their spinal cords were cut at the same time?

I sense if you stare long enough into darkness, you begin to see shapes. The next night, as my eyes squeeze shut against the wailing from a nearby basement, I lift myself to the window. If I bear these tests willingly, and move toward the pitiable howls, *then be it done unto me, according to thy word.* If I resist this, or act unwillingly, my load will only expand, and if I put it down and refuse, for sure only worse things may come.

CLAUDE'S RED NOTEBOOK:

Feeling, from which everything emanates, must keep its complete spontaneity and all its freedom for putting forth experimental ideas. Just as in other human actions, feeling releases an act by putting forth the idea which gives a motive to action, so in the experimental method feeling takes the initiative through the idea. Feeling alone guides the mind and constitutes the "primum movens" of science.

§

Spring, and our tiny darling boy, Claude-Henri, is born. The Napoleonic cult of the heir makes a son a prize, given to a woman's care as the capital of the family's estate. But just nine months later, he starts to weaken with fevers and stops keeping food down—gray and shrunken, barely able to cry. I call for the priest to do a rough baptism, with ablutions but little ceremony. The baby has the cutest smile, but he's crawling less than he should. I spend many hours rocking him. *Open thy mouth for the dumb… be merciful as your father is merciful…*So what's Claude doing? He tells a long tale of how he gave some milk soup to a dog and killed it while it was digesting, the blood coming from the liver sugary. The liver didn't destroy sugar? He feeds dogs nonsugared food and kills them and looks at their liver; the blood still has sugar. He does this a thousand ways, and always the blood has sugar from the liver. But a hundred more tries and he sees that animals fed sugar have sugar everywhere, and animals just fed meat only have sugar in the vein leaving the liver.

When I sneak past his cellar to catch a glimpse of the man, I find only the
stained wooden trough, bloody water, nothing to clean the rancid floors.
Claude: "What do you want? Labs are the tombs of scientists."

Claude often amuses his audience with this fable:

> "One of my dogs with a fistula in its side disappeared from
> my lab. Not an hour later the bell rang, and the police com-
> missioner wished to speak to me—his wife and daughter were
> lavishing attention on it—'Do you know this poor animal?'
>
> 'Certainly,' I replied, 'and I also recognize my silver cannula
> which I am happy to get back.' The dog recognized me too,
> and greeted me in a friendly way. Then the commissioner gave
> a stern lecture in which he said I had placed myself in a serious
> situation by taking his dog, and his wife and daughter burst into

grief-stricken reproaches over my cruelty. I hastened to cut short this scene with a firm denial of the accusations made against me...

I first assured the commissioner that I did not pick up dogs, that the animals I used in my experiments were supplied to me by people whom the police employed to collect strays. I reminded him (for it was July) that the walls of the quarter were covered with posters to the effect that no dog was allowed out unless muzzled or on a leash, and that his dog had probably not been so equipped when it was taken...

At the end of the week the wound was completely healed, and no trace of the operation remained. From that time I enjoyed the protection of the commissioner and the approval of his wife and daughter. More than once the commissioner was of use to me in getting at the truth of the complaints which were frequently made against me, and I stayed on in the quarter behind the Medical School because I knew that no hostile move would be made against me without warning."

§

There are wars people say they don't want, though while they are still coming, who prevents them? Victor Hugo saw beaten and exhausted horses, and penned common scenes of suffering and compassion:

"The donkey who, going home overloaded and weary,
Dying, feels his poor flat hooves bleeding,
Takes an extra step, strays and puts himself out
So as not to crush a toad in the mud,
This abject donkey, soiled and bruised by the stick
Holier than Socrates and greater than Plato..."

But it's Baudelaire's Paris lamenting its cacophony, beside itself as one whose forms cannot match its dreams—the basis of nausea being the separation of what is felt and what is seen, a qualm, or the feeling of motion when one is still. Horses, whipped in the streets to pull harder, emit ungodly grunts, 'tools' screaming as cart wheels split on the pavers; wood-cracking clatter; intolerable *quartier*. Buildings heave to the ground, parted off. Families share walls, fountains, every small patch of stone to put laundry on, or a tomato. The ground hangs open wide, and detours overland, to lost destinations sunk in muck. Baudelaire: "The cannon roars, limbs are flying...the groans of victims and the shrieks of those who conduct the sacrifice can be heard...it is Humanity, in search of happiness." Sidestepping the spray of an enormous coach, we're supposed to exalt new public transports despite what everyone plainly sees: the carriages are a horse's hell, overcharged with people and bags tossed on—followed by whips and screams. Victor Hugo:

> "And the cart-driver is now a storm of blows
> Striking this convict who drags on under halter
> Who suffers and knows neither rest nor Sunday.
> Should the rope break, he will strike with the handle,
> Should the whip break, he will kick with his foot..."

A doctor, Dumont de Monteux, reports an old mare savaged by its driver to the Prefect, who has no choice but to ban the use of the handle of the whip. Dr Monteux convenes a meeting at 4, rue de la cité Trevise, where Dr Etienne Pariset is elected the first president of the *French Animal Protection Society*, modeled on its English counterpart. Claude: "In order to understand how men and animals live, one has to see a large number of them dying."

§

No sooner has the last revolution washed from the cobblestones then
cholera resurfaces in the rain and open sewers, and a new crusade ensues,
this time against rats. Glove-makers pay 20 cents a head, and into this
mess Claude invites his mother for a visit. They take the girls to sit for a
portrait in a studio using photo paper, the latest technique:

Claude proudly walks his peasant *maman* through the Tuileries, showing off the marionettes and carousels, all the tainted Paris, where thanks
to his old mentor, Professor Rayer, he's just won the Physiology Prize
from the Academy of Sciences for his discovery of the role of the liver
in producing sugar. He scrawls in his notebook, "I am the leader of the
current physiology movement." But to my astonishment, a critic, Mr
Figuier, publicly faults Claude's findings—based on his own work with

dead animals from the stockyards that shows a stomach substance, albumine, which masks sugar, which is why Claude only finds it in the vein coming from the liver. Figuier asserts there is no sugar except from food. To settle the matter a commission is appointed, and they ask for more proof from Claude, who sets about killing monkeys, cats, moles, porcupines, bats, and birds. He kills geese, hibernating bears, fish, mollusks, clams and muscles, lobsters, and crabs. He looks for sugar in insects and butterflies, chickens and chicks in the eggs, sheep and the lambs in the wombs. Claude's Red Notebook, "You need not hesitate to say aloud that my adversary is wrong and that he is an imbecile." The commission confirms Claude's theory, summarizing that "Mr Figuier hasn't put all the force of battling such adversaries into his work. He should recall that, since Magendie, Claude Bernard is the premier living physiologist, and he deserves to be always discussed seriously. Even when he is wrong, and we don't believe that to be the case in this instance, we can say that his talent, his wisdom, his marvelous facility with experimentation and induction, leads him almost always to be right."

Needless to say, Claude's mother's visit does nothing to bring us, the Mrs Bernards, closer. Mrs Bernard finds me too sophisticated, I'm sure. This is the difference between Paris and the country, yet Claude dotes on this bumpkin in every way at my expense. Humiliation may be a dish served cold, but I refuse them both the pleasure of seeing me eat it.

"My mother-in-law,

Your behavior toward your son's wife hasn't been that of a mother-in-law; I should write your priest about the way you've acted toward me! Your son is a spoiled brute from whom you demand things that don't belong to him…You've driven him to behave toward me in a reprehensible manner. If I didn't have children,

I would make him return my dowry that has served mostly to pay your creditors. You want a scandal, you'll get a scandal...I'm going to consult with people about my rights. Your son had only debts when I married him, and it was I who paid them all. Everyone knows your son had nothing and that he still has nothing.

—Fanny Bernard"

Between the philosophers, the scientists, the government, and the students, there's no one left in this city to care about a soul. My father once promised that the restoration of the throne would bring the restoration of church as state, but I feel more isolated in my devotions than ever. Proudhon: "Everything is in one conspiracy against the priest, even Mr Foucault's pendulum. Unless conservatism succeeds in rehabilitating society from bottom to top, in its body, its soul, its ideas, its tendencies, Christianity has not twenty-five years to live. Perhaps in half a century the priest will be chased out of his profession as a swindler."

Claude's friend, the chemist Marcellin Berthelot, writes in *Revue des Deux Mondes*:
"Positive science doesn't pursue first causes or ends and goals, but only establishes facts and their immediate relations—following a series of 'whys' based on the simplest givens...To run society based on the foundations of positive science is the goal...People will be convinced by the Public Real, the only certitude that is not a dream—as reality becomes more and more manifest, there will be fewer moral dreams and more enduring worldwide public facts."

§

After Claude goes out one warm November night, I dare follow in my nightgown, and catch him stalking a pile of palettes near the corner, massed of gray but in the progress of ruin. I fumble, fall out of the doorway while trying to get a good look, and a pair of dogs disappear with a graceful leap. Claude curses me for being outside. Any normal doctor's wife would be outlining the next day's meals, listening to children read while embroidering, getting the servants for evening prayers, welcoming seamstresses, making lists of accounts, and hosting lavish entertainments. Some seasons have laundry, others canning and making liquor. Remove candlewax from tablecloths, freshen a chamber pot with angelica, shine the silver, change chair covers and drapery with the seasons. A normal doctor's wife would have four or five dresses, updated regularly. Account books exact, kept in columns, tallied weekly. Numerous servants supply the impression of a lady at ease. Inside the house, the wife doesn't think of the world outside—the politics, science, none of it. Disagreeable news makes a proper wife faint or swoon or stumble to a couch. She's fixated on her family, the home. Winters she should gather socially. Mass daily, often twice; confession, offerings, daughters to school with the *sœurs*, where they learn penmanship, social deportment, arithmetic, but not novels because, well, too much *individualism* there. I remember the rule of thumb: self-expression limited to five minutes per day. "In other words, Fanny, a good wife wouldn't look at her husband the way you do, or inquire about his doings. A good wife hears without listening, or listens without hearing, anyway, she is as deaf as anyone who wants to sleep."

CLAUDE'S RED NOTEBOOK:

Sew the two ears of a rabbit together, then having fused them, cut one below in order to watch the reestablishment of sensibility, and see if the action of the sympathetic might then pass from one ear to another.

"Fanny!" they hiss, "Never think of yourself, except to renounce the thought!" But all my money goes out with Claude and doesn't return, while the wife of the poor scientist is asked to live in a perpetual spiritual connection to his sacrifices. The chiffoniers are the bitter reminders of my respectability, their ransom my costumes and housewares. I can't help it—I was told to reject my story, so now his story is all I can think about. Everything he talks about is livers and kidneys, blood and nerves, and there is no pew at the church in my name, so I think about nerves and livers. This marriage is hardly between people, but between me and his *big idea*. A fashionable martyr minces her barbed crown hand to hand, while studying the pains in John Foxe's *Book of Martyrs*. Here's Saint Peter on his anonymous cross. Saint Lawrence toasted on a spit. Adalbert chained to a post and poisoned with arrows. Waldenses plowed off a cliff. And cursed Saint Stephen, his streets of blood. People laugh, but even the most self-denying martyr stands straight in the crowd's derision—rejecting comfort and calm for the fray. I look Claude straight in the eye and then slowly return to our apartment. Yet for this mouthful of fire, martyrs soak their words in humble brine. From here, though, I scan the embers as they strive toward flame, and resist the snickering—for all of us locked in this situation forever, slack as marionettes dropped in a box. "Kids should not be cooked in their mother's milk." Yes, but, "Do not yoke together the ox and the ass"—right?

Would it have been so hard to give me my own tomb? I finally got that personality I was warned against, and it doomed me just like they said.

§

When I confront him, Claude says that pain exists only in conscious creatures—lacking thought, there is no suffering. Animals, Negresses, Jewesses, are all said to have less of it. One thing I know, even in sleep, distress and pain bring lost parts back, demanding to be experienced as a *part*, rather than the 'it' of 'get it out of me'! Claude's Red Notebook: "To gain an idea of the functions that are called organic, one can say that these are those which persist when the individual sleeps. Those that have ceased are the functions relating to the outside." But every scream makes night impossible: barricades quoting barricades, a mess of gestures; turn over a carriage, add some stones, roll up a cannon and stand ready. Is that a man or an animal? Corpses make effective props. In the Tuileries, they shout, "The anger of the people is the lesson of Kings!"

In the bookstalls, amid the mayhem, literary 'physiologies' are advertised to describe 'things as they are,' meaning: 'very ugly, without softening or embellishing.' It's popular now to follow Feydeau and call stories 'stud-ies,' with their fleshly passions and violent subjects, dragging all that once was hidden off-stage, the *ob*scene, now front and center. "The ideal is lacking in the naturalist," says Hippolyte Taine—who studied at the Medical School and is fast becoming the Great Philosopher of the realist movement—"he is as eager to dissect a doorkeeper as a minister of state." Monseigneur says that a wretched fate can be unmade by gaining a wider view, a longer perspective, an infinity in a moment which conquers trag-edy through God's eyes. But the moment one is in pain, the soul cleaves to its mortal body and nothing else, and the mind struggles, unable to free itself to look even a few feet around. Up and still awake, it doesn't take me long to stand at the window and track where Claude goes. About Balzac, Taine writes: "With such a litter of tools and variety of repulsive prepara-tions that when he emerges from his cellar and comes back to the light, he retains the smell of the laboratory in which he has been buried. He is armed with brutality and calculation; his roughness frees him from fear of shocking people. In this capacity he copies the real, he likes the monstrous on a large scale; he depicts baseness and force better than other things."

I can't tell if it's for the sake of the animals, or for the reputation of Paris, but after so many complaints, the city announces the Grammont Law against abuse of domestic animals—though it doesn't address vivisection, and pertains only to abuses witnessed in the streets. "The Grammont Law is formal in this regard and declares that only cruelty committed publicly is punishable. This means that when the offense is committed in a private residence or its outbuildings, even if multiple people are present, this event, however reprehensible it may seem…is not legally punishable." With a member card to the Animal Protection Society (subscription at 10FF/year) someone can call the police if they see an infraction in a public place. Covered under the law:

—overworking or overloading an animal

—withholding food, air, light, or movement

—brutal methods for getting a fallen animal to its feet, without taking the simple measure of unburdening it from its charge

—any action to get from the animal efforts that are clearly beyond its strength

—heaping up or hanging any animal (calves, sheep, chickens and others intended for market) either in the carriages or in the slaughterhouses, or markets

—all games that could cause mutilation or death to an animal

Which animals does the law protect? "All animals born, living, growing, nourished, or reproducing under man's roof and in his care… horses,
donkeys, mules, cattle, sheep, goats, pigs, dogs, cats, rabbits, pigeons,
chickens…" How will the accused be punished? "Will be punished by
a fine of five to fifteen francs, and up to five days in prison… Prison will
always apply to recidivists."

Tonight the open window reveals a city alive with noise, as sound by
sound I catalogue hundreds of actions in progress. Claude goes out to
make his quota. I don't know what mechanism or force upends my paralysis, but I rise and dress, stomp down behind my husband, and there in
the courtyard I meet his eye, just as his boys are handing a pile of puppies
back and forth. Ensues between us a new species of ferocious moment. I
am unbound like a fury, all hands grabbing and kicking at knees: I refuse
to allow even one puppy out of my arms, though they're struggling and
upside-down. I'm screaming bloody murder until Claude nods to one man
and they depart into the night. I take the pups upstairs and pack them
safely. I go to the church parish where I know the woman who cleans, and
I hand them to her, with a promise to help find them homes the next day.

Denis Diderot: "Woman carries within her an organ subject to terrible
spasms; it dominates her, and arouses fierce phantasms of all kinds in
her imagination…Nothing is nearer to her than ecstasy, vision, prophecy,
revelations, fiery poetry, and hystericism…It was a woman who walked
out into the streets of Alexandria with bare feet, her hair unkempt, a
torch in one hand and an ewer in the other, proclaiming 'I want to burn
the heavens with a torch, and extinguish hell with this water, so that man
may love God for his sake alone!'"

§

Morning, exhausted, I pick through life's messy top layer—up close, a view is rough; outside, workers yell for beams falling, stone hoisted; the complete collapse of plaster. I try to clean the dust and soot from the house-surfaces, organize the pantry. Our little bishon follows me from room to room, and the girls follow him. Noise can't quiet itself; it must stand higher and higher on its own shoulders. I'm so tired I can't start a new fire. The wood is cold, wet, indifferent, heavy, and unreasonable. Nothing happens even if I feed in a hundred papers. Nothing but smoke, acrid and nauseating. My throat and nose burn, but nothing else.

Claude-Henri, our cherished boy, dies at 15 months. Never for one moment did he seem to think his life a curse; he'd smile weakly and play with small toys in his hands as though they were all the blessings in the world. Unimaginable pain when I picture his face, his big eyes and sweet smell, eyebrows raised as he drank his cup on my lap, gazing at my worry with something almost like curiosity.

CLAUDE'S RED NOTEBOOK:

How can one not believe in God, for I have knowledge, and this knowledge can not come from matter because matter does not know itself, otherwise, it would become its own master (Bienayme).

Where does materialism lead? To absurdity.

A forest, it is a mass of cells. This dryad, hamadryad, it is a cell. Thus, certainty of God, through mind, faith and reason. Uncertainty, through the senses, which prevents determinism.

Such is the state of man.

Make these ideas bear fruit.

I can see Claude suffers the boy's death, even as he rejects the stares of his daughters. I'm not as horrible to look at as they say, but in a mirror I see a sour face that shrill complaints deplete of joy. Soon, time spent at home feels aberrant and artificial, and Claude manages to sneak in and out with as little sense of belonging as possible; avoids even pretending to deal with me. "If you'd taken care of our sons like you care for your dogs, our little boys wouldn't be dead."

§

By the next week, he's yelling that he's been forced to forgo his Commerce Saint-André-des-Arts laboratory when even the sympathetic commissioner can't stem the anti-vivisection tide of protest erupting outside the door when he enters and leaves. The flood of noise complaints, and the construction that has everyone on edge, has left the local commissioner no choice but to confront Claude. Now he arrives later and later, only to sleep. He rarely speaks, and if he does, it is to question the girls who hesitantly mumble. The writer, Jules Michelet, describes a dinner table at which wife and daughter attack or refute the husband's every utterance: "They are on one side of the table, you are on the other, and alone."

CLAUDE'S RED NOTEBOOK:

The experiment is always the termination of a process of reasoning, whose premises are observation. Example: if the face has movement, what is the nerve? I suppose it is the facial; I cut it. I cut others, leaving the facial intact—the control experiment.

Claude continues hosting his mangled animals, to observe without getting out of bed. The moment he lies down, I am awake, hearing his breathing as it slows into snoring. I hate his sleep. The girls and I increasingly share these rooms with post-operative creatures, sitting all night at the dining table giving drops of water, swabbing blood and pus. Claude is trying to keep the animals alive for another day's lesson; we are gladdest for them to die if they can. In his notes, the girls and I read about frogs fastened into holes in dogs' stomachs and digested alive, while their desperate attempts to escape are carefully recorded. There is nothing to explain how a fragile peace becomes a violent conflict overnight, but it does. Thanks to Church teachings, I know we should arm ourselves not for quick skirmishes, but for a long war, to battle the inferno we will be forced to face, the resounding wall of madness. Ill, something calls for attention, begs to stand off and accept care, the poor little things who cannot stop their confused pleading until we achieve a small comfort. Going along with this, we succour illness. But refusing to give up the whole for the cries of the little parts, we say, "Part, come back." Returned to health, the afflicted part loses its partness and fades quietly back.

Charles de Remusat, in *Revue des Deux Mondes*:
"To raise a hand involves all sorts of actions one must explain, not to leave anything in the dark, the reason which leads, the will which decides, transmission of the will which contracts the muscles. We can separate physical from mental phenomena, explaining some with physiology and leaving reason and thought for philosophy. We're going to look at the successor of Mr Magendie, Claude Bernard, and his work on the nervous system..."

Claude lectures and demonstrates to his audience how ablation and poisons are the best tools for exploring the mess of live bodies. Once you slice the deceptive placidity of skin, everything you think you know vanishes, and the hand must lead where eyes would be useless.

Even for a character hidden away in the crowd, an action sneaks up, a deed, more than just an idea. Maybe this is how you always felt, little girl with courage, but I stayed a pretty good coward until one night I found myself stepping into the street with an extra end of rope, dressed to move faster because a slice of fat to fold into a handkerchief makes all the difference to the nose of an animal. What about the girls sleeping upstairs? What about my own dog, jealous and excited by the fat and the rope? What about the duty to stay at home and guard the house, sleep in it, to sleep at all times as its caretaker? Which was the first dog I caught, and how did I manage it? Was it a little one, lost and alone, rather than already mixed up in a pack as some quickly get? Was it friendly and immediately smelled on my hands the treat it gets for wagging and jumping around my knees while I'm fumbling to tie the right sort of knot? Too loose, and the whole rope slides right out as the dog bows backward and pulls away. Maybe this happened a few times, and the little thing got its reward and escaped. Finally, there must have been the first dog I triumphantly led into the courtyard and up the stairs. I must have bathed and toweled it, locking it into the girls' room with a dish of water.

Balzac, *The Theory of the Bed*:
"The hand is essentially an instrument of touch. Now touch is a sense that, in a case when it has to take the place of other senses, gives the fewest wrong impressions; no other sense can take its place...Jesus Christ performed all his miracles by means of his hands. It is through the pores of the hands that life itself passes; and, on whatsoever they touch, the hands leave the mark of a magic power. Again the hand has a share in all the delights of love. It reveals to the doctor the mysteries of our bodies. From it, more than from any other part of the body, exude the nervous fluids, or rather that unknown substance which, for lack of a better term, we must call 'will'....A man may be saved by the stretching out of a hand. It serves as the gauge of the various conditions of our feelings...To be accused of want of tact is to be condemned irretrievably. We speak of the 'hand of justice', 'the hand of God', and again of a 'coup de main' when we would describe some brave deed."

Awake and organized inside the house by noon, I prepare the meal despite light-headedness and weak legs. After the next time I go out,

I'm so unable to rouse myself and make anything to eat, I hand the girls whatever cold salted food there is, or some jam, and take to bed again. Melodramas are popular but exhausting; good and evil clashing in dangerous places, the characters all so instructively *certain*. The Goncourts: "I am foreign to that which is to come, to that which is, and a stranger to these new boulevards that go straight on, without meandering, without the adventure of perspective, implacably a straight line, without any of the atmosphere of Balzac's world, making one think of some American Babylon of the future. It is stupid to live in a time of growth; the soul is as uncomfortable as a body in a damp new house." Tonight's plan was to go on a short walk around the Odeon, but the dogs I'm tracking tear fast to an unlit street at the hill just above Jardin des Plantes, farther from the apartment than usual, and here I run right into Claude, walking-stick in hand, accompanying his brigade. There's no denying what I'm up to any more—I stare and count the church bells. Ten. Where there was a wall of flame there will be cold ash—he clears his throat and points his stick forward, and his minions seem relieved we will part without further ado. I cut toward the garden marching loudly, and split off around a corner street that will put me back in front. But a broken railing leads to jumping as I slip across wet stone, fall forward, and injure my leg badly. This time it's "Aoh!" from behind some kiosk, and two young men holding a medium-size hound leap a mile at the sight of me. I'm still the boss's wife. Maybe not for long, but bent over here bleeding, dress ripped right in two, I must be a sight. I can't get the brown and gray dog they clutch between them, and I limp down a side street as they stare. My feet burn and I imagine they barely feel theirs.

Every fire tells its story, though fire is the rare element that takes form as the illusion of form, accomplishing what we can't: total transformation. But I say war, like illness, like pain or confusion—you're either in it or you're not. And if you're not, you can't quite imagine it. In the bonds of fury, I could almost invent many things to improve the home: boiling hot bath, fetid clothes, blocking up the chimney so the smoke would choke him, feeding him rancid milk, or blood, or sewage. Not ignoring digestive and physical differences, Pharoahs knew that to find out if food was poisoned you fed it to the cook, not the cat. Here, the *secularism* spreading through Paris ominously describes priests working "diabolically through women like a serpent through Eve," and "women fanatics filled with devils" whose sole purpose is "tormenting their husbands." They say these priests gain access to men's homes by using wives like trojan horses, while weak-minded girls provide fertile ground in which fanaticism grows. Yet a *fanatique* fails under any flag—her emotions only lead to error. On a good day, our house contains slammed silences of silver, cold hot meals, the extremity of minor glances, and the costly depletion of all one can put into a jab at the back of a head or a turned body in a bed. The Goncourts: "And then, women are on their way out. Today, as we stand here, a woman is no more than a bit of venereal gymnastics, dished up with a touch of sentimentality. And, that's all. No salons, no meeting place, no polite society...."

Still, an intimacy more powerful than any intimate act has started to connect my husband and I. My dog-stealing of his dog-stealing drives him into rages, and even though our network of safety might seem to a stray as just another form of prison, I persist in the slipping of ropes and the binding of jaws, the calming and holding and transporting across bridges, to dim courtyards on the way to other courtyards, the loading into carriages bound for secret places and handed to hands roughly. But my plan, fervent and steadily enacted, has for its counterpart the clueless boys who fear his wrath at their inability to outwit the black-clad lady.

§

Finally retired from the Collège de France, Magendie leaves Claude the post. Claude's old professor, Rayer, has joined the Emperor as personal physician and connives for Claude a chair at the Sorbonne that had been for botany. But what I know, and others will soon find out, is that lately Claude isn't feeling fine. His kidneys give him blinding pains, he says, and his intestines cramp to a bed-ridden extreme. I stare at him blankly and unswayed. He is the one who teaches a false form of medicine without doctors or hospitals. In bed, comfortless, he curses because I give him nothing to relieve him, and his lab's so damp and frankly unhealthy he can't find a moment's place to rest. He's feverish and mad as a hornet, so I hold out some cold tea. I wish I could take credit for this onslaught of misery, but mine are simple mental crimes. Okay, I say, I won't bother you and will let you rest—though I don't know why I should.

Irritatingly, to say the least, the owner of the mansion behind which Claude's parents spent so many struggling years, decides to sell house, presses, wine-cellar, pigeonière, and six hectares of vines sloping down to Saint-Julien. As a little ember can carry an entire wildfire in its clutch, Claude jumps at managing the vineyard, with the help of local farmers to clip and tie grapes the rest of the year—and because he can journey from Paris quickly on the new train, Claude buys the estate for 60,000 francs, inviting his mother to move into this folly just as his health worsens, saying she will care for him there. He requests permission to stop his Sorbonne and Collège de France courses in 1862, 1863, and 1864, giving him the excuse to devote himself to writing, the passion of his youth.

"Subject: Leave given to Mr Claude Bernard for health reasons:

Mr Administrator, Thank you for informing me by your letter of 4, January, that Professor Claude Bernard has been afflicted by something whose treatment will take some time. I would let you know, Mr Administrator, that I will grant this professor a leave, conforming to his request and your opinion....

—M. Duruy, Minister of Public Education"

He'll start with a *Revue des Deux Mondes* article on curare, and another on the general progress of this new 'physiology.' Amusingly, he cites Goethe, Molière, and Pascal. Writing, he boasts, will become an extension of his experimental work. I restrain myself from comment. In a laboratory, big questions are made small so that they fit in that space and become visible; maybe he thinks this is how writing works too? When the results are transferred to the world at large, the tiny actors appear heroic, the unnatural events inevitable, the partial answers obvious. I am never, not once, invited to that house I bought him in the Beaujolais. He lives there only with his mother, the occasional assistant, and Mr Davaine, who comes for long stays. The precise empirical thinking of the grape harvest exhilerates Claude, who appreciates in winemakers what he loathes in doctors. Attention to the sugar content and to the color of the stems—all this and the tasting of the fruit—lead to decisions about when to pick. Daily, even hourly evaluations, create a relationship with the laden vines. Grapes swell, practically sing with secrets, until caught at the right moment.

With Claude out of town, my nights grow arduous, competing with his young men who continue to supply not only his ongoing experiments, but the growing number of incidental and competing ones around the neighborhood. I'm one, they seem numberless, and exhaustion drives me into flights of near panic over the tiniest loss. I start to confuse times and errands, disoriented enough in the daytime I can barely feed myself, or dress. You know, as I do, that we can see darkness the closer we look into it, but how can the flow of time be reassembled or analyzed if you take it apart like this? Nights must have a different purpose—to be ignored, forgotten, slept through—not to be so unrelenting. In the plot, when excess is removed, and whatever deformity is purged, there we may find *katharsis*; excess spleen exhausts itself, excess purging calms us down. I decide to start a campaign of words, unexalted as mine may be:

"My dear friend, your mother won't leave her maid for more than fifteen days because she is scared of bothering her.

But you, you don't even worry about leaving us alone for more than three weeks. Do you think one should have more respect for one's maid than for one's wife? The children send hugs and say thank you, the grapes arrived this morning.

Goodbye, I wish you all the pleasure you can find far from us and I send kisses.

P.s. You have so many friends here who, luckily for us, seem to want you to return to Paris."

I must be eloquent since I get no reply. I continue:

"Aren't you ashamed to have left your wife and children to live with a vicious mother who has persuaded you you're better cared for by a mercenary than by me! I can see from here that vile servant who is using this base opportunity to become your spy.

You want to push me to do something my religion prohibits! You want me to appear to all the world as an immoral woman with whom her husband can no longer live. I haven't once overlooked my spousal and motherly duties, despite your behavior toward me.

Despite it all, I could have had what you reproached me for lacking, and you might have been willing to dine out with me. The alarming state of your health and the worries I've had for so long

about my money have prevented me from sleeping and eating...You
may have forgotten that only a few months ago you thought you
had only a few hours to live.

—Your desperate wife"

When in the city, it's true he gets worse, don't ask me why. I pass behind
him, touch his sleeves, bump his back in the chair as he sits among papers
and pamphlets, trying to be slender, trying to be slight, trying not to
notice how much he makes us tiptoe and whisper. This is the form of
a torment, like a temperature just warm enough in which insects are
invited but can't settle, do nothing but swarm, slowly and without effect,
lost as to the open door or window, lost as to how to ignore him as he
does us. I admit to a bit of screaming. It's ingratitude for the gifts of
family, the pathetic way he can't be bothered to eat dinner when we eat
dinner, his lips so loud later when he stands in the cupboard devouring
meat and wine. It's just too damn much to explain the empty seat and
the congealed food. It's way too much to be bothered with the look of
his daughters when they would like to see even the possibility of a smile.
That look which turns into small caustic sadness, something I must then
work out from their bodies as I sponge them and lay out their dresses
for bed. It is not nothing to keep a fire alive. Apollo falls in love with a
nymph, who, having been shot by Cupid with lead, vows never to marry.
Her father changes her toes into roots so that Apollo can't take her, and
her arms became branches when he tries to grab her, her head the crown
of the laurel tree. But inside the trunk, Apollo hears her frightened heart,
so he tears twigs off to make a wreath upon his head, saying, "You won't
be my bride but you can be my tree!" But that girl would rather be a
tree than the bride of even the great Apollo. Sick in his armchair with a
blanket, coughing and aching, Claude asks for food, and I set him a plate
like to a prisoner.

§

CLAUDE'S RED NOTEBOOK:

There are those who say that science is entirely objective;
it is in the mind and not in reality. This is absurd.
Without doubt the form of science, as we conceive it,
is in our mind, but facts exist. In a monument, for
example, one can say that style and form and art are
in our mind, but the stones exist independently of
the form of the monument, when all is said and done.
Science is the same: facts are the stones, the scientist
chooses them to make his scientific monument, which
is the fact of his mind.

What perverts the judgment of physicians is that they
are followed and listened to. The credulity of sick people
makes a pedestal for them, which is taken seriously, even
without their knowledge. It is the same for many other
professions that are associated with the weaknesses of
humanity. The ancients were right when they hid their
priests and their physicians in the depths of the temples....

Today authors initiate us into their privacy. They
tell us how they go to bed, how they get up, how they
sneeze, etc. This is a false point of view because when
a man is a great man, it is not when he goes to bed,
when he gets up, sneezes, etc. It is when he writes,
when he thinks, and this is only at times, like an actor.
For in these moments, the man is truly great, and we
have him by his works. It would be better to ignore
the rest; that adds nothing to the man, and for those
who do not understand these things, it can only make

him smaller and destroy art. Art vanishes because it
is that mysterious something which moves you without
your knowing too much why. There is a certain pleasure
in not knowing, because the imagination can go to work.

In the course of 1865, Auguste Compte dies, and Baudelaire's *Les Fleurs du Mal* is taken up in court and condemned. Jules Verne astounds the crowds with *Five Weeks in a Balloon*. After two years of illness, Claude publishes his *Introduction to the Study of Experimental Medicine*, writing of the ideal scientist: "He doesn't feel that he is in a horrible carnage; under the influence of a scientific idea, he pursues with delight a nervous filament inside stinking and livid flesh that for any other person would be an object of disgust and horror."

Poe: "…but why will you say that I am mad? The disease had sharpened my senses—not destroyed—not dulled them. Above all was the sense of hearing acute. I heard all things in the heaven and in the earth. I heard many things in Hell."

Edgar Poe's tales line the bookstalls and reading rooms. Madmen join ideas that alone make sense but joined are strange. Then, mistaking this strangeness for something true, the madman argues rightly, even persuasively, from his beliefs. And his actions? Today's lunch sits untouched and then, just as I'm going to remove the dishes, a lab assistant appears to let us know that Monsieur Bernard will stay in his foul laboratory for his meal. Hell is noise and noisome, yet Orpheus's song stops even Sisyphus in his routine. Shamans of this sort survive under the earth in the muddle between life and death, on their mission-retrieval of lost or stolen souls. The girls look at him. I look at him. We all look at this pathetic little assistant and pretend we don't know him from the night before when we tripped him coming around rue Clotaire. He fell right into a puddle, and a small cat jumped practically into our arms. Helping him stand back up, I think Marie-Claude gave him a genuine smile.

CLAUDE'S RED NOTEBOOK:

In physiology there are always two things to consider: 1. The organism, 2. The environment. The same consideration can be repeated everywhere. There are: 1. The materials that come from without, 2. The organic force. There are: 1. Man and his genius, 2. The circumstances in which he finds himself. There are: 1. The tree, 2. The earth in which it grows. There are: 1. The cow, 2. Her nourishment. There are: 1. The fact, 2. Their explanation. There are: 1. Man and his genius, 2. His work and perseverance. There are: 1. Man and his genius, 2. The nature of the science with which he is occupied, which makes him more or less reproachable.

There's only so much distance I can manage on foot while leading several impetuous beasts. I'm not old, but travel is hard through the mounting evidence of our dear Emperor's ambitions. The hauling and shouting are loudest at Ile Saint-Louis, and huge work lights reflect in the water. Rush under Pont Neuf, and the shadows escape up the banks. Nomad workers stumble across me. Easier to run in men's clothing, but I can't bear that. Shit mixes on our shoes until we pay the *decrotteurs* their small fee to brush us clean. Curiosity is man's first temptation, but it is every dog's birthright, to seek each smell, to dash in pursuit of unseen quarry. We humans may cherish science as an idol, an evil Moloch even, putting discovery in the palace of love— but don't say animals lack similar appetites. The rain makes the mud slick, and our boots suck it as we tumble into each other, hands down in the sticky mess, the cold breaking our skin. At night the streets need no names, the rivulets change, running along until stopped, go around this plaster pile, choked in the plumbing, the waterways, the sewers, the cemeteries. For every night despite us all, there is Mr Haussmann. His loyalty, more than consideration of birth, status or inheritance, is what defines this new bureaucrat. Everyone says Paris is sick, suffocating, blocked up, intestinally cramped—all digestion and stomach, disease and organs. Thus the government guts it all. Baudelaire: "…all that a great town contains of living monstrosities," the city and its "new palaces, scaffoldings, blocks, old suburbs, to me all becomes allegory," a "setting like an actor's soul." Athena had her city, and we will have ours, finding mythology more comforting than history. I hear they've wiped the Boulevard du Crime clean of theaters. Where the first Napoleon started the military extension of the rue de Rivoli, ours wants to offer his puppet Senate an opulence conceived by triangulating from high wooden lookouts. This conceptual Paris-space, abstract above all, allows engineers to construct what writers can't: a city of functions, zones, some industrial and dirty, others sparkling. "Paris suffers from an aneurism of the heart." No arteries lead to the vital and dying organ, and the more the city sweats and turns feverish, the more I would like to hide myself from the shredded streets and open pockets of waste.

CLAUDE'S RED NOTEBOOK:

Ideas develop spontaneously in the mind, and when one yields to his thoughts he is like a man at the window watching the passersby. In some such fashion one watches his ideas. This requires no effort, and it even has a great charm. Where the work is, and the

fatigue, is to collar the idea like one stops the passerby,
despite his desire to flee, and then to retain him, and
give him character, etc.

Haussmann hates that the corner of the street he's standing on has
a thwarted view. He hated the six thousand barricades, and palettes
of bodies; "Barricades and boulevards would not coexist." Fountains
must be pulled from walls, marshes dried and drained. Hôtel de Ville
and the Place de Grève, dislodged and controlled. Heavy or dirty
industry moves to the outer "red belt." Despite all that's removed,
people fumble by touch and feel through the sinuous rubble whose
never-ending dampness infects the bottom floors. Haussmann promises to divert the water along sixty-three kilometers of underground
sewers, with boat tours for royalty and a mirror world of walkways.
Victor Hugo's Javert chases Jean Valjean: "The sewer is the conscience
of the city. All things converge and confront one another there...One
can say this for this refuse heap—it is not a liar...." Haussmann, like
his imagined Roman predecessors, "wants to give to the king a city
of marble after receiving a city of wood." Budgets and timetables are
a bureaucrat's poetry, and the new Opera and museums are as gaudy
and hollow as a Paris measured in tons, materials, acres. The city
finally has its limbs, arteries, stomach, even lungs (Bois de Vincennes
and Boulogne), but is it alive?

Haussmann: "I had to safeguard the great work that my efforts had
placed in my hands. I had to prevent it from being undone. I climbed
often into the breech to repulse the constant assaults; and my energetic
but calm resistance, always supported by new and precise arguments,
exasperated the equally energetic adversaries who accused me of stub-
bornness."

At the end of the day, he will face every building with stone.

Baudelaire: "We are each of us celebrating some funeral."

§

Faust: *Do you see the black dog coursing there, through corn and stubble?*

Wagner: *While back, yet thought him not important at all.*

Faust: *Look closer—what do you think he is?*

Wagner: *Why, just a poodle who has lost his master, and scents about, trying to track him.*

Faust: *It spirals all around us, as you see it approaches, fast and faster...A fiery eddy around it.*

Wagner: *I see the poodle, as I said already; and that's all there is to it.*

Faust: *It seems to me that he winds magic traps around our feet—future traps.*

Wagner: *He jumps around unsure, and our presence scares him, two strangers he doesn't know at all and not his master.*

Faust: *The circle narrows, he is near!*

Wagner: *You see a dog and not a ghost! He growls and lies on his belly, he wags his tail: all canine habits.*

Faust: *Come here and walk along with us!*

Wagner: *He's a poodle—silly beast. You stand still and he waits too; you talk to him and he climbs on you; drop something, he will fetch it back, even if you throw it in the lake!*

Faust: *You seem quite right, I find his skill to be no spirit; all is drill and habit.*

Wagner: *A dog expertly trained can even the wisest man entertain. Still he deserves your favor: it is prudent to cultivate the students' noble student.*

Faust enters the study with the poodle beside him.

Faust: *Behind me, field and meadow sleeping, I leave in deep, prophetic night, within whose dread and holy keeping, the better soul awakes to light....Be quiet poodle! Stop that racket! Why are you snuffling around the door? Go lie next to the stove and stay quiet. As you ran and leapt and amused us before, so now we have taken you to our breast—but only if you stay a silent guest.*

Don't snarl, dog! That noise is out of place. We're used to seeing men despise what they don't understand, but do dogs too snarl at what's beyond them?

Faust reads from a book:

'Tis written: "In the Beginning was the Word."
Here am I balked; who, now, can help afford the Word?—impossible so high to rate it; and otherwise must I translate it, if by the Spirit I am truly taught.
Then thus: "In the Beginning was the Thought."
This first line let me weigh completely, lest my impatient pen go too swiftly.
Is it the Thought which works, creates, indeed?

"In the Beginning was the Power," I read.

Yet as I write, a warning is suggested, that I the sense may not have truly tested.

*The Spirit aids me: now I see the light! "In the Beginning was the Deed,"
I write.*

*If I must share my chamber with thee, Poodle, stop that howling, would
you! Cease to bark and bellow! Such a noisy, disturbing fellow I'll no longer
suffer near me. One of us, you hear, must leave! No longer guest rights shall I
offer you; the door is open you are free to go.*

*But what do I see in the creature? Is that the course of nature? Is it pos-
sible Fact, or Fancy's show? How long and broad my poodle grows! He rises
mightily: a canine form that cannot be! What a spectre I've harbored thus—
resembles a hippopotamus—with fiery eyes, teeth terrible to see: for all of thy
half-hellish brood The Key of Solomon is good!*

*Now to undisguise, hear me exorcise with a query: art thou, my happy one,
Hell's fugitive stray before whom bow your cohorts of Hell?*

*Behind the stove—see it! An elephant expands! Fills the space entirely mist-
like melting, faster and higher.*

Thus, Mephistopheles emerges from the smoke.

Faust: *This was the poodle's real core, a traveling scholar, are you?*

Mephistopheles: *...Dream your dreams, O Faust, until we meet once more.*

A few minutes later,

Faust (waking): *Am I so foully cheated? Is nothing left of that lofty spirit but
a dream the devil counterfeited? And that a poodle ran away?*

§

As public awareness of our nightly stray-snatching grows, Tony, Marie-Claude, and I steel against hostile students griping about their professor's professional and domestic *torment*. Claude tells everyone I have "made his home a living hell"—as all the while he "keeps the doors of his laboratory closed against the winds of doctrine"—where doctrine is his word for conscience. Balzac, from *Pinpricks of Married Life*: "Civil War. Never was war waged of a more truly domestic nature...two contrary, hostile interests is an exact definition of marriage...for three-quarters of the French people."

"When we have a friend with whom it is very nice to walk in the evening because he knows many actresses and other women, we suddenly don't have money or time for our wife... I am certainly humiliated leaving the building manager's office. And I will be even more so telling my laundry woman I can't pay her."

Claude has been named Senator of the Empire, and the French Academy gets around to naming him one of the forty Immortals of France, entrusted with guardianship over the purity of the French language, as preserved in constant revising of the dictionary. His Academy seat number 24 is the same seat Flourens had warmed, and Victor Hugo before him. At the reception, Claude takes a moment to say of Flourens: "In his marriage he found the peace and quiet necessary for a working scientist. His devoted companion understood and appreciated him, identified with his intellectual life, which she supported by hiding from him the little troubles of existence."

Meanwhile in his private rants, Claude recounts tedious dictionary ses-
sions at the Academy, while the Emperor and his Haussmann are building Great Museums to display the world's treasures. Claude grouses that
the scientific exploration of the body should also receive monumental
funding—for labs, not hospital beds. Anything observed in the clinic is
anecdotal until produced in his lab, yet where is the government support?
If a disease cannot be recreated, it doesn't exist. Claude: "Even a city in
Germany with 6,000 people would have its library, its schools, but also
its laboratories—and yet Paris, our grand Paris, watches her scientists
hiding in caves, unable to read from the big book of Nature."

CLAUDE'S RED NOTEBOOK:

*One must first set forth the principal idea and sacrifice
all the details; without this, interest is distracted and*

boredom intervenes. Have only one idea to prove and make everything converge upon it. One should take only the flower of anything.

Well, the higher Claude's star rises, the more smuggling his animals away from him nationally offends, and people start arraying themselves for or against us, looking from their doors and windows, pointing in the direction of stray dog or man, or conspiring to do the opposite, misdirecting us with obvious insult. It is in these little details, however, that the people of Paris, whose city is tattered or in progress, need to decide what they want. Pain, after all, brings awareness of a contrary thing—an agon—agony personified: a statue carrying weights. The girls and I hide near the quai and watch as Claude makes his morning stop to buy frogs. What would he do if we rushed out and greeted him? Would he even smile? Claude's Red Notebook: "In a word, the spontaneity of living matter is just a false appearance. There are always external principles, foreign stimulants that provoke the appearance of properties that are otherwise inert by themselves."

On a sleeting winter day, we flee his gang into the Church Saint Sulpice, with the Blessed Virgin immaculate and standing with Jesus on a big bald globe, floating in sculpted clouds pouring immobile from the recess toward a gilded lamp curled nearby, candles in metal baskets, and Mary's determined foot crushing a snake. It's a world of stone figures—each more tormented than the last—until their most agonized finds himself at their lead, head hanging loose but never moved to give up struggling. Lying on a pew, napping in God's house, my thoughts are formless and free as shadows released from their objects. Recently in Lourdes, a mountain girl saw the Virgin—undeniably signaling the return of miracles. Does the Holy Father love statues at least as much as people? Christ suffers in all his senses—including profound grief at his betrayal. Smote with every variety of pain, he burned with visions, smells, sounds, tastes of bile.

Our family has lost even the most tentative sensation of love. The girls have never known a time without war, silent or in preparation, raging or recuperating. The charade of home—I do errands, and Claude walks to his lab—and some days the girls sit and talk together for a moment and seem almost normal. Locked away from one parent by the annihilation of the other, and our lack of will to reconcile, means I no longer tolerate his contact with them: any time they so much as hint at going to an event at which he might be present, I give them an earful. His attempts to pull them aside and hastily talk "sense" into them aren't lost on me either. It is no pleasure to be a child inhabiting a world of allegiances. Homeless wanderers like the strays who run these streets; only outside, and at night, does our family connect.

CLAUDE'S RED NOTEBOOK:

Everyone follows his own path. Some are extensively prepared and follow the furrow that has been traced out, etc. For myself, I arrived on the scientific field by devious paths, and I freed myself of the rules by cutting across the field, which others would not perhaps have dared to do. But I believe that in physiology this has not been bad, because it led me to new vistas.

What about my boys? Wouldn't I have sacrificed everything to have saved them? The babies are gone, yet every day the same question: to what length for one's life or the lives of others, to what length?

In a good drama, *recognition* signifies the shift from ignorance to awareness, pointing to a state of enmity or blood relation, best when a reversal
of roles begins to take place. In daylight, when the girls and I see women
walking their dogs, we stare at them and take mental notes—sometimes
we stare so hard we are hurled a glare in return. Yet we persist because
more than once we've restored a dazed animal into the tearful embrace
of that same lady later.

§

Claude, from a public lecture at Collège de France:

"Gentlemen, in the last lesson, we showed you that an animal that has
mostly used up its oxygen in a confined space could live in conditions that
would kill a healthy animal. I've called your attention to this because we
might think it's odd to see a weaker animal resisting harm better than a
healthy one.

Experiment: this bell jar, put over mercury as we normally do, encloses
a finch who has been there for two and a half hours and is already very sick.
I introduce another bird that you can see fighting for life, convulsing and
collapsing. The newcomer is obviously sicker and succumbs quickly. But if
I lift the bell jar, the newcomer immediately perks up and flies, even though
it appeared almost dead, whereas the physiological milieu of the first bird
hasn't improved measurably though it passed two and a half hours in the
bell jar and could have lived another half hour. This finch will also recover,
but not for a very long time."

At home, Claude paces room to room, reading monographs from scientists around Europe. From his grumbling, I know that he disdains everything that is not in his influence. He marches around banging on tables,
pronouncing his hate for Charles Darwin and his *Origin* because it cannot be tested under controlled lab conditions, and therefore cannot be
"knowable." Claude's Red Notebook: "False scientists have a great thirst to
explain everything, but are not very ardent for proof. They explain every-

thing, but never prove anything. They hasten to explain, but not to prove." At church there's much ado about Darwin's evolution as well, and I laugh at how many times a day Claude sounds more Catholic than the priests, though publicly, Claude admits: "Everything is evolution. The evolutionary idea is now dominant in all the sciences. We do not know a being, a phenomenon, or a history, except through its evolution. No one period can characterize a being or a phenomenon absolutely."

By the end of this dramatic exposition and rising action, our hero sits high in the French firmament: the Academy of Medicine, Academy of Sciences, Chair of General Physiology at the Sorbonne, Professor of Medicine at Collège de France—and yet—if this be tragedy, good fortune may reverse. If a comedy, what seems like bad luck might start to change. That pain in his gut is destroying him—and no one he knows knows why. He thinks enteritis, perhaps cholera. He vomits. He doubles over, and can only hobble for walking. He supervises the laboratory, but finds it difficult to stand in front of an audience. As a connoisseur of the stories fires tell, I hear sounds instructing what to do next—if it's rushing air and energy that moves too fast—time to tamp down a bit, step back, this fire hasn't need of you, though its freedom is illusory, just as in the end, plot is immobile without conflict. Conflict, one senses, is found in every situation, an array of tensions that pressure time forward. They say a great talker is a great liar, so the turning point may well depend on who best constructs an argument. Within an hour, I return with fuel and lay it into the bed just right, so it's accepted quickly and takes flame like a drink.

§

Claude returns to Saint-Julien and to his contemptible mother. In front of the mansion, Claude plants a grove of six yew trees, *six ifs* (a pun on "sees-eef" or Sysiphe/Sisyphus). In the grove, he places a stone bench, and calls it his "Bench of Sisyphus."

Here on this bench, Sisyphus steals a moment as he has stolen many things, not least among them Death, tricked and tied up. How has he managed to capture the most elusive predator in all creation? Death: *"Here, put on these chains, Sisyphus, I've been sent to carry you to Pluto's realm."* Devising the deceit of proffering himself as a gentle helper, Sisyphus pretends to care for Death in the face of death, concerned that the job be done right: *"O, Death, I'm not sure those chains are so strong— Perhaps you should try them first to be certain they will hold me?"* Smooth talk tricks even those who know him best or have been warned; as a king he'd already been a thief, taking from his poorest subjects. So Sisyphus binds Death in his own chains and parades him through the streets before sealing him in an airtight closet. Jubilant cheers rise from this newly immortal day, yet not even the oldest and sickest are truly happy, because without Death, the increase in pain grows thousand-fold—and gravely injured soldiers on the battlefields wander decapitated or mutilated, hauling their bodies to knock at their loved ones'

doors, unable to die. Mothers, wives, and sons scream in fear and ask the Gods what to do with these would-be corpses. Chaos descends on the crowded planet until finally Zeus commands Ares to take his weapons and go pay Sisyphus a visit. *"Unchain Death from his prison and punish Sisyphus once and forever."*

Zeus: "There's no way for war to determine a battle, if Death cannot be present to tally and remove the soldiers. No death is far worse than violence." And so Death is freed.

§

"Oh by the way, Fanny, we saw your husband at a ball the other night." "Oh Fanny, have you heard that your husband's courses will start again next month?" "Fanny, what do you think of the Princess' new Salon? What! You haven't been!"

Dining at Princess Mathilde's or going to the Opera, Claude complains, "I realize how tiring it is to have fun. Wednesday I went to Garches, yesterday to the Princess's at Enghien, today at the Baronne's in Boulogne."

Is it normal to lie in bed and wish a husband dead? The sort of normal that has no season, no calendar, no weather, no growth or diminishment; really just picture him hanging there, my body focusing the desire like a pulley through my chest, tightening iron chains as I choke into the middle nothingness of the ceiling, hung on this sinful hatred in which I picture his offal weeping. His footsteps, real or imagined, sound in the other room, and cause me to tingle with fury. Every breath, every step, every bite of food, his whole existence such a waste of money.

CLAUDE'S RED NOTEBOOK:

A general tendency to reconcile everything: physicism,
vitalism, solidism, humorism, materialism, spiritualism,
etc. A comedy. Set down the arguments in a separate
book.

"Miserable man! You left me more than seven months ago, and you
dare to tell me that when you return to Paris you won't be coming
back to the conjugal home! Why don't you just get rid of me as you
threatened to, using one of your poisons with whose subtlety you
are so familiar? You would be less cruel than making me endure
so many evils! You've been making me suffer for ten years, pushed
by your parents...I see that, knowing how horribly you have acted
toward me, you think you can alleviate your guilt by fleeing me. You
should be so unhappy with a conscience like yours. Your mother, by
replacing me with that maid I can't even think of without losing my
mind, has found the way to completely master you and my fortune,
which is the sole motor of all her actions...I am sure the advice of
Mr Davaine has unduly influenced you, and I attribute most of
what's happened in our marriage to his influence. Everyone in the
world deserves your friendship and respect except your unhappy
wife and your young children. I'm writing this to Saint-Julien even
though you may already be in Paris.

                                             Fanny Bernard

Maybe I will see you next in another world, where I hope to be
less unhappy."

George Sand: "The horse, the cow, the dog cries; they have tears
of despair as a stag in distress; but they also have cries of pain and

of tenderness." For Aristotle, pain was an emotion, the opposite of pleasure, but not a physical thing. All senses, including thought, have a painful dimension to them. Finally realizing their father is leaving us, Tony and Marie want to stay in the flat, but we are forced to move. The increasing number of animals that the girls are caring for makes staying put hard. A hoopla erupts over my request for two francs for the *Animal Protection Society* as part of my expenses—while no one misses the irony of Claude's membership appearing in their listings for *1865, 1st Jan., Bernard (Claude), physiology professor, Collège de France.*

"So I am a schemer to whom you don't deign respond? Aren't you evil to completely hide my own affairs from me! Don't you think I know you aren't giving me rent from a house of which I own a third! In a few days it will have been eight months that you left me to live with your servant whose care you prefer to mine. But you must have other reasons to stay apart such a long time, for I just read in the "Course Review" that your health has returned.

You don't deserve the effort I make to write this. Mr Davaine gives you advice you only follow because it fits your emotions.

I'm going to find out what a woman whose husband has left her can do, and I'm going to try to regain what you're refusing to give me."

I demand to know the state of a building in Faubourg Saint Denis left to me by my father. I return a fruit basket to Saint-Julien that Claude had sent the girls, and I include through Davaine a demand for the reimbursement for the expense of sending it. My daughters are henceforth forbidden to accept fruit from a father who dishonors them.

Claude and I enter a fancily tricked-out *formal separation* on the day he moves to rue des Écoles. The girls and I hoped to live at the convent at Sacré-Cœur, but the Mother Superior won't allow our dogs. I am forced to hire a lawyer— Mr Boinod—to go after Claude for monthly payments and supplements for finding apartments, and also the return of the furniture belonging to me. I'm asking 1,500FF/mo plus 1,000 per apartment. He's a Senator after all, with salary of 30,000FF/year—not to mention his academic posts and book sales. Claude: "When one does not know what he ought to want, he should know what his enemy wants and want the contrary." He asks for half the silver and linen, an ivory Christ, a carved-oak stoup, pictures of the children, some of the books (especially one which had been a gift of the Empress Eugenie) and "various little things which belonged to my last child."

"I've just had Mr Davaine here, who you dared send to my house with the key to your desk, which he didn't know how to open. I gave myself the pleasure of letting him try for a long time. He'll tell you himself what I told him about you. Your behavior toward me is still that of a boor who treats his wife like a slave. It's clear who your mother is."

The girls are grown enough to reject being treated as children in Claude's memory when he can't address them in person. In Claude's opinion they have practically ceased to exist, as he assumes them under my influence, and in agreement with my views. Mariette Rey has stayed with him as cook and cleaner, though I'm sure begrudgingly. His work on the Sabbath is a constant source of irritation, and his habits at the house both unreasonable and offensive. In France, divorce is considered republican and revolutionary since it was first made legal in 1792, when couples could divorce with only a six-month waiting period, and without expense or guilt. But has marriage ever been more than politics? Was divorce ever the private disregard between former lovers? The first Napoleon's civil code made divorce restrictive—the whole family had to give consent. Since incompatibility was eliminated as a justification, and adultery only counted if a woman committed it, control of wife and daughters was heartily reestablished—and divorce was abolished entirely in 1816. Legislators tried to reinstate it in 1831, 1832, 1833 and 1844, voted down each time by the Chamber of Peers. And so indeed, radical women's clubs promote the issue in their journal, *La Voix des Femmes,* and the Vésuviennes, a quasi-military organization of Parisian working women, stump for it. Still, we are stuck, and the girls' lives stay in his control. They wonder why wives and daughters join convents or change religions. The injury to a father's right to the disposal of daughters is called *rapt de seduction.*

I should hate to say it, but I can't help smiling even now—it seems at least possible, at the least coincident, that the failure of our marriage was the final blow that killed the elder Mrs Bernard, found in an unhappy contortion a few steps from her house. Claude's old friend, that loathsome Pelouze, and his dear Professor Rayer, also die within a few months. No doubt Claude will now not hurry to Paris until spring, when he will surely be welcomed at the elbow of every salon hostess. He will renew the company of the literary establishment, Ernest Renan and the Goncourts and the rest. A mother such as he had wouldn't have cared for any of that. She had her grubby hands on the only thing that mattered, and now it's all his.

Charles Brook Dupont-White, in *Revue des Deux Mondes*, "The Philosophical Inferiority of Positivism":
"No,' say the people, 'You don't do! You reduce me to the visible and to the tangible. But I have thoughts and aspirations above what I can touch and see. The origin and goal of the world attracts my attention. I won't say, 'Who cares about humanity!' 'To be or not to be' is still a grave issue. I am

a religious animal, so says Fenelon. 'You are more than I could ever learn, but less than I could want to know.'... But the agony of the dying man—what do you understand of this? The suffering that fills every being—what do you learn that will take away five minutes of that pain? Do you have any solution at all? ...Guessing and Imagination aren't always wrong. Columbus guessed America. The Greeks guessed gravity. Says a physiologist: *nature non facit saltus.*"

2.

AUTHORS | SPECTATORS

It's not just Claude, or the gossips at church, but the whole world seems to be arguing about Mister Darwin. I imagine him in England, motion-sick, lying in his shadow at the end of the day. It disappears. He grows larger. He frets at an iron garden table, housebound with geraniums and tea, his life a private agony despite the froth of applause. The last survivor of a certain evolutionary zigzag, he fusses over his wormy plot and the worms it contains. In this vastness, his imagination attempts to see an image of its past—which to an imagination offers up the losers and survivors of life's gambles. Survivors, blind to their pasts, or at least shocked to have outlived them, proceed aggressively—for it seems time does not support being looked at (*It might not have been this way, time might have been an exhibitionist*, he thinks)—until, in the center of attention, he hesitates and hulks back.

Darwin, letter to Asa Gray:
"...By the way, one of my chief enemies (the sole one who has annoyed me) namely Owen, I hear has been lecturing on Birds, & admits that all have descended from one, & advances as his own idea that the oceanic wingless Birds have lost their wings by gradual disuse. He never alludes to me or only with bitter sneers & coupled with Buffon, & the Vestiges..."

History wants to come alive, Darwin insists, as a way of explaining change, as a way of putting people inside the whole story—but his dragon-hunting peers only seem to stack up fossils—and Darwin refuses Richard Owen's fashionable word *dinosaur*—unsure how anything but nonsense can yet come of it. The fossils found thus far are meager, and to tell anything coherent out of such a mess? Fragments where there should be skeletons, one-offs where major theories should coalesce, parts and pieces from beasts who lived millions of years apart entangled as though they were the best of friends? Even finding the bones for one entire skeleton is a fool's game of sorting and sifting through parts of a hundred other skeletons. The most complete collections have scarcely a whole beast between them. Darwin: "That our paleontological collections are very imperfect, is admitted by every one." And then, in the unlikely scenario that enough material surfaces to piece something together, the artistry of wire and plaster and putty needed to cobble it demands another set of skills entirely. Skeleton parts get invented, or lumped to the wrong creature. Poor Edward Cope sticks a skull on the butt-end of a spine and publishes this monster to roars of mockery. At the end of the day, there's still next to nothing of eyes or skin or colors, nothing of movements through the water or the jungle, nothing of speed or sound or habit. For these things have fallen away into the elements which absorb and renew the living. People don't even believe animals can go extinct, Darwin despairs, or admit that extinction and ancestry connect at the root. But if not extinct, where would these enormous animals be hiding? And if fossils are recent carcasses, why isn't every rock, desert, and crag filled to bursting? Fossils one day will confirm my suspicions, whispers Darwin to Emma, as she hurries from the kitchen to help him upright: we're all mixed up together.

As a boy, Darwin pursued the hunt, and even athletics—but once he saw a dog abused, and it made him vomit. In the medical school anatomy theater—corpses hacked like chickens—he ran from the room, quit his studies, and ever after avoids even speaking the word *blood*. The invitation to join *The Beagle* released him from Seminary, which wasn't working out either: his hands too busy in the garden, and no interest in God. But on board ship his hands fell numb, as tropical illness killed many of the crew. Darwin:

"I trust and believe that the time spent in this voyage, if thrown away for all other respects, will produce its full worth in Nat: History: And it appears to me, the doing what little one can to increase the general stock of knowledge is as respectable an object of life, as one can in any likelihood pursue."

Back in England, his cousin Emma provided him with walks, reading, company, and ten children—though his extreme sensitivity to pain and blood made her pregnancies anathema—and she kept each birth to herself. "She has been my wise adviser and cheerful comforter throughout life, which without her would have been, during a very long period, a miserable one from ill-health." So there's a proper wife! Though even she must have tallied her losses when their nine-year-old died of fever. Darwin rejects church, and can't take séances or prayers, so I can only imagine how God must sit in an awkward seat between them.

Darwin, from *The Expression of the Emotions in Man and Animals*:

"When the sensorium is strongly excited, the muscles of the body are generally thrown into violent action, and as a consequence loud sounds are uttered, however silent the animal may generally be, and although the sounds may be of no use. Hares and rabbits, for instance, never, I believe, use their vocal organs except in the extremity of suffering...We have also seen that intense pain, like rage, leads to violent outcries, and the exertion of screaming by itself gives some relief; and thus the use of the voice will have become associated with suffering of any kind. The general law that a feeling is a stimulus to Muscular Action."

As Darwin grows older, regrets lead to insomnia, floating images, and dread. His health, and that of his whole family, obsesses him:

"Children are one's greatest happiness, but often & often a still greater misery. A man of science ought to have none,—perhaps not a wife; for then there would be nothing in this wide world worth caring for & a man might (whether he would is another question) work away like a Trojan."

He is hard-working and rumored to repeat, 'it's dogged that does it!' each day as he hauls stiffly to the ground. His dog Polly—joyous tonic—jumps around his head as he peers through his glass at the worms. An hour's conversation with a friend, and that night is all diarrhea and shivers. Retreat from the world is a form of death.

Darwin:
"What I shall soon have to do, will be to erect a tablet in Down Church 'sacred to the memory &c', & officially die, & then publish books 'by the late Charles Darwin.'"

§

CLAUDE'S RED NOTEBOOK:

Pathology adds nothing to the organism; it only disturbs it. The pathological state does not create any new vital property; it merely enhances, depresses, or deviates those that exist.

Ever since the triumphant day when Claude paid off his Saint-Julien estate, unburdening himself of wife and daughters, he relaxes in the country, even as his assistants loiter around his Paris door. The physiology that Magendie, and now Claude, have seeded, is flowering throughout the city. Yet, practically without my noticing, my cause, too, has massed a gang: faces bundled in scarves, hands thick-gloved, lugging sacks and crates of meek and terrified animals to transport away. Meetings, speeches, people step into lines behind or beside us—and the girls wave as if they know them all, exchanging nods and solemn looks, sometimes laughter. It's an odd feeling, this swollen crew, as what had been my private battle gets a very public push from the English anti-vivisection movement, in the form of a complaint against vivisection made straight to the Emperor by the *English Society for the Prevention of Cruelty to Animals*. In response, the Emperor sets a commission to look into the matter, headed by none other than France's top scientist, Claude Bernard.

Six months later, we gather anxiously around the *Bulletin* of the Animal Protection Society that has reprinted Claude's official "Report on Vivisection":

"...The two pamphlets (*Bell's Life*, and *Vivisections, or Atrocities Committed in France*) to which the Academy's attention was drawn, attack: 1. Experiments of every kind on any living animal used by physiologists for scientific ends; and 2. Operations made at the veterinary schools...According to these accusations, you would think that the scientists, professors, and students engaged habitually, or even momentarily, in vivisections, wear the hypocritical mask of science either to serve their egos or to excuse their atrocities, and that they prolong the vivisections to satisfy heinous pleasures...

Experiments on living animals have always caused a terrible feeling, true for all the people of the world. We limit ourselves to general practices, performed within restricted limits, and conditioned by appropriate forms, at least in our schools, which the authors of these articles have ignored. Additionally, we always seek to shorten suffering as much as possible, and to soften pain through diverse methods which science possesses, such as chloroform, ether, narcotics, cold, compression, sectioning a nerve... Unfortunately, in certain studies, for example in those that explore the functions of the nervous system, pain itself is often a display, an absolutely necessary guide.

What surprises us is to see people, enemies with no experience or understanding of physiological operations, approving of bullfighting, hunting, cock-fights, forced work, to which animals are often condemned in public! In the schools, each cut of the knife is done for science; in the circus, the injuries, anguish, exhaustion, and death are presented without complaint. Those are the spectacles that should be forbidden in every country; useless and dangerous spectacles, cruel and immoral! But let's get back to our subject. In research on living animals, the goal justifies and legitimizes the means, in the same way that a gifted surgeon, when he amputates a limb or removes a tumor, is supported, encouraged, calmed by the thought of the happy ending which will result. 'Kill an animal,' said Plutarch, 'but with compassion and regret, not for fun or pleasure, nor with cruelty.' And anyway, cruelty toward animals is punished in France by the Grammont law.

Experiments on living animals are indispensible to physiology. Services rendered by vivisection are immeasurable; just ask all the doctors, the surgeons, the naturalists. Vivisection has proven itself against old absurd fantasies, baseless systems, and nameless hypotheses that have reigned for too long in science. Physiology, experimental and positivist, has given life science a new certainty that it never had. Its conquests are now counted by the hundreds.

Physiologists have been criticized for haphazardly applying results obtained on living animals that don't resemble man. This critique, on first glance, might seem just. It would be right, if we always operated on invertebrates, even though these too can provide immense help in a number of cases. But even more help is true when studying animals with cerebrospinal nerves, equipped with five senses and four limbs, possessing a four-chambered heart, two kidneys, two lungs, a diaphragm…Secondly, it's been alleged that what we observe based on bodies stimulated by pain could never be exactly the same as what happens in the normal state of organs in ordinary life conditions. 'Torture asks and pain responds.' This objection is far from accurate. For if it's true that suffering engenders a disruption in the working of certain parts, this disturbance is rare and minimal, and we can always take it into account. But normally no derangement happens, and the results are rigorously identical to those we'd see in the normal state. Let's not dwell more on this truth. Experiments shouldn't be permitted except by master physiologists, competent professors, and elite men of science who have a well-determined goal and who know how to use proper method, quickly and expediently…It is right to say, 'One should never capriciously spill blood or produce pain, and he who interprets life's mysteries should have an elevated mind, a forgiving soul and innocent hands.' (Littré)

Finally, we address the last question: what is the purpose of repeating in public demonstrations those physiological operations on living animals that show students previously established facts? The Commission believes these operations are not absolutely necessary, and we could abandon them. Vivisections, above all, are laboratory experiments. It's therefore useless, possibly even dangerous, to offer them as a show: studious curiosity doesn't gain much, and the public's sensibility can lose a considerable amount."

I throw the *Bulletin* crumpled into the fireplace, where smoke takes a tentative interest and swirls mysteriously, as though biding its time. After a while it seems there won't be ignition, even though the smallest spark can make a city burn. This smoke's too alternately aimless and frantic, and the damp paper won't catch.

Mr Bouvier, 'Follow-up on the Vivisection Discussion':

"We heard, gentlemen, that there were abuses in live animal experiments, and that there were urgent reforms to make in the practice of vivisections. We were given the example of public demonstrations of experimental physiology. This public instruction, gentlemen, should not need to justify itself. It is one of the glories of French science, and, as such, is undying. Magendie, who created this form, would have quoted Horace: 'I've raised a monument more eternal than bronze: *monumentum exegi oere pèrennius.*' Do you realize, gentlemen, who is the one French doctor on everyone's lips across all of German science? It's Magendie's successor: the professor of experimental physiology that we've seen come and take his place among us. And we want to mutilate his teaching? We want to interfere and ban all public experiments that support his demonstrations? We want to reduce him to the *dissertations ex cathedra*, in black cap and gown, like an academic at the Sorbonne?"

§

If an ancient hero committed an unwitting error, this was called *hamartia*, the miscalculation during which types of events are confused, where big and little change places, and judgment misses the mark. Wanting desperately to achieve something, the hero achieves the opposite, and half the audience ends up laughing at the other half. What is the best way to see this mistake, the origin of the wrong turn, the twist in phrase or idea that in twisting, twists the hands and the mouth? Pity is that pain one feels in knowing how easily we are fooled, the fool always in us to rush in the mistaken direction of crowds. For Christians, *sin* is the word for the wrong turn, and the tools used against Christ were reed, cross, nails, holy sponge, holy lance, ladder, hammer, pincers, and chains. Jesus was offered wine and myrrh to anesthetize him, even a little, but he refused because somehow the pain was speaking, and he didn't want to silence it.

A revival of the works of Goya—*Los Desastres de la Guerra* (1810-1820), depicting Napoleon's invasion of Spain—brings well-heeled crowds to the museum to admire the difficult 'truths' of war. The backgrounds of the tiny etchings are so dark and unspectacular that each image forces us to lean into the frame, while the captions keep us reminded how hard the looking is at the boundary of *voir* and *savoir*. The girls and I walk through the rooms, but later we can't help wondering if there had been even one sound coming from these pictures, could all those people tolerate them in a museum like that? Aristotle: "They pity their acquaintances, unless they are very closely connected to their own household, in that case they feel for them as they feel about their own future suffering...for the dreadful is something different from the pitiful and capable of expelling pity." So which is it—what we dread or what we pity? What we see or think, or finally, what we hear that determines what we'll do?

Darwin, from *The Expression of the Emotions in Man and Animals*:

"Claude Bernard repeatedly insists, and this deserves especial notice, that when the heart is affected it reacts on the brain; and the state of the brain again reacts through the pneumo-gastric nerve on the heart; so that under any excitement there will be much mutual action and reaction between these, the two most important organs of the body..."

Claude, from *Revue des Deux Mondes*, "Physiology of the Heart":

"This is the study of the heart by the scientific experimental point of view, but will this overturn the poets? The novelists? The philosophers? Physiology should take away our illusions and show us that the sentimental role that for all time has been attributed to the heart is no more than an arbitrary fiction. In a word, should we indicate a complete contradiction between science and art, between feeling and reason? I don't believe in this contradiction. The truth wouldn't know the difference, and the scientist's truth wouldn't contradict the artist's. On the contrary, I believe that science coming from a pure source will illuminate everyone, and that science and art should hold hands while interpreting each other and explaining each by the other.

For the physiologist, it's not the animal that lives and dies, these are organic materials made of tissues. Similarly, when a monument disintegrates, it's not the ideal of the statue that deteriorates, but only the stones that form it...Expressing feelings happens through an exchange between the heart and the head, the two perfect gears of the living machine. All these explanations, one might say, are only from the materialist side. To this I would answer that that's not the question. If it wouldn't separate me from the goals of my research, I could easily show that, in physiology, materialism leads to nothing and explains nothing; when you say you have a broken heart, it is a real physiological condition! Is the concert any less beautiful because a mathematician explains all the vibrations? The physiologist merely provides an explanation for the material basis of things. The physiologist can interpret everything the poet says—all the sayings about the heart are all true!

Science doesn't contradict the observations of art, and I'm not of the opinion that positivism should kill inspiration. It's the opposite that should happen. The artist should find in science a more stable basis, and the scientist should find in art a more assured intuition."

§

After Claude's commission, nothing but a *suggestion* against amateur vivisections changes in the Grammont law. Physiology has spread even to the medical school now. Without a husband in bed, and with my daughters older, my nights are relays of large and small dogs—caught before the lab boys have wiped their chins from dinner—packed into crates and carts, communicated at drop points, given to the drivers. It's easy to see why the self-proclaimed *writer* in this family could think that by moving out, he's successfully eliminated my role: I'm so tired during the day, I am barely visible against the backdrop of city life. "What reasonable person would do all this work, Fanny, pushed by folly, tossed from the boards?" In a fast-paced vaudeville, new characters can even appear mid-scene—for just after returning to his bachelor's life in Paris, Claude meets a young woman, Sarah Raffalovich—an ardent Republican living under the Empire—who sits in on one of his courses at Collège de France. Approaching him afterward, she asks if he can help with a medical issue (which of course he can't). Taken with her intelligence and beauty, however, he promises to find out about it, and thus begins their *intellectual* correspondence.

Claude, letter to Madame Raffalovich:

"You described the sad picture of your sufferings which, luckily, seem not too serious. I told you I don't practice medicine; but because you believe my advice might be helpful, I would be glad to listen when you would like and see if science mightn't give some small hints to make you feel better."

Jewish, from Odessa, and married to a banker relocated to Paris, Raffalovich's articles on intellectual goings-on for the St Petersburg newspaper give her reason to be out and about, and her dinner Salon is an important one to which our hero is soon invited—despite her husband's dismay that Claude wears the costume and attitude of an Imperial Senator.

Claude, to Madame Raffalovich:

"For four years I have refused most dinner invitations, and this year I also have decided not to leave my schedule that, perhaps with time, might deliver me from my intestinal affliction.....I should warn you that you'll have a pathetic guest, as I'm not allowed to eat much in the evening, and sometimes not at all. "

Claude starts dropping in on Madame Raffalovich from five o'clock until seven on Thursdays, on the pretext of needing scientific articles translated from German and Russian. His endless letters to her, often affixed with little purple flowers, bear witness to his thirst for her attention. Yet Madame Raffalovich's replies are nowhere to be found, burned on some discreet fire before this one. As I've said to myself many times: a character may be shoved offstage, but they can still be present in the audience's thoughts. Offstage is a very big place.

Claude, to Madame R:

"Dear Madame, you contain every perfection, every fine quality, every talent. You find yourself equally at ease in the highest regions of philosophy and in the most intimate details of running a house and a family. Nature has endowed you as richly as possible. As someone said: I am a soul that has chanced upon a body, and he added that it was a stupid encounter *because he found his soul so poorly housed. With you, dear Madame, there is complete harmony, beauty of the soul corresponding with beauty of the body..."*

The Goncourts, 1869, April 30: "Funny things happening! Claude Bernard's reception at the Academy keeps being put off because Patin, who is to receive him and eulogize him in the customary speech, does not know what to say. Every day poor Patin forgets at the bottom of the stairs the bit of physiology taught to him a moment before by the great physiologist in his study."

Claude to Madame R:

"What a shame that I'm not a pretty woman; one could compare me to a tender flower that can't live except with the ardent kisses of a blond Apollo and the caresses of fragrant zephyrs. Instead of that, I'm only a doddery old Academic who shouldn't even leave his room. I'm in for three or four

days as usual. I hope that the God of flus permits me to keep my promise to you for Sunday."

Letter I am forced to send to Claude through my lawyer, Boinod:
Monsieur, It's important that I tell you that I've received the details of the new demands by Madame Bernard that the alimony be fixed at 1,500 francs per month, or at least at 1,200. In general she claims a food supplement of one thousand francs, with the authority to choose an apartment to her liking, and the return of her personal furniture.

Claude, to Madame Raffalovich, New Year's Eve, 1869:
"It is three minutes to midnight. In a moment all will be changed, we will be in another time, and an everlasting barrier will separate the two eras. What will ensue from this passage from one year to another? Nothing physical, it would seem, and the hand of the clock couldn't possibly have consciousness of the great event that it is bringing about....The separation of years unquestionably bears a relation to the slow succession of astronomical phenomena, which we perceive only when their effects are accumulated in time, without their having been speeded up for it, nor their having deviated from their course. I think that it is the same for everything. All events that seem sudden and instantaneous to us are never anything but the sequelae of slow and gradual effects accumulated beforehand.

Examples: in the physiological domain, a living being falls, suddenly killed by a poison or some other kind of agent. During a certain interval, which one can lengthen as one wills, the poison accumulates without producing any effect, and it is only at the moment at which the quantity is sufficient that the effect comes—suddenly, to all appearances, but not in reality. In the mental domain: A passion suddenly explodes; no, it is only the result of effects accumulated beforehand, often, it is true, in an unconscious manner."

Madame Raffalovich invites Claude to her box at the Comédie-Française:

"*Dear Madame, I suffered greatly today, and I still had to teach my class in front of the Emperor. I would have liked to be in better shape. I hope this downturn, which happens every 7 or 8 days, will pass; that means that I hope to visit you at the Théâtre Français around 8h1/2 loge no 16—first on the side. I'll only ask your pardon for not staying until the end.*"

Later, in yet another letter:

"*Beaumarchais correctly said that life is a battle. When we're far from the crowd where the world lives, it's hard to go back to it, and when we're in it, we have to fight not to get uprooted from our ground and taken with the current. I'm now in this second phase of the fight. I must defend myself against all sorts of reports and commissions that are trying to absorb me...*"

And again:

"*I was horribly bored and tired last night at the Tuileries ball. You were right to tell me not to follow these deceptive worldly illusions and to get back to work. Science, after all, isn't a coquette and isn't capricious; she always pays back the suffering you suffer for her.*"

In April, Claude gets invited to Compiègne, the country castle of Napoleon III and Empress Eugenie. While there, he maneuvers a private audience with the Emperor, at the end of which he has succeeded in winning a salary for one assistant. The next time Claude catches the Emperor alone, he convinces him, in a brief awkward monologue, that since laboratories provide France the cradle and proving ground of modern science, they need a significant increase in government funding to reverse the dominance Prussia has built through the steady endowment of their laboratories—and more importantly that they are placed above ground, in the full light of day and with public support. Claude: "Our illustrious physiologist possesses, at Collège de France, a situation which even the worst assistants of a German university wouldn't abide; for many years, this sort of underground hovel, humid and diseased, has served as his laboratory for twenty years, has nowhere in it where one could walk with a dry shoe…Physiology has no place here, no laboratory in France, where we await a definitive installation such as they have organized abroad. Nowhere other than Germany, as reported by an eminent source, where there exist many universities with beautiful and good laboratories, many foreign and national students cultivating the science of experimental physiology." The Emperor decrees that Claude be built a laboratory at the Jardin des Plantes. Claude: "Science absorbs and devours me; it's all I ask of it, that she will let me forget my existence."

§

Anna Kingsford, I knew you'd arrived in Paris because people rushed to tell me you'd come to *kill* my husband. What a beguiling possibility! Yet given that rumor is at least half a truth, I wondered what sort of accomplice you would prove, and was glad to learn…you didn't mind being stared at up on your lecture platform, trying to save our country from its shame.

From the *Bulletin* of the Animal Protection Society:
"Madame Algernon Kingsford, medical student, member of the *International Society for the Total Suppression of Vivisection*, proposes to translate and publish, in the Bulletin, extracts of documents produced by that Society."

Anna Kingsford, if we'd met, wouldn't I have badgered you with questions? How did you possess such courage? How do you ignore the jeers and taunts? Edward Maitland, your companion-biographer, says you were weak at birth, that your parents laid you out exposed, another mouth to feed, you barely cried—but lived. Later, garden flowers became your companions, and from your first years you read dreams. Anna Kingsford, dreamer, what do you see? Unconscious cerebrations, clothes in clouds? Garments of intertwining threads? You can't breathe—or can you? You were never quite made of skin. You told your story through a man's mouth, or did you?

Above the crowd, you argue that pain is pain, no matter the subject; injustice, injustice, no matter the victim; you know the experience of the hunt on the fox. In Stratford-in-Essex you were born Annie Bonus, John's 12th and last child, precociously devouring the literature of persecuted heroines, collapsing like hounded beasts. Woman with horns, the beauty of an animal, the weakness of an animal, the strengths of an animal strapped to a table. A moon rises blood red sometimes, and you wrote a book of poems—and then at seventeen, a novel of Saint Beatrice, "left almost alone, an orphan and a Christian, in the midst of a pagan people." Even then you had the habit of freezing the narrative, to study Beatrice in a striking pose: the "motionless figure" tinted by moonlight "with a hue that made her appear rather like...a piece of exquisite statuary than a living form." You set your precocious epic in Christian Rome, seized with the martyr of the primitive Church. Beatrice reclaims her beheaded brothers from the Tiber, burying them Antigone-like, and by your pen takes her prison sentence with rapture, while pagan Lysias is punished with "all the terrors attendant on an evil conscience." A review of your book said: "[Annie Bonus] displays great research and a depth of religious feeling, which is the more pleasing because wholly free from exaggeration. Although in these days it is rare that any are permitted to win the 'bright peculiar crown' of martyrdom through the baptism of blood, yet in the most quiet uneventful life there will ever be found occasions for stern self-sacrifice..." You chased oracles after dreaming, then wrote of a girl whose visions are mistaken for fits. "The nighttime of the body is the daytime of the soul."

By twenty, a suffrage campaigner and editor of the *Ladies Own Paper*, you argue women's rights under the name Ninon Kingsford, describing the fate of an aspiring woman doctor told she cannot pursue medicine: "This aim frustrated, her only design crossed, she is thrown on her own resources for her enjoyment, and because these, through defective education, are shallow and superficial…she stands, another Andromeda, bound to the rock on the sea-shore….shackled by the chains of ignorance, a helpless prey to that terrible monster whose name is 'Ennui.' But to the educated man, what heights, what depths, are accessible! Like Perseus, he leaps from the edge of the high cliff…When will Perseus come to deliver the fair Andromeda, to loosen her fetters, and to set her free?" As an editor, you "combine aesthetics with the ethics of the liberal school in the world of women"—to show a better view of the "new women" most often depicted as "a hard, unlovely crew, contemners of art and taste, barbaric, implacable Gorgons, in whose vicinity no fair or graceful thing can endure, but whose very aspect freezes into stone all living forms of beauty." Under pressure you marry your cousin Algernon, a pastor at Shropshire who promises you can use your father's inheritance as you see fit, if you will only write his sermons. You and your daughter Eadith worry at each other, and motherhood's obligations stifle you.

Your friend Florence Miller recalls, "Mr Kingsford, assisted by a buxom and capable young woman (who was called, I think, Belinda) as cook-housekeeper, did the housekeeping; he ordered the meals, and arranged all the details of daily life. On the other hand, as we sat at dinner in the evening of my arrival, and my hostess was planning what we should do the next day, Mr Kingsford quite simply said,—'You know, Nina, tomorrow is Saturday, and that sermon is not altered yet.'"

Anna Kingsford:
"If I take a bird out of a wood and cut its wings, what wonder that it cannot fly? And when, after a while, I let it go about the house,

and it begins to understand that it cannot fly, what wonder that it ceases to attempt flying, and is content to hop about from room to room and from stair to stair? Well, my friends see the bird, and they say it is tame. It has lost the use of its wings, and so it goes on its legs, and is tolerably content. But one of my friends looking on—perhaps his name may be Mill—says, 'I think your pet would be happier if it could fly.'

But it is not for the actual privilege of voting itself that I would so much plead, but for the benefit that the extension of the franchise to women would bring to the whole sex. It would give women a higher place in society; it would raise them in the estimation of men; it would lift them from the level of goods and chattel to the position they ought to occupy, of citizens and responsible beings."

Florence Miller: "When Belinda, the maid, brought me my hot water on my arrival, and helped me to unpack, there came at her skirts little Eadith, 'sole daughter of the house and home.' She and I soon got on good terms…She was not at all a pretty child, totally unlike her beautiful mama; rather of the practical stodgy order, indeed—Anyhow, she was much enjoying the changes of headgear and coiffure, when her mama, hearing our chat and laughter, looked in at the door to say coldly, 'Don't take much notice of that child; if you encourage her she will be bothering you all the time.'"

The guinea pig, Rufus, will stay with you instead. "I am compelled to be a wife without a husband and mother without a child and to have a home in which I cannot dwell." Your daughter Eadith won't grow up thoughtful like you; she will be average and uninterested. How can this dreadful homelife satisfy? Spurred by a dream of Mary Magdalen, you request Catholic christening as *Maria Johanna* in the next town. You pick another name—*Colossa*—under which you publish a novel, *In My Lady's Chamber: a Speculative Romance, Touching a Few Questions of the Day*. You write still more books: vibrant women living in Greece, Gaul, India,

Venice—weaving the garment of piety across time and cultures, while your own England boils: abolition of slavery, rights of women, treatment of animals. Your essay against the growing practice of vivisection makes an impression on Frances Power Cobbe who contacts you directly, and with whom you begin to collaborate. On a visit to your older brother, you see him abstain from flesh food, a cause that becomes "the only effectual means to the world's redemption, whether as regarding men themselves or the animals."

In fine clothes, by carriage and cart, you tour the lecture platforms, distributing *An Essay on the Admission of Women to the Parliamentary Franchise*: "And now, as Mr Mill tells us—no second Miss Garrett may pass the wicket—medicine is shut henceforth upon all aspiring women. But what a grave mistake is this!—even setting aside the injustice of the act itself! How can the grand science of medicine be fully developed and appreciated by the human race, unless both sexes study it alike?"

Anna Kingsford, letter to Florence Miller:
"I think of all your papers I liked best those in which you showed by the examples of Mendelssohn's sister and Merschel's what women might be if they were not everlastingly suppressed and bullied into silence...It is the Bible and child-bearing that quenches us all and dries up the flame in our spirits. What is to be done about the babies?...Ought we all to swear virginity or adopt Malthusianism? All the shops today are full of Easter Eggs. As I looked at them I reflected on how much better it would be if we laid eggs like the happy and decent hens. I know I would take care not to hatch mine!"

You've run your paper, you've written and spoken up, but now you want your hands in the practical mess: "I am completing my education by studying medicine," you announce. "Not that I believe it will be complete even when I have my diploma; for the subject is limitless, and really leads to other subjects. For all things are related."

In England, Frances Power Cobbe has been building the anti-vivisection crusade, writing how "the smooth, cool man of science....stands near the torture trough." It's Magendie she described, first. While London won't train women doctors, Paris boasts. But your husband sees your frequent seizures, and so asks an older widower to join you and the guinea pig in France. Ed Maitland originally met you in a lecture against vivisection, and also believes "the world has but to be informed of the facts of the case as regards the practices of the physiological laboratories, to rise in overwhelming indignation against them." Later, Maitland has you descending like an apostle into hell in order to combat great spiritual evil. Where you are called "Annie" or "Nina" or "Ninon," Maitland calls you Mary, writes you as Mary, for you are her re-incarnation. You will die at 42, defenseless against the world's arrows, and as your hagiographer, this is exactly the story he wants. French so fluent, and such a charming girl—you will go to Paris! You won't touch flesh, to wear or eat. Vegetarianism becomes the outward sign of your faith. Io, lithe and beautiful, makes love with clouds. Too much a woman, you are hidden in a cow. Never enough mother, you cross the rivers. A horned virgin, naked in a clearing sky. But other women fall jealous; here's a beautiful cow lecturing on ugly things. You will sit in the back to avoid notice, you will pretend men's names and dress. You will find a small flat, rue Jacob.

Anna, letter to Florence Miller:

"Last night I attired myself in my husband's garments, screwed my hair up tight and came into the boudoir, where I lit a cigarette, sat down and awaited results. My husband, coming in with the lamp, failed at first to

recognize me. In his boots I was exactly his height: a little padding about the shoulder and waist would make everything complete."

Professors assail your senses, lecturing over the yelps and whimpers, struggling to keep down the beasts, to hold their limbs, goading you in the demonstration theater, expelling you from each lecture when you cry out.

"Look here—in my Apothecaries' Certificate they have taken 'Ninon' to be a male name and have reported themselves satisfied with 'his' proficiency. Now, Ninon is a male name. Can't I go to St George's as Mr Kingsford on the strength of that certificate?

Yours sincerely, Johann-Maria Kingsford."

Anna Kingsford, what is your rule of life? Everywhere men accost the beautiful beast, but to become an instrument of divine hands is to overthrow materialistic systems, so you said you needed an education first in the Christian churches, and then in the philosophy of science of the world's "most materialistic school, the University of Paris."

Anna K:
"My medical training is mostly to pound out of me all awareness of others as sentient creatures, to deafen me to my own conscience, and to their needs and lives, to elevate my self-regard so that I stand above all others, unmoving, unmovable. This scientific education is also, sadly, a philosophic one, a mental one."

To win against this "modern inquisition," Anna with tongue and pen out, didn't you long to hear the words, "Death of…Richet. Bert. Bernard. Pasteur"? "A method which is morally wrong cannot be scientifically right. The test of conscience is the test of soundness," Anna Kingsford. Seizure, rue Jacob. Living as the niece of this unrelated man—"My malady has resolved itself into three symptoms: bleeding from the lungs, sickness, and weakness." You fall dead to all appearances. Zoroastrians revered the despised dog as much as a murdered low-caste man, so their emperor, Ashoka of India, stopped the hunts. Other kings founded hospitals for sick and injured animals. Da Vinci buys caged animals from the market to free them and is vegetarian. You hold these images in your fever dreams where all times meet.

Florence Miller: "No doubt it would have been good for Nina if I had accompanied her, for, as it was, Mr Kingsford (who, of course, could never leave his parish work for very long) invited their elderly friend Mr Edward Maitland to take some sort of charge of Nina during her residence in Paris, and it was Maitland's influence that led her into the strange medley of so-called inspiration, mysticism, and revelation received by dreams, passive writing, and intuitive listening to spiritual voices, that was (and is) regarded by a certain number of people as her chief claim to remembrance, but that greatly diminished confidence in her wisdom and respect for her professional learning in the world at large...The drawback that all this 'inspired utterance' was to her professional and social influence she incurred as an addition to the unfortunate scandal to which her close association with Maitland, growing more continuous and open year after year, inevitably subjected her, notwithstanding her husband's sanction to this intimacy. She met Maitland soon after I first knew her. He was already an elderly man (55, or more, I should think) and physically a plain and heavy one and dull and unattractive in conversation..."

According to Edward Maitland, your *New Gospel of Interpretation* started in your asthma or your neuralgia, from sciatic and facial nerves numb over the body, or the cautery, red hot iron—or injections of laudanum leading to horrors so intense they try chloroform to subdue it—the combination knocks you out. Spasms and fainting. They try to keep you asleep, in a coma. They can't keep you from dreaming.

§

In exile on Guernsey, a saddened Victor Hugo sits beside Aeschylus, Molière, Shakespeare—even a restored Satan himself—at his séance table. Bored by even this conversation, he invites others to chime in: Sappho, Homer, the Wandering Jew. Isn't he lucky to converse with such timeless souls? Wanting to push his séances farther, he holds the spirits longer, asking the Archangel *Idea* to interpret their words and thoughts, while he walks the garden with his beloved Juliette, leaving his spirit to write out his questions.

While Victor Hugo makes séances, you never believed such faddish things, preferring to study the elements common to all religions: "The Perfect Way seeks to make peace between Science and Faith...to bring together East and West...to unite Buddhist philosophy with Christian love, by demonstrating that the basis of religion is not historical, but spiritual."

But poor Hugo lost his favorite daughter—drowned boating on the Seine—and he clings to finding her, and perhaps gaining wisdom, maybe even a little understanding, from those who have come before.

Hugo's *Doctrine of the Table*:

Man is an alien who comes from and returns to the sky.

We go to the sky by the union of love and thought where love includes and gives soul to all animals, plants, pebbles; the dog is our comrade in exile, the tree our kin, the pebble our brother.

The tables add thought and doubt to Christianity.

Man doesn't start on earth, but expiates his sins committed in other lives.

We don't therefore suffer for the crimes of others, generations gone suffer because Adam was bad—God becomes just.

There is an eternity of souls but not an eternity of punishments.

This is a bigger truth than all the religions.

§

Why do you compare yourself to Io, Zeus's lover-cow tied to a tree, with Argus, hundred-eyed, to guard her? Maybe it's because when Io finally escapes, she becomes a wanderer unknown even to her family. In jealousy, Hera sends a gadfly to bite the grazing beast, chasing her to foreign shores in loveless exile. Paris is a city of enemies in a country of enemies, a place which should break apart but won't. Shopping or just strolling, factions hide in plain sight. Family not speaking to family, neighbor to neighbor, suspicious that each is the cause of all that's wrong for everyone else. How could your father recognize you, a cow lowing ankle-deep in mud? The only way to make yourself known is to scratch your name as a hoofprint in the silky river sediment, an inscription that lasts less than a moment.

In class, the *Elementary Book of Physiology* instructs you how to shave animals and cover them in shellac to suppress the function of their skin. You learn that they die of asphyxiation in 6-12 hours. But really, you spend your time stalking Professor Bernard, to witness his activity in the laboratory where there are no furies, no vengeance, and the audience regards all this as they would any theater, set apart from its consequences, uninflected, unimpeachable, impervious to blame. And what does he do, Rufus, your red-brown guinea pig, always in your arms or a custom basket? Maitland says you call yourself anti-humanist—"and if that means that I'm against the positioning of humans above all else, I am an anti-humanist and proud."

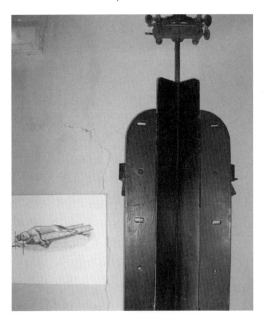

Anna Kingsford:

"Very shortly after my entry as a student at the Paris Medical School, and when as yet I was new to the horrors of the vivisectional method, I was one morning, while studying alone in the Natural History Museum, suddenly disturbed by a frightful burst of screams, of a character more distressing than words can convey, proceeding from some chamber on another side of the building. I called the porter in charge of the museum, and asked him what it meant. He replied with a grin, 'It is only the dogs being vivisected in the laboratory.' I expressed my horror; and he retorted, scrutinizing me with surprise and amusement—for he could never before have heard a student speak of vivisection in such terms—'What do you want? It's for science.' Therewith he left me, and I sat down alone and listened.

As much as I had heard and said and even written before that date about vivisection, I found myself for the first time in its actual presence, and there swept over me a wave of such extreme mental anguish that my heart stood still under it...It seemed as if suddenly all the laboratories of torture throughout Christendom stood open before me, with their manifold unutterable agonies exposed, and the awful future the atheistic science was everywhere making for the world, rose up and stared me in the face. Then and there, burying my face in my hands, with tears of agony I prayed for strength and courage to labour effectively for the abolition of so vile a wrong, and to do at least what one heart and one voice might to root this curse of torture from the land."

At the base of the stairs of the main medical school building stands the statue of a lovely girl disrobing for all to see. She holds folds of a cloth immodestly above her torso, with the carved words: *Nature Reveals Herself to Science.* The central courtyard is sealed from the street, and students fill it busily. Still, it is the marble girl who silently invites attention. Claude: "The nature of matter does not determine the force which directs it or the effect which it produces. Example: a church or a monument produces in us a particular effect that depends on its form, on its architecture, etc. But the nature of the stone is unimportant."

Goethe's Faust:

"Mysterious in the light of day, Nature in veils, will not let us perceive her, and what she is unwilling to betray, you cannot wrest from her with thumbscrews, wheel, or lever."

Claude, from *Introduction to the Study of Experimental Medicine*, "...the experimenter doubtless forces nature to unveil herself by attacking her with all manner of questions...[he] must note her answer, hear her out, and in every case heed her decision."

When you visit him to speak out, the chief of the University of Paris hospital, Leon Le Fort, argues that vivisection is "necessary as a protest on behalf of the independence of science against the interference of clerics and moralists. When all the world has reached to the high intellectual level of France, and no longer believes in God, the soul, moral responsibility, or any nonsense of that kind, but makes practical utility the only rule of conduct, then, and not until then, can science afford to dispense with vivisection."

You reply: "If torture were indeed the true method of science, then would the vaunted tree of knowledge be no other than the upas tree of oriental legend, beneath whose fatal shadow lie hecatombs of miserable victims slain by its poisonous exhalations, the odor of which is fraught with agony and death!" To refute the vitalists, and to display the animal-machine, your professor, de Lanessan, shows the "beating of a fish's heart, grafting of a rat's paw, decapitation of a dog, development of a tadpole's tail—all continuing after the deaths of the *'original'* creatures." Original creatures? You laugh—looking around—what does that mean?

Socrates: "The bodies of men and beasts are warm and living as long as they breathe, and as soon as the breath leaves the body, not only do warmth and motion cease, but the body begins to decay. Life, therefore, is breath, and breath is air, and as air is eternal and inseparable in its very nature, therefore the soul or portion of air which gave animation to the body will not perish at the dissolution of the body."

You repeat the notion that any new creature taking a breath of life inhales a new soul, the same particles that animated some other body. Plato told of souls traveling ten thousand years to take rebirth depending on their actions. You quote Menander who, when asked by Credo what to transmigrate into, says: "Make me anything rather than man, for he is the only creature that prospers by injustice." But in your anti-vivisection speeches, you forgo philosophy and describe instead the animal experiments you've seen, until the audience covers their ears and shouts "Stop!"—all to the amusement of medical students who come to disrupt. Frances Cobbe calls this tactic of quoting the scientists, *realism*, for "Nothing has been inserted save verbatim extracts with reference in most cases from the actual reports of the vivisectors themselves, as published in their own books and in the scientific journals, or abridgments of the same." On the street corners, your speeches compete with the collapse of buildings, and evenings of last-minute markets. Above the cacophony you stand and shout: "Citizens and Women-Citizens of Paris! An abominable crime is every day committed in your midst…"

§

Paris also becomes the city of your dreams: "Dry air, high levels, and a crisp, calm, exhilarating atmosphere favor its activity….It is not, therefore, surprising that the greater number of these dreams, and, especially, the most vivid, detailed, and idyllic, have occurred to me while on the continent."

Anna Kingsford, *The Bird and the Cat*: "I dreamt that I had a beautiful bird in a cage, and that the cage was placed on a table in a room where there was a cat. I took the bird out of the cage and put him on the table. Instantly the cat sprang upon him and seized him in her mouth. I threw myself upon her and strove to wrest away her prey, loading her with reproaches and bewailing the fate of my beautiful bird. Then suddenly someone said to me, 'You have only yourself to blame for this misfortune. While the bird remained in his cage he was safe. Why should you have taken him out before the eyes of the cat?'"

Even René Descartes (the scientific 'Our Father' invoked by your professors) was no stranger to the power of dreams. In a state of "enthusiasm" (which he imagined could have only come from 'on high') he limped along a crowded road of ghosts. In a second dream, thunder and sparks from the fireplace threaten to burn everything around him. Finally, asleep a third time, he dreams he is confronted by a dictionary, and a book of poems, and the question of how to lead his life: which is the way? The pages open but the important ones are missing. A poem begins "it is and it isn't" and suddenly all resemblances between events in the world and human lives aren't what they seem—in fact, he realizes, meaning is only made by the human mind—and 'nature' is only the mind's seizure of the world as an object of thought; it is not real. Thus Descartes becomes a doubter, beset with fears of the all-powerful delusion that he might be dreaming when he's actually awake. His *Meditations* feature a hero distancing himself from the world, an observer able to ignore the spectacle of the senses. The hero's body (and its "ressorts, leviers, canaux, filtres, cribles, pressoirs") exists only as a machine, toward which the mind sits detached, guiding when it can.

"How can the immaterial soul influence the material body?" the Princess Elisabeth of Bohemia challenges Descartes in her first letter, attempting a dialogue. Theirs turns into one of many of his *amours intellectuels*—intercourse through discourse. Elisabeth's challenges sharpen his ideas, and she becomes a leader of the Cartésiennes, women rationalists championing intellectual exiles. Preferring books to heirs, the women take literary pseudonyms: "Sapho," "Theodamas," "Acante"—and yet despite the equality dualism promises, Elisabeth opposes Descartes' sequestering of the mind from its body. She writes to him of the "responsibility of enunciation" by which the enunciating subject must be responsible for the status of the objects of which it speaks.

Descartes, from a letter to the Marquess of Newcastle, 1646:

"In fact, none of our external actions can show anyone who examines them that our body is not just a self-moving machine but contains a soul with thoughts, with the exception of words, or other signs that are relevant to particular topics, without expressing any passion. I say words or other signs, because deaf-mutes use signs as we use spoken words; and I say that these signs must be relevant, to exclude the speech of parrots, without excluding the speech of madmen, which is relevant to particular topics even though it does not follow reason. I add also that these words or signs must not express any passion, to rule out not only cries of joy or sadness, but also whatever can be taught by training to animals. . .

Now it seems to me very striking that the use of words, so defined, is something peculiar to human beings. Montaigne and Charron may have said that there is more difference between one human being and another than between a human being and an animal; but there has never been known an animal so perfect as to use a sign to make other animals understand something which expressed no passion. . .This seems to me a very strong argument to prove that the reason why animals do not speak as we do is not that they lack the organs but that they have no thoughts."

§

Limping home after a rough night, my hands feel brittle. Beyond the high walls of private homes, I imagine the candle-lit windows of exquisite salons where illustrious appetites serve themselves a savory feast. "To life!" they toast, "whatever it is!" The guests smile and raise their goblets. "Of what is life made?" they wonder, as tauntingly they turn toward the darkness. "Fanny, what is your idea? What do you think life is?"—bursting into laughter at my silence.

Buffon: "Life is a minotaur eating the organism."

Poe: "Have I not told you that what you mistake for madness is but over-acuteness of the senses?"

Claude: "Anyone who says, 'Well, that's life!' is merely explaining darkness with still greater darkness."

Poe: "A low, dull, quick sound such as a watch makes when enveloped in cotton."

"Life and death, are they the same?" Claude gives the example of a girl, beautiful one day, dead the next—and her body giving in to the same forces—air, humidity, heat—that it was surrounded by in life—but in death can't fight—can't resist—so the living body becomes united with the outside elements. Only with a superior vital force do living creatures not succumb to what's outside.

Bichat: "Life is the ensemble of functions that resists death."

Poe: "Observe how healthily—how calmly I can tell you the whole story."

Blainville: "Life is a double internal movement of decomposition both general and continuous."

Claude: "It's not worth defining life—everyone knows it when they see it and you can't separate them—what is dead, lived, what is alive, will die. The first thing is to know it; the definition can only be given afterward."

Spencer: "Life is the combination defined by heterogenous changes both simultaneous and successive."

Claude: "If we wanted to express that all the vital functions are the necessary consequence of an organic combustion, we would repeat what we've just said: Life is Death."

Kant: "Life is the internal principle of action."

Claude: "The organized matter of the brain which manifests the phenomena of sensibility and intellect peculiar to the living state has no greater awareness of the thought and the phenomena that it manifests than the brute nature of the inert machine, a clock for example, has awareness of the movements that it manifests or the hour that it indicates; nor any more than printed characters and paper have awareness of the ideas that they recount. To say that the brain secretes thought is equivalent to saying that the clock secretes time or the idea of time."

It is rumored that Descartes' wife stormed in to stop Descartes' use of their family dog, Monsieur Graf, for his experiments, screaming that the poor thing was just springs and hinges to him.

Claude: "Life is only a word that means ignorance."

Yet the girls and I know how an injured creature says "stay away," communicating danger to the group as it devises its best way free. Being able to recognize death increases survival in those who see it clearly—to stay away in deed and thought and avoid its source.

In Euripedes' Satyr play, Sisyphus asks, "Why invent Gods at all?" He reasons it is to make visible our secrets, and thereby enforce morality. Without gods, who would ever know our thoughts? What would ever make us do the right thing? Secrets are why Sisyphus was visited by Death in the first place—because he told things that were not his to tell.

In the censorious context of 5th century Athens, only the theater could allow anyone, especially a hoodlum like Sisyphus, to speak atheism so directly.

Claude: "A created organism is a machine which necessarily works by virtue of the physico-chemical properties of its constituent elements…. But the term 'vital' properties is only provisional, because we call properties *vital* which we have not yet been able to reduce to physico-chemical terms; but in that we shall doubtless succeed someday."

Descartes: "But though I regard it as established that we cannot prove there is any thought in animals, I do not think it is thereby proved that there is not, since the human mind does not reach into their hearts."

After releasing Death from his closet back to Ares, Sisyphus has so thoroughly angered Zeus that Zeus hastily sends Death back for him. There Sisyphus rests on his bench, admiring how beautifully Orpheus charms even the stones, and how he snuck in and out of the underworld alive. Seeing Death approaching, Sisyphus devises a new trick. Running home, he dares his wife Merope (whom he knows doesn't love him) to throw his naked corpse into the town square once Death claims him, a sacrilege he's sure she will gladly perform. Later, in the underworld, Sisyphus makes a great show of how wronged he was by her profane act, until Persephone is forced to release him to earth's surface to avenge his improper burial. Unbound from Hell, he henceforth refuses to leave the upper world, prefering life as a fugitive.

CLAUDE'S RED NOTEBOOK:

One of the finest achievements of modern science is to have proven that forces are never lost; the same for matter. There is only transformation of energy of one kind into another. Motion, heat, light, electricity, etc.

Is there something analogous in physiology? When, for example, the spinal cord of an animal is cut so that its heat diminishes and its muscular irritability increases, there is then a more intense muscular and nervous electricity. Reflect on its application to intellectual and other faculties...

Do sleep and wakefulness represent supplementary states in which there is a transformation of one force into another?

§

More and more people mock us in the streets as we try to manage our unruly ménage. They yell "Zoophilists!" and think we are no more than outcasts, though the girls have friends now and even go partying. I wonder what my daughters say about me when they're out, or hear said, but anyway I tell myself I'm no better or worse than the average sinner, offering hasty confession and minor indulgences so that saintly martyrs, washed completely in their fires, may move upward through the gates. Saint Francis who shook hands with a wolf in agreement for no more violence. Saint Neot who saved hares and stags from huntsmen. Saint Godric who saved birds from snakes. Saint Aventure who stole a stag from hunters. Saint Carileff, too. Saint Monacella who protected a hare from the hounds, as did Saint Anselm and Saint Isidore. Finally I give some extra *sous* for the Hermit of Eskdale who saved a boar and was killed, Saint Anthony, patron of lower animals, Saint Francis, brother ant, and Saint Nannon who established a Sanctuary for Fleas in Connaught, Ireland.

In the changing political winds, a street switches names from rue de Dix Decembre to rue de Six Novembre, but smells don't know dates, and the dates don't mean much to the dogs we hand off at these meeting-points. Many anxious nights begin this way: all the familiar streets replaced by billowing steam and piles of rock. There is no clock in the forest where Paris was. The river is brown and swollen with the run-off of last night's storm. I'm fleeing into the center of the flooded grove, wild-eyed and frantic to catch any creature before it is snagged by the soldiers surrounding us on the last patch of dry land. God punished the corrupted, violent earth with a flood to set everything back to the beginning. I see bizarre dragons, leathery and feathered, as I come within arm's length, and they hop off hissing along the bank. Iridescent greens and pinks, a large blue patch, yellow tails and spots of red along each side—their eyes blink slowly before they spring to the tip of the island where others gather. They are hunting our souls, or they are indifferent, I am dreaming or just mental, I can't be sure.

§

Francis Bacon: "For like as a man's disposition is never well known or proved till he be crossed, nor Proteus ever changed shapes till he was straitened and held fast, so nature exhibits herself more clearly under the trials and vexations of art than when left to herself."

Francis Bacon, our hero's hero, believed that a novel might best express the goals of experimental science. So he set *A New Atlantis* at Solomon's House in an imagined Bensalem, and cast a lost ship of European explorers ashore, where they find a magnificent university. In this fictional world, the scientists are constrained, as one character explains to the castaways: "We have three that try new experiments, such as themselves think good. These we call pioneers or miners. Then we have three that take care to direct new experiments, of a higher light, more penetrating into nature than the former. These we call lamps. We have three others that execute the experiments so directed, and report them. These we call inoculators. Lastly, we have three that raise the former discoveries by experiments into greater observations, axioms, and aphorisms. These we call interpreters of nature." The castaways witness a "feast of the family" headed by "the father of the family, whom they call the Tirsan." The mother is kept behind a wall of glass "where she sitteth but is not seen." Parks and zoos are full with animals: "We also try all poisons and other medicines upon them as well as chirurgery and physic."

CLAUDE'S RED NOTEBOOK:

Mental anticipation, as Bacon says, depends upon a fact or an idea.

In physiology it depends always on the idea that there is a use for everything. Today we still look for the use of the parts.

Like Descartes, Bacon worried that the rational mind can't fend off illusions, which he described as Four Idols: *Idols of the Tribe*, crooked mirrors which distort external things; *Idols of the Cave*, beliefs which seem true despite all evidence; *Idols of the Market Place,* images and senses; and *Idols of the Theatre*, traditional philosophies, which, like plays, render fictional worlds that are never experimentally tested.

§

I kneel in St-Sulpice among the statues and paintings, and I can't help but wonder if we should think of Saints as examples of behavior, or if they only serve to remind us to see everything we do from God's point

of view instead of our own. In our lives, we have opinions and prefer-
ences, we like and we hate, we care or don't, we think and we do and we
believe. But God's perspective? Knowing everything, being everywhere
and nowhere? How are we different from inert substance in his sight?

Claude, from *Introduction to the Study of Experimental Medicine*:
"The experimenter who finds himself facing natural phenomena is like a
spectator watching silent scenes. He is in some way the magistrate of nature,
only instead of being in the grip of men who want to fool him with lying
confessions or false witness, he's working with natural phenomena which
are (for him) characters of whom he doesn't know either the language or the
customs, who live in circumstances which are unknown to him and which
he still wants to understand the intentions. For that he uses all the devices
imaginable and, as we might say, he lies to know the truth. In all this, the
experimenter reasons in his way and gives nature his own ideas."

Then the girls and I pass through the Tuileries, and the colorful box
stage of the marionettes. We watch, but we are big-headed simpletons
dressed in our rag-clothes. Piousness is indicated by the presence of a
puppet-priest who follows us around, occasionally shouting orders as we
rush to make prostrations. Claude is a larger-headed puppet, dressed in a
laboratory smock, followed by puppets carrying wilted bouquets of rabbits sewn to their hands. Side to side they bend to collect rabbits that
sprout from the stage. There is no dialogue in the puppet show, there
is nothing left behind. But grabbing the puppets from the puppeteers'
hands, the girls and I fling them straight at the crowd, who, children,
pull them on their hands and dance.

Bernard de Fontenelle, *On the Plurality of Worlds*:
"Nature is a great spectacle, which resembles an Opera. From where you sit
in the Opera, you don't see the Theater exactly as it is. The decorations and
Machines have been arranged in order to create a pleasing effect from afar,
and the wheels and counterweights that create all the motions have been hidden from your view. So you don't have to bother guessing how everything is

done. Only some stagehand hidden in the orchestra might perhaps be interested in the extraordinary Flight and might want to know exactly how it was executed. You see, the Stagehand is rather like a Philosopher. But what increases the difficulty for Philosophers is that in the Machines that Nature presents to our view, the cords are so perfectly hidden that we have taken a long time to guess what causes the motions of the Universe.

Imagine all the sages at an opera—Pythagorases, Platos, Aristotles, and all those whose names are drummed into our ears. Suppose that they watched Phaeton lifted by the winds, but they can't discover the wires and don't know how the backstage area is arranged. One of them would say, 'Phaeton has a certain hidden property that makes him lighter.' Another: 'Phaeton is composed of certain numbers that make him rise.' Another: 'Phaeton has a certain attraction to the top of the theater, and he is uneasy if he's not up there.' Still another: 'Phaeton wasn't made for flying, but he would rather fly than leave a vacuum in the upper part of the stage.' And there are a hundred other notions which I'm astonished haven't destroyed the reputation of the whole of Antiquity. Finally, Descartes and some other moderns come along, and they say: 'Phaeton rises because he's pulled by wires, and because a weight heavier than he is descends.' Nowadays we no longer believe that a body will move if it's not affected by another body and in some fashion pulled by wires; we don't believe that it will rise or fall except when it has a spring or a counterweight. Whoever sees nature as it truly is simply sees the backstage area of the Theater.'

'In that case,' said the Marquise, 'nature has become very mechanical.'

'So mechanical,' I replied, 'that I fear we'll soon grow ashamed of it. They want the world to be merely, on a large scale, what a watch is on a small scale, so that everything goes by regular movements based on the organization of its parts. Admit it! Didn't you have a more grandiose concept of the universe, and didn't you give it more respect than it deserved? Most men esteem it less since they've come to know it.'"

Bernard de Fontenelle wrote poems and a play that failed miserably when produced. He burned the play. He wrote an opera that also failed, and some more bad poetry—but he achieved renown with *Dialogues of the Dead,* in which both living and legendary people hold far-ranging debates. Fascinated by the immensity of the universe, and by the moral implications of expanding empires, Fontenelle wrote *On the Plurality of Worlds,* dialogues between a teacher and a female student, a popular genre. The mixing of amateurs in both science and philosophy was feeding a booming market of cords, weights, boxes, and bell jars—the stagecraft industry of salon theaters that provided anti-academy havens where discourses could unite in improvised conversation. The salons fit easily with the 'notebook method' of learning, until Descartes began arguing for systems, consistent in method and materials. Because Descartes included women in his systems, said the Countess, "we owe him honors." "Without him men might still take us for machines." Galileo was born of salons, though he worried about spies who might denounce what they heard. Montaigne: "Conversation is born free." Madame de Scudery, writing as Sapho, advised, "Speak too much or too little is how you must speak." Like Fontenelle, she set her dialogues in gardens, and in her books there is no protagonist, no consistent narrator or authorial voice, just a sequence of entertaining verbal adventures: *Conversations on Diverse Subjects*.

Fontenelle, second evening's dialogue:

"We want to judge everything, and we're always at a bad vantage point. We want to judge ourselves, we're too close; we want to judge others, we're too far away. If one could be between the Earth and the Moon, that would be the proper place to see them well. One should simply be a spectator of the world, not an inhabitant." On the third evening, the Marquis responds: "I confess my weakness; I'm not capable of such perfect impartiality; I need to believe."

Salons these days are pure politics, and barely imitate those old salons. Educated people no longer engage in 'scientific method'—the natural world increasingly handled only by experts in their dank *theatrum mundi*. Yet there are plenty of Dinners to keep Paris occupied, and Claude is admitted to the popular Dinner of Upstarts (for people without inherited wealth) where he consorts with Delacroix, Dumas, Saint-Beuve. The competing salon is the exclusive Dinner Magny on rue Contrescarpe-Dauphine, with its very few members: Gautier, Taine, Renan, Berthelot, Flaubert, les Goncourts, and George Sand. Claude is a popular guest there, too. Other salons include: Dinner des Gens d'Esprit, Dinner du Vendredi, Dinner Bixio. The Goncourts: "He is interesting to listen to and agreeable to look at, this Claude Bernard. He has the handsome head of a good man, the scientific apostle. Then he has a 'we have found' so distinguished when speaking of his discoveries."

The Goncourts: "—seen tonight, rue de Courcelles, Claude Bernard, looking just like a ghost of science." Rue de Courcelles is the Princess Mathilde's house—where on Wednesdays the intelligentsia gather. Claude is brought by Saint-Beuve, the literary counselor to the Princess. The Goncourts: "Courcelles. The salon is lively tonight. Among the guests, two returning: Gautier, very pale, his lion eyes even more caved in; Claude Bernard, who has the face of a man just pulled from his grave... The conversation gets around to modern marriage, this marriage without courtship, without even flirtation, this brutal, cynical form of marriage that we called 'rape in the presence of the mayor with the encouragement of the parents.'"

Contemplating the wisdom of the pious can only help lead my girls to virtue, and with the temptations to care more about one's clothing than one's soul, the lives and examples of saints couldn't be more timely.

By the fourth evening, the Marquise submits:
"Finally, whatever the sun might be, it seems entirely unfit for habitation. It's a shame; the location would be ideal. We'd be at the center of everything, we'd see all the planets turning regularly around ourselves, instead of which we see an infinity of peculiarities in their paths because we're not in the proper place to judge well, that is to say in the center of their movement. Isn't it pitiful? There's only one place in the world where the study of the stars would be extremely easy, and precisely at that point there's no one." Fontenelle: "The sun would be a home only for the blind."

The Goncourts: "—Tonight, great praise for the Princess to be able to carry on chatting with stupid women and fools—and, even more curious, staying on topic about a painting of Guerchin! But nothing was weirder than how crucified she seemed in turning from our conversation with the great and seductive scientist Claude Bernard, obliged to respond to two blatherers. Once they'd left, she cried, 'Really! It's enough to dawdle in the world until thirty years old, but then one should retire and never bore society to death again!'"

In 1666, the Academy of Sciences was founded to challenge the salons and caused a split between experimentalists and conversationalists. The Jacobin clubs closed to women in 1793, along with the possibility of suffrage. The interests of the state increasingly aligned with the frontiers of knowledge, until states and knowledge grew so roughly together, the old salons were emptied of both women and conversation.

Fontenelle:

"The logic of mathematics is like that of love. You can't grant a lover the least favor without soon having to grant more, and still more, and in the end it's gone awfully far. Well, if you grant a mathematician the least principle, he'll draw a conclusion from it that you must grant him too, and from that conclusion another, and in spite of yourself he'll lead you so far you'll have trouble believing it." By the fifth evening, the Marquise's perspective is radically changed: "But here's a universe so large that I'm lost, I no longer know where I am, I'm nothing."

"And as for me,' I answered, 'this puts me at ease."

"You offer me a kind of perspective so vast that my eyes can't reach the end of it... And in effect, aren't all the inhabitants nearly annihilated by the phrase you have to use in speaking of them? You're forced to call them: 'inhabitants of one of the planets of one of these infinite vortices.' We ourselves, to whom the same phrase applies—admit that you'd scarcely know how to pick us out of so many worlds. I'm beginning to see the Earth so frighteningly small that I believe hereafter I'll never be impressed by another thing."

Fontenelle:

"I'm satisfied to have taken your mind as far as your eyes can see. I have only to draw the curtain and to show you the world."

Returning home, I can imagine how dearly Claude values the devotion of his energetic new assistant, d'Arsonval, who cheerily risks my wrath mounting my stairs to claim or deliver things. Claude eventually wills his unpublished papers to this man because he's so intrepid. The girls and I have grown used to these bit-part players entering and exiting our scenes, providing our remaining link to the hero we never see in the flesh again. Claude's wild neglect of his family is evidenced in thinning cupboards, and an increased community of animals play-fighting under the tables or lounging on the beds.

Marquise:

"The other worlds may make this one little to you, but they don't spoil lovely eyes, or a beautiful mouth; those have their full value despite all the possible worlds."

§

Not far from where Claude and I first lived, Émile Zola and his girlfriend take a small apartment on rue de l'École-de-Médecine. When Alexandrine first met Zola, he hadn't published a word, and was a clerk at the publisher, Hachette. She was a model for Cézanne and shared studios with painters, but now, she tells her friends, living with Zola is different—dark to dawn at his desk without a break, some manic spirit never ceasing to drag his pen forward. When he's not editing an article, he's working on a book, and the rest of the time he's writing letters, dozens of pages long. He spends his whole night at the desk. What sort of future, she wonders, to love a writer?

The Goncourts, the first time they meet Zola, bluntly say he's "an inde-scribable being, deep, confused, after all: pained, anxious, troubled, doubting." Zola quits Hachette and his paycheck; he will live by his writing alone. Alexandrine says nothing and maintains the chores. He's different than painters, she gossips, more industrious, without playful intervals between sittings. He requires silence for his daily rituals and rhythms. With meals prepared and quiet ensured, she makes his home like a perfect wife should. Entering his room of piles and scraps, her job is to help and protect. He writes 178 articles that first year, and even invites his widowed mother to live with them. But only twenty articles sell the next year, and their budget tightens. As surely as one unpaid bill becomes another, Alexandrine cheerfully makes potatoes and soup, and they host a weekly dinner, no matter how meager. Zola: "I've been suf-fering these past days from a rude attack of spleen. This disease takes a particular form with me: panic mixed with worry, physical and emo-tional suffering. Everything seems veiled in black; I belong nowhere, I exaggerate every pain and every joy." Zola continues writing vignettes such as *Love under the Roof*—for here they are, grisette and artist. It is asked—after Balzac—what can the new generation of realists do? Balzac announced he would write the 'natural history of man'; the new authors can delve more deeply into the senses and the physiological causes that determine them, like Madame Bovary's "animal awakening," where "we can feel [her] quivering and shuddering under Flaubert's pen."

Gustave Flaubert: "It is time to give it [art] the precision of the physi-cal sciences, by means of a pitiless method." Flaubert writes to George Sand, "I expressed myself badly when I told you that one should not write with one's heart. I meant to say one should not put one's personality on stage. I believe that great art is scientific and impersonal. One should, by an effort of the spirit, transport oneself into the characters, not draw them to oneself. That, at any rate, is the method."

Émile Zola's first book, *Claude's Confession*, is not just steamy bildungs-roman, but a self-proclaimed "physiological novel," a "naturalist novel" conforming to the "reality of life." Some small money is made on its success and he, Alexandrine, and his mother, all move to rue de Vaugirard just past the Odéon, sixth floor with a terrace overlooking the Luxembourg. To research another book, *Le Ventre de Paris,* Zola makes nightly forays into Les Halles, accompanied by Maurice Dreyfous—his editor and friend—to study everything about the fruits and vegetable markets from the first hours of night until dawn. Not wanting to miss the adventure, Alexandrine tags along—a woman invited and welcomed into the night. *Le Ventre de Paris* mimics the physiological interest in stomachs and digestion, foregrounding bodies and body-functions, and for this, critics accuse Zola of "digging in the trash and chamber pots." Zola: "People should realize that if our analyses are inevitably cruel, it is because they probe deep down into the human cadaver. Everywhere we look, we encounter the brute. To be sure, there are more or less numerous veils; but when we have described them all, one after another, and lift the last one, we always find behind it more things that repel us than things that attract us."

A friend who shares his passion for science and the positivists gives Zola a copy of Claude's *Introduction to the Study of Experimental Medicine.* Zola: "It was necessary to start with the determinism of inert bodies in order to arrive at the determinism of living bodies; and since scientists like Claude Bernard now show that fixed laws govern the human body, we can assert without fear of mistake that the day will come when the laws of thought and the passions will be formulated in turn. One and the same determinism must govern the stone in the road and the brain of man…From that point on science will therefore enter into the domain of us novelists.…"

To be sure, not everyone's so smitten with all this science. Not everyone wants to change what novels are talking about, or expose what imagination hides, tearing open nerves and brains, probing why we act or what we do. Baudelaire: "In spite of his admiration for the fiery phenomena of life, never will Eugéne Delacroix be confounded among the herd of vulgar artists and scribblers whose myopic intelligence takes shelter behind the vague and obscure word *realism*...Those who have no imagination just copy the dictionary. The result is a great vice, the vice of banality, to which those painters are particularly prone whose specialty brings them closer to what is called inanimate nature—landscape painters, for example, who generally consider it a triumph if they can contrive not to show their personalities. By dint of contemplating and copying, they forget to feel and think."

Saint-Beuve, of *Madame Bovary*: "Anatomists and physiologists, I see you everywhere!"

Flaubert to Maupassant: "Don't talk to me of realism, naturalism or the experimental! I'm sick of it. What empty platitudes."

Appalled at the accusation that he exaggerates facts, Zola writes: "Don't try to contradict me with sentiment. Take a look at the statistics for yourselves. Go and investigate the locale yourselves. And then you will see if I have lied or not. Alas, if anything, I have attenuated the facts. When the day arrives when we can finally bring ourselves to recognize poverty for what it really is, with all its pain and degradation, it will not be long before something will be done to improve the condition of the poor.... Why would anyone suppose that I would calumniate the unfortunate? I have only one desire, to show them such as our society has made them, and provoke such a great outpouring of pity, such a great demand for justice, that France will finally stop letting herself be devoured by the ambition of a handful of politicians and pay attention to the physical and material well-being of her children." Zola's novel, *Thérèse Raquin,* brings critical comparisons to the paintings of Manet and Courbet: "The school monstrously confuses the eloquence of the carnal with the eloquence of the nude, and appeal[s] to the most surgical curiosity, displaying the diseased so we can admire their blotches, inspired by cholera, his master, exciting the pus of his awareness."

Zola: "Is experimentation possible in literature, where heretofore observation alone seems to have been used?"

Claude: "In the conduct of their lives men do nothing but make experiments on one another."

Zola: "It will be sufficient for me to replace the word 'doctor' by the word 'novelist' in order to make my thought clear and to bring to it the rigor of scientific truth."

Claude: "Science works by substituting reason and experiment for feeling, and by showing us clearly the limits of our present knowledge. But by a marvelous compensation, in the measure that science thus reduces our pride she increases our power."

Zola: "Since medicine is becoming a science, why should not literature itself become a science, thanks to the experimental method?" He will look into social ills and bring their facts into the open. "The problem is to know what a certain passion, acting in a certain environment, and in certain circumstances will produce as regards the individual and society. And the way to solve it is to take the facts in nature, then to study their mechanism by bringing to bear upon them the modifications of circumstances and environment. Just as Mr Claude Bernard transferred the experimental method from chemistry to medicine, so I transfer it from medicine to the drama and the novel."

Claude: "The experimenter is the examining magistrate of nature."

Zola: "We novelists are the examining magistrates of men and their passions."

Later, a critic attacks: "Almost too easily, he continues to hide his literary insanity under the cover of a science to which he claims, shamelessly, to be the most zealous servant."

Zola: "I put men and women through things."

Diderot, father of naturalism, displayed 'exact truths' in his theater and novels—followed by Balzac's truths, and then Flaubert's 'dissecting' of Emma Bovary. These were no longer sentimental romantics with their lofty symbols, but "the hard-hearted analysts of the social organism, coldly laying bare the aberrations and pathologies of their characters."

Zola: "One day physiology will no doubt explain the mechanism of thought and passions; we shall know how the individual machine of a man works, how he thinks…"

Ferragus, from the *Figaro*, "Putrid Literature":
"Let's recall how the touchstone, Balzac (the shit in which all the mushrooms grow), put all kinds of corruptions into Madame Marneffe, and yet, because he never put Madame Marneffe in a grotesque or trivial situation, her image can amuse or be of good taste,

and she has thus even appeared onstage in the theater. I defy anyone to do the same with the Comptesse of Chalis! I defy anyone to stage Germanie Lacerteux, Thérèse Raquin, or all these impossible ghosts who skirt death without breathing in life, who are nothing but nightmares of reality...

In love with disgust, pleased with what's horrible, it's an ordeal which unfortunately responds to the basest, most bestial, least admirable human instinct. The crowds at the guillotine or who peek at the morgue, is this the public one should court, encourage, or keep in the cult of the awful and purulent?

This said, I should admit the special nature of my anger. My curiosity slipped in a puddle of mud and blood entitled *Thérèse Raquin*, authored by Mr Zola, passing for a young man of talent. At least I know he's aiming for fame. Lover of vileness, he's already published *Claude's Confession*, the love story of a student and a prostitute; he sees women like Mr Manet does, and paints them mud-colored with pink make-up. Intolerant of criticism, he gives out intolerance himself...titling his pretend literary essays, 'My Hates!'"

Zola, preface to *Thérèse Raquin*:

"We begin, I hope, to understand that my aim was scientific above all else; I attempt to explain the strange union that can come about between two different temperaments, and the profound difficulties of a sanguine nature in contact with a nervous one. If you read the novel carefully, you'll see that each chapter is a study of a strange case of physiology. In a word, I only want one thing: given a strong man and an unsatisfied woman, to find in them the animal, to only see the animal, to throw them into a violent drama and note scrupulously the feelings and acts of these beings. I've simply done on two living bodies the analytical work that surgeons do on cadavers.

I admit that it's hard, when one finishes such work...searching the truth... to hear people accusing you of having the goal of making obscene paintings. I've found myself in the same position as painters who copy nudes, without a single desire of touching them, and who remain deeply surprised when a critic is scandalized by the living flesh in their work. When I was writing *Thérèse Raquin*, I forgot the world, I was lost in the exact and miniature copy of life, giving myself over to the analysis of the human mechanism, and I can assure you that the cruel passions of Thérèse and Laurent held nothing immoral for me, nothing that could engender negative behaviors... I've waited in vain for a voice to respond: 'No really, this writer is simply analyzing, forgetting himself as a doctor forgets himself in his operating theater.'"

Claude: "...it is the experimenter who always doubts and does not believe that he has absolute certainty about anything, who succeeds in mastering the phenomena which surround him and extending his power over nature."

Zola: "The true work of the experimental novelist is there, to go from the known to the unknown in order to master nature; whereas the idealist novelists remain in the unknown by prejudice...on the stupefying pretext that the unknown is more noble and beautiful than the known..."

The Goncourts: "Dining at Magny's. They were saying that Berthelot had predicted that a hundred years from now, thanks to physical and chemical science, man would know of what the atom is constituted and would be able, at will, to moderate, extinguish, and light up again the sun as if it were a gas lamp. Claude Bernard, for his part, had apparently declared that in a hundred years of physiological science man would be so completely the master of organic law that he would create life in competition with God. We made no objection, but we well believe that at that moment, good old God with his white beard will arrive on earth, with his bunch of keys, and will say to humanity, as one says at the bar at five o'clock, 'Messieurs, we're closing up!'"

"My *Docteur Pascal*," Zola announces, "will be barely disguised, very transparently a biography of the illustrious scientist, Claude Bernard.

This great man was unhappy in life. And the anguishes of his private life, the setbacks, the discouragements, all these household miseries that come with the scientist's profession, make a disorienting mix with the tranquil pleasures of the laboratory that I am planning to depict. Claude Bernard was a martyr of married life."

3.

SIEGE | DEMONS

Hard to admit there are battles more awful than the ones we're still fighting with these cat-snatching assistants in their torn coats and poor shoes. I mean, who cares about barroom brawls or parliamentary debates while the animals still need us? Yet when bullets start flying, other battles go to hide. As easily as one situation overtakes the rest, the Prussian Army threatens to come right to our door. Claude: "Paris is anxious...the Senate and the Legislature are still holding session...I try in vain to work...my body is on one side and my mind on the other. If I had something mechanical to do it would be a great distraction." Marechal LeBoeuf, Minister of War, makes all sorts of predictions about France's might, but he's only sustaining an empire of his ego. This isn't the first of his blunders in grandiosity (think of Mexico); then comes Napoleon III's defeat at Sudan by Bismark, Thiers surrendering Alsace/Lorraine, the surrender of Paris, and the Prussians invade, surrounding our city and stopping all flow of food and supplies.

Claude: "Invasion and Revolution at the same time. I leave the Senate meeting, the last one I'm sure. The legislature is invaded with cries of

'Decay! 'Vive the Republic'; the deputies are cut off and can no longer deliberate. The madness begins..." After the Senate adjourns in panic, Claude prepares to escape the city, dispirited over the fall of France's capital. "We were defeated scientifically," he concedes.

Our soldiers are trained to unthinkingly withstand horrible circumstances without running away, to await command and put aside fear. A log sits in a fire like that, without complaint and immobile, as it slowly falls bit by bit away from itself, submitting to the element that steals every semblance of its name. As the battles grow loud, I imagine Claude hopes that physiologists, tucked tight in their *milieu intérieur*, will remain independent of fortune. The same priests who've been yelling all these years that Darwin has murdered Adam and put us all in the same place as the animals, are now in open rebellion against the "materialists" whose ascendency they believe has brought on this defeat. For their part, every young Republican howls against God and the Empire. Zola: "Civilization will not attain to its perfection until the last stone from the last church falls on the last priest."

Claude, to Madame Raffolovich:
Dear Madame, Events march on and follow the course of my somber predictions. The surrender at Metz contains impenetrable mystery, the bombardment of Paris is imminent or already started; Lyon, the South, the Center all are threatened; here is the present waiting on the future. And all this is framed by the revolutionary committees forming to save the homeland revolutionarily, that's the word in fashion.

I've heard: They'll only proceed 'revolutionarily.'

They dress, drink and eat 'revolutionarily.' They speak, walk and fight 'revolutionarily.' I'll stop because it's better between us to leave politics out of it.

Darwin, from the *Expression of the Emotions in Man and Animals*:

"When an animal is alarmed it almost always stands motionless for a moment, in order to collect its senses and to ascertain the source of danger, and sometimes for the sake of escaping detection. But headlong flight soon follows, with no husbanding of the strength as in fighting, and the animal continues to fly as long as the danger lasts, until utter prostration, with failing respiration and circulation, with all the muscles quivering and profuse sweating, renders further flight impossible..."

Claude, to Madame Raffalovich:

"Going out yesterday was not a success; today I'm obliged to stay in my room despite the splendid sun glistening everywhere. My prison is only sadder for it, but luckily the mind can detach from the body and conquer space. I'm walking at the moment in my fields at Saint-Julien."

And:

"I read with surprise that courses are continuing at Collège de France. I admit not to see what the zealotry of these new Archimedes can do for the advancement of science or the future of France. For me, it seems impossible, in a besieged and bombed-out city, to be preoccupied with any thought other than its deliverance..."

A few days later:

"I never thought I was destined to be the witness to all the misfortune of my country that an odious conqueror can insolently run through without encountering any obstacle. It's done: France is facing an implacable victorious enemy who, not satisfied simply to ruin her, wants to dishonor her. But I hope that my homeland will die rather than survive such insults. In vain would those who so cowardly left her overwhelmed like to call her back to life to rejoice in her humiliation. When the German monster that dares still speak in the name of civilization will have released its prey, after ravaging, trampling, and dismembering it, it will be really dead; it will never live longer than the time it takes palpitating flesh to go cold and go out. The internal tears will achieve the final destruction, and in the 20th century, people will say 'here was France, there was Paris...'

Please burn my letter and pretend I said nothing. If I'm given to see things in black, you must blame my intestines. My health already was bad the last days of my stay in Paris, disorganizing me more and more with anxiety, displacement, changing regimes, etc."

Why does only the past provide material that burns—from the trunks of trees, to letters and clothing and gunpowder and houses—yet not our thoughts or our cowardice, our dreams or regrets, what we don't do, won't do, will never do, even if we say we must? Burning destroys time's illusory solidity, freeing the air from holding ideas in place. This ashen outline is now stark, as the animals we chase are losing their status as pets, and appear as nothing but steaks and stews. Our network of transport, the houses where they shelter, the people dedicated to their safety, are fast becoming unsure. We can barely keep another creature with us for fear of losing our lease. We share our rations cooked and uncooked, but within a couple of weeks there are barely any rations left.

Claude, letter to Madame R:

"...Events are still dark and the future obscure. I promised not to talk to you of this again, but ever since the shameful surrender at Sedan, I see everything in darkness. How many meditations this war has given birth to! How the differences in character between the French and Prussians are well drawn, especially, if you ask me, in the relationship between Jules Favre and Bismark...And these neutral powers that contemplate, with sublime selfishness, this crushing of France who has spilled, too chivalrously I'm sure, her blood for several of them! As for me, looking at things purely philosophically, I admit my deception.

I believed that the progress of science would enlighten people and lead to communal progress and a growing civilization. Where will they be, these barbarians who return to exterminate one nation and make it disappear? I discounted the barbarians of Berlin for whom science has become a brutal form of progress rather than an instrument of civilization and liberty... And this is enough to see how much our governments are, in general, strangers to the rigor of scientific minds and how much importance we give to lovely discourse which leads to illusions and gives birth only to unhappiness...

...How I've come to envy those who are dead!...

In the meantime, I continue my solitary walks, and to calm the anxiety and nightmares I get from the newspapers, I take to bed the *Pensées* of Pascal and the *Pensées* of Nicole and his *Treaty on Peace between Men*. How disillusioned I am with these words: Honor. Patriotism. Glory, etc. Here, for example, the third pensée of Pascal, art. IX, which I happened to read yesterday: 'Why are you killing me?—and what, don't you live on the other side of the ocean? My friend, if you lived on this side, I would be an assassin and it would be unfair to kill you, but since you live on the other side, I'm brave and it's fair.'"

In the revolution of 1848, Collège de France was damaged by fire, so Claude frets about his laboratory, even as hunger is our enemy's preferred weapon, and the flocks and farm animals that filled every park, stair, and courtyard, the geese and goats and cows, are now all gone. Rat sellers fight with dogs over rancid scraps. The girls and I talk only of leaving Paris at the first chance. Cannon fire marks invading soldiers, the syrupy river reflecting nothing but blood, mingled beyond all the faces. We aren't penning letters to our distant loves, or contemplating the order of the stars. An escaped kitten, and ten people on its trail, is what we see of the appetites perverting the menu. "Cat steak in mushrooms," "pigeon chop with peas," "shoulder and filet of dog braised in tomato." In the Beaujolais, Claude strolls and pens and contemplates, waiting "in the current we call the river of life, in the hope either to drown here or receive the arm of salvation."

Letter from Davaine to Claude, January 19, 1871:

"My dear friend, I've just received word that you are sick. If any part of this is the worry you may be feeling about your daughters, I would hope to calm your nerves on this subject. Our neighborhood was not bombed; it is unlikely that it will be targeted at all. The forts on the right bank would need to be breached and they've barely been attacked. I've been to see your lawyer; he hasn't had a visit from your wife or your daughters. I often see Dr Martin, who asks their news and yours, and who told me he was fully disposed to help if they needed anything at all. Your elder daughter came to see me in November about the money your wife should be receiving each month. I told her you hadn't given any instructions on that subject, probably because you didn't expect the siege to go on for so long; that if they needed money, I was sorry I wasn't able to advance them any, not having any at all myself; but if there was an emergency, Dr Martin had instructed me to tell him and he would take care of it. To this she responded gratefully, adding that they didn't need money. I haven't seen her since, and Dr Martin, who I have seen a number of times, hasn't seen her either.

I will write your daughter that you are sick and that, if they need anything, you have instructed me to provide it. If we are bombed in your neighborhood, I will go personally to check on her. We are in a very difficult situation, though it is tolerable. What do you think of the German scientists? What people! I will have the pleasure of your news soon, for the current situation can't go on much longer; everything will improve. I have no news of my family.

Your friend, Davaine"

Bulletin of the Animal Protection Society, March 7, 1871:

"Mr Behier, I have the honor of proposing to the Academy of Medicine the following: 'All associated or affiliated foreign members of the Academy of Medicine who live in Prussia or the countries who helped this power in the last war are barred from the list of the Academy.'

I know, sirs, that one might reply: 'These are scientists, and it is as scientists, not as Germans, that they are associated with the Academy,' and I foresee all the discussion on the independence of science, etc. I've taken all that into account, but we mustn't forget that there are scientists in Germany who, in the midst of the painful trials that our country has suffered, haven't held back their insults and rejoicing over the misfortunes of France, and this even in their roles as Professors who practice as well as teach science. Witness the discussion of Mr Reymond Duboys, excusing his French name. Another, Mr Mommsen, went so far as to say that if our soldiers were brave, if Paris were well defended, it's because the French still have a little German blood left in their veins. In my opinion, if I thought my veins enclosed even a little of the same blood as they have, I would bleed myself dry to get rid of such a liquid.

No, sirs, this is about the honor of the Academy, this is about all of our honor, to break all ties which could unite us with these sons of Vandals for whom the process of methodical plunder displays the lessons of the famous Cartouche."

Claude: "Never in all my life have I been in a moral situation this disturbing; then again, I've never seen my country invaded."

In February, to cement their burgeoning friendship and mutual admiration, the young Louis Pasteur travels from his vineyard in the Jura to visit Claude, later writing: "His personal quality, the nobility of his face, his likeable beauty, seductive at first: no pedantry, no shortcomings of the scientist, an old-fashioned simplicity, the most natural conversation, as far as one can get from all affectation, but nourished with good and profound ideas, such are some of the external merits of Mr Claude Bernard."

Claude to Madame R, Saint-Julien, 1871:

"You'd be surprised by the indifference of certain areas with regard to Paris. I, who am at the moment a provençal, can tell that even in the Rhône area, which certainly has done its homework, there persists an antagonism deep and deaf between Paris and these outlying areas. It happens despite itself. Many people even seem happy about the suffering in Paris and would like to see them suffer more. This comes from their thinking Paris is the cause of all their political misfortune and they are loathe, they say, to submit to a dozen 'Faubourgians' who turn over the government and impose it on the rest of France... There is no way, I think, to see the political horizon without clouds for a long time..."

Again, to Madame R:

"...In other good news, we should be housing the bombed-out from quartier Mouffetard. I saw in the papers that they're requisitioning the apartments of people who are absent. You must have been requisitioned before me because your house is much more comfortable and safe. I'm still in the area of bombings. I anxiously read all the news of bombs and I saw that on the 22nd of January there hadn't yet been anything at Collège de France or rue des Écoles. But I fear these stories aren't complete or that the bombs are just waiting for my return; I'm not without worries here. Finally, if by law I must have the happiness of fraternizing with the bombarded, I only hope they won't heat themselves using my books and papers and that they will allow me to return home when I return to Paris. I guess I can't come back during the armistice; still I wish they would allow letters to pass."

Saint-Julien, 17 Feb:

"You're right, Madame: under the Monarchy, we had republican elections, under the Republic we had monarchic elections; and now, when we'll be under the Monarchy, we'll redo the republican elections, and on and on until extinction. That's the consequence of this revolutionary spirit blowing across France that goes against whatever exists and makes it so that for the past eighty years France is like Jerome Parturot searching for the best form of government. I think the illness is very deep."

Claude, letter to Madame R:

"As the human Horace, I drag around with me an undefined sadness; I have what one might call the todium vitae. I don't understand where it came from, who knows, maybe it's politics and the result of my first accomplishments as a Senator? In this case, I hope that science will soon lift me out of it. I've brought several books with me but I don't know if I have the will to work."

Saint-Julien, 26 February, 1871:

"This is, in fact, a shameful and disastrous peace that has been signed. Whatever I was expecting from this sad document, I couldn't feel anything more painful. I've been walking all day with a malaise that indicates a new health crisis. You see where France has fallen, through the negligence of Europe, the ineptitude of the Republic, and the odious hypocrisy of Prussia. And if that weren't already enough, the French people save up, to really humiliate their country, the horrors of a civil war to display in front of the Prussians. Poor insane people! They deliver themselves to these lunatics, who, because they know how to say a sentence, think they are soldiers or politicians. This belief in innate knowledge, and the absence of scientific sense in the masses, has lost France vis-à-vis Germany. Only the scientists can extirpate these false ideas and prepare for the vengeance of the future."

To Madame R:

"I'm a bit calmer now about the shame and humiliation inflicted on my poor country; only the agitation is transformed into sadness that will never go out. What a pity, I thought to myself in last night's insomnia, that I can never be young again. Now that I've lived through all the difficulties of existence, that I've known all the physical and mental pains of life, how my choices would have improved! I think I would have been a perfect man, and I could have changed the destiny of my country. But no, I'm condemned to feel the cruelest of pain, that of regret and impotence. Most likely in Paris I'll find many obstacles to my future scientific projects, so I'll try to isolate myself in books and experiments and to absorb myself while waiting to be absorbed, in my turn, by the rigid laws of humanity."

30 March, 1871:

"An irresistible attraction calls me back to Paris and combats the excellent reasons you've given for me to put off my return. I think I would be happier to be doing any physiological experiment in a dark laboratory than to see flowers fading in the sun. You'll likely respond, why don't you do physiological experiments in Saint Julien? Oh well, I can't, because it was always impossible to do things outside their natural milieu. I'm not defending this, I realize it's a fault, only proving that I've more of a passive than an active character, since the milieu acts on me much more than I on it.

You know I'm a man of dark foreboding and I never think I'm allowed to change the way I feel. I consider France stricken with a terrible illness from which she will only recover after many sufferings, if she recovers ever....

They know that the committee of the National Guard and the Commune will never pay the billions they want, so they'll reestablish order and occupy Paris without resistance I hope, because the bravura of these gents from the Commune shows itself against the French and not against the Prussians. Next will come a Restoration, and then a throne which will last as long as thrones have lasted in France for the past 80 years. But what shame to swallow and what pain to endure for France! And no one feels sorry; she's fallen this low and only inspires disgust from other nations. Where does this profound French decadence come from? From a great number of social causes, but all stemming from a single moral cause, the absence of principle or belief. The series of events that have unfolded gives us the obvious proof. One must have a criterium in this world, otherwise we don't know where we're going, and France is there, deprived of principle, she is tossed to the bottom of the waves like a rudderless ship. She hasn't believed in divine rights since '93; she no longer believes in constitutional government; nor does she believe in the Republic..."

Claude eventually begins experiments on flowers and anesthetics—for even the most devout man will fall off his chair while praying—and that is the law of gravity, as they say. Claude: "In my research on the feelings of plants, I've seen that it's possible to stop the growth and the flowering through anesthetics...We created the problem of Sleeping Beauty. Couldn't we stop human flowers just as well; their charms would be less fleeting and doubtless their feelings too."

To Madame R:
"...it's hard to realize the effects when one is staring right at the cause; the biggest difficulty is to recognize the depth of thought that results

from the emotions. There's no way I would be able to resolve this problem physiologically: it would take at least Mr Chevreul to show us the right Ariadne's thread to get ourselves out of this Daedalus (dédale=maze?) called the human heart."

§

Beyond dreaming, even each waking moment felt to Descartes like a systematic duping: "If there is an evil genius who makes me believe I have a body when I do not, and that there is a world when there is not, it nevertheless would be true that I seem to have perceptions of the sort that an embodied subject in the world has." Is investment in the physical world an error, made possible through foolish consensus, specific experiences, gullible minds—in other words, despite appearances, are we essentially brains in jars in dark rooms in silence, fed sensory hallucinations with little we can do to wake up and know the truth? I wish that an evil demon fools me that I'm dreaming when I'm not, that I'm imagining the screams and the smells and the colors of the day, that I am walking as a dream-woman walks, and that if he simply commanded it, it would all dissolve. Perhaps these words are dream words, and all the ways I feel are just the hyperactive ravings of a madwoman in reverie. This jar is cut off with no possible exit. There exists nothing but me and the evil genius. His only purpose is to deceive me. My sole purpose is to prove nothing can be proved. And so the demon makes a chimera of everything I care for, work towards, love. Against the evil genius, does Descartes identify the perfect weapon? "…At last I have discovered it—Thought; this alone is inseparable from me. I am, I exist, that is certain. But for how long? For as long as I am thinking…." But between cannon shots and children crying, between dying young people and a city in flames, I'm not sure Descartes didn't have the important parts backward: maybe thoughts are what deceive us, and our sense of the world that might wake us from dreaming?

Claude, Saint-Julien:

"I trim my roses, I cultivate my periwinkles, I read the papers, and the hours flow, taking with them my inertia. For I have become an entirely passive being, incapable of any mental work, that's to say, any initiative. These are the thoughts that drive me; I don't control them. I will follow your advice, and like Mr Raffalovich I won't set out for Paris until calm is reestablished and Paris will have returned to eating properly from its plate."

After putting flowers to sleep, Claude sets up experiments on his grapes, to prove his friend Pasteur wrong. Pasteur, working with his own grapes, believes alcoholic fermentation requires the presence of living yeasts, while Claude thinks soluble yeast enzymes are enough—that it's an entirely chemical, and not a biological process. He's gotten himself into this because, following Magendie's strict determinism, Claude doesn't like theories about germs and bacteria causing illness or physiological change. For him, all diseases are just extensions of normal health, caused internally via an increase or decrease of what's already there. His Red Notebook: "I would no more admit that disease can produce something new than admit that a physician can guess the future." This being just one of many professional disagreements bothering him, he rests on his Bench of Sisyphus in the afternoon, past the hour of work and before supper.

"I don't know why but winter has made all the birds disappear; we don't see a single one. The country appears desolate; a mournful silence reigns in the fields. And to add even more to the sadness of this solitude, I hear almost every night the visit of an owl who perches on my chimney and makes me listen to his plaintive cries that hold on in the darkness of night like a long harmonious groaning. Under the influence of that sad music, my thoughts bound to the present, the past, the future. My memories bring back involuntarily a variety show I saw in my youth, at the Palais-Royal. Where has the time gone? A character in the play is still in my mind, a romantic poet who wrote a verse which started:

What more touching

than the song of the owl

that hoots from the height of the silent tower?

I was stunned to recall this silly verse stuck in my skull for all these thirty years. What a singular machine is man!"

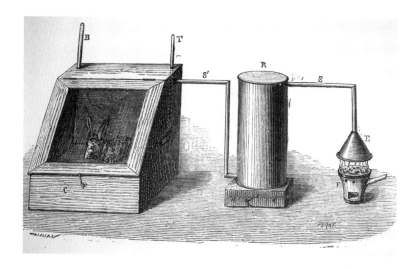

Free of spectators, Claude devises other ways to use his spare time, and begins studying the mysteries of hibernation and animal heat, using marmottes he traps in the fields. Lacking an assistant, he employs the town's children to bring him buckets of frogs from the pond, and pays good bonuses for rabbits and larger animals.

CLAUDE'S RED NOTEBOOK:

The external temperature, the sun, act on the (cold-blooded) animal as on the plant. In the warm-blooded animal friction prevents the heat from being lost except when the animal is cooled too much. Then it becomes a cold-blooded animal and for it to become warm-blooded again, it must be rewarmed, without which it will die.

In Claude's ovens, the marmottes, rabbits, and dogs bake to death in eight or ten minutes, depending on the position of the heads within the ovens. In his notebook: "Count the pantings. At last the creature falls into convulsions and dies—uttering a cry." But rural life has its own problems: a snake takes a bite of him on his way through a field, and on his way back from a conference on "The Feelings of Plants," he catches a rain shower and ends up back in bed.

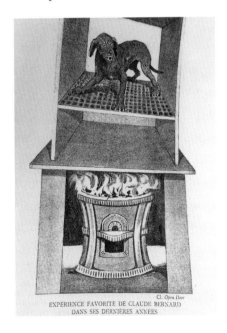

Cl. *Open Door*
EXPÉRIENCE FAVORITE DE CLAUDE BERNARD
DANS SES DERNIÈRES ANNÉES

§

You've all heard, we've all heard: the Paris Commune proclaimed itself "the communal revolution, begun by the popular initiative of 18 March, inaugurating a new political era: experimental, positive, scientific. It is the end of the old governmental and clerical world, of militarism, of monopolism, of privileges to which the proletariat owes its servitude, the Nation its miseries and disasters." Louise Michel, dressed in kepi and men's uniform, leads the women's battalion, fighting barricade to barricade from Boulevard de Clichy to Place Pigalle, where they surrender. Louise is going to blow up the Butte Montmartre but she's too late. Haussmann's unfinished Opera House is surrounded on three sides. We hide and we steal, for seventy long days of radical reform: reformed schools, some neighbors getting their homes back, workers' associations collecting in the bars. But on May 21st we're warned back inside, as the army of Versailles comes murdering house to house, and more blood is the rebuttal of the Communards, killing hostages in thousands of executions.

In all this, the critic, Ferdinand Brunetière, finds it crucial to remind theater-going Parisians that there were more plays given during the Terror of 1793–1794 than before or after. Are people really going to the theater? If they are or aren't, the Commune's "revolutionary theater" gets proscriptive: no *Madame* or *Monsieur* unless a play is set before 1792; never the name 'Louis.' Zola: "Either the theater will be naturalistic or it will cease to be: such is my formal conclusion." Following suit, we hear that the entire troupe of the Comédie-Française is arrested for plays with kings and aristocrats, and for insulting the revolutionary government by depicting the Empire. "The committee is especially charged with illuminating and forming opinions that the theaters have been neglecting in the present circumstances. They are too much in the service of tyranny; they must serve liberty instead."

Claude, letter to Madame Raffalovich:
"Do you remember last year, when you were in Trouville with your mother and children, I wrote a letter after the revolution of 4th Sept? In my dark forebodings, I saw France desolate, torn apart by internal conflicts...I said you might flee and that I would never see you again. You responded that you would never flee a free country and that the Republic would give birth to prodigies. Today, I'm shocked at my sad perspicacity."

In the mayhem, the girls and I are too afraid to leave the apartment. Doesn't anyone notice that blood is losing its power? Even the cruelty of mythological beasts—the ogres, dragons, and giants—relied on their salvageable ignorance, and only the ones who cannot finally learn to stop killing are the true monsters. Gratuitous violence is pure excess, "description without end," an accumulation of words or actions for their own sake. All we see before us now is a city that contains no relationship precious enough to protect, every person fully armed or cowering in their home. I mother my daughters as the cat, the dog mother their own—our frightened faces crouched at the window. The dog cowers; I cower. I have met the modern citizens we hear about, so desperate they forsake their church, forsake their God for trinkets and tidbits of power. All I can say is it's up to us to make heaven or hell. You can take the arms off, legs off, cut the nerves, cut the flesh, the bones, and the soul still is there—you cannot touch it, or find it, you cannot see it, or measure it—and until the man is dead, you can cut his every part, but the mystery of life remains visible in God's eyes, even after you cut out the eyes, it is there, because it is not equal to any eye. Even destroying a wicked city was proscribed by God: *For we know that the whole creation groaneth and travaileth in pain together until new.*

Darwin, from the *Expression of the Emotions in Man and Animals*:

"As soon as the sufferer is fully conscious that nothing can be done, despair or deep sorrow takes the place of frantic grief. The sufferer sits motionless, or gently rocks to and fro; the circulation becomes languid; respiration is almost forgotten, and deep sighs are drawn."

When the Commune is finally cleared, killings nonetheless continue—now as the expiation by the Versailles army. Louise Michel sends her two dogs and six cats to Madame Dolon in Montmartre, where she knows they will be safe when she is taken to prison. The Tuileries have caught fire, rumored to have been set by mythological women, *les petroleuses*. Rue de Rivoli, Ministry of Finance, Louvre—it is said their plan is to burn all of Paris, but it's the National Guard who leave the Hôtel de Ville in flames behind them.

CLAUDE'S RED NOTEBOOK:

Aristotelean entelechy. Every being works for itself. It makes itself the center of everything. It utilizes everything for itself that it can from the external world. From this results the law of the strongest, which dominates and subordinates to its profit all that is below it. Christianity reacts against this law. Charity is anti-entelechic. All the virtues are anti-entelechic.

As girls at church we studied *surrender*, and learned the position to take when confronted with His overshadowing. But do war and violence compel obedience? Claude: "Activity in war is movement in a resistant medium." The situation we place our opponent in must be more costly to him than what we are asking him to give up. He must be entirely disarmed. Yet even though war requires physical duration, it is only the will of the enemy which, when given over, marks the end of hostile conflict. Holding enemy territory only hobbles him. I got Claude and his young scientists to lose ground along their habitual paths, for example, but war is also the domain of chance, though this should be minimized in battle as much as possible. If the good warrior finds things different than she expects, she is ready. We have lost thousands of animals in the past year.

Claude, to Madame Raffalovich:

"In great unhappiness one should recall men who are right and strong, as Horace says, 'et si fractus illabatur orbis, impavidum ferient ruinae!'...I noticed that the social paroxysm we're experiencing has shaken or extinguished a great number of lives; I don't think I've ever lost so many friends and acquaintances in one year. I don't even know where I am anymore, it's a general dispersion. I received a letter from my friend Davaine who is taking refuge in the North, and I know that Mr Dumas and Mr Deville have left for Geneva, etc. You spoke of Madame Renan and her fourth escape, but her husband should be in Versailles as a deputy. I read recently he's put up a new electoral law. How can your friend, Mr Lanfry, who is also a deputy, circulate freely in Paris? I hope his arrest was only false news. With all the false news printed these days, I wonder how future historians will figure out the truth?"

"Dear Madame, we have every right to say that when man, most noble in creation, degrades himself, he descends lower than the animals. These horrible savage beasts have devoured that poor Bonjean, so loyal and good, so courageous in danger. Sadly, he justified these words: Qui amat periculum peribit in illo. I thank you for your letter, which helped me sort out these atrocities.

I'm still nursing my sadness like a sick child, because in fact I am sick. I wasn't always like this, I didn't let myself get beaten down, I had more will power. Today, my resolutions disappear in the frenzy of my acts and ideas...I want to follow your advice and re-immerse myself in science. Inspired, I wrote the director at the Jardin des Plantes and at Collège de France that I would be back in two weeks. I've ordered everything prepared in my labs and at my house. I heard news that nothing has happened to my apartment except a few broken panes from the explosion of the munitions building in the Luxembourg."

"In my garden I have a family of hedgehogs with whom I'm making relations, though these animals seem unfriendly. I want to tame them to bring them to Paris."

§

Paris smolders until the bodies are cleared, even as summer tourists arrive with their colorful hats and bags, moving through galleries of ghosts. It is announced that Sacré-Coeur will commemorate and atone, and exiled leaders return as Senators of this now-themed Third Republic. Does Claude find his laboratory intact? I'm sure he would love to celebrate, but are the Raffalovichs in town? He walks the city staring at charred monuments. The regular movements of shopping bring optimism to the survivors, no matter their previous roles. Does Claude worry that he might be investigated as a Senator of the Empire? No one seems to care about that old Empire now, the violence creating a sort of abyss. But whatever happened to the lovely Princess Mathilde? To all the people, parties, salons he knew from before? Taking a carriage to rue de Courcelles near Parc Monceau, and seeing her house closed, does Claude fear she may have met the worst revolutionary fate? An attendant at the house answers that she is only gone for the summer.

The girls and I take advantage of the first quiet morning to pack the apartment, and our few remaining animals, and move out of Paris for good. Guarding them in the chaos has put a hole in my strength, not to mention the madness of starving, and that the ransacking of churches, the feeling that no neighbor, no friend, could be trusted, has turned the city, which was always my home, into a remote transaction. In Bezons we can have a few hectares, close to Paris with a ferry and a bridge, and yet we are left alone. Marie-Claude is particularly inventive and stubborn in fortifying our home, as she can't forget the recent fate of the animals— how she cried and fought with everyone not to eat them. Tony and I will rouse ourselves back into the activist fray—keep up contacts, and assist at night with particularly difficult transports. The laboratories haven't put off getting back to their vile business, and we can't either. The good news is that what was in disarray is again shaping up, and from the count of heads, our cause is popular. Tony is articulate and passionate in her youthful leadership, and I'm proud of the girls, though I still have to drag them to mass, reminding them it's a support, not a distraction. The pretense of keeping house no longer worries us, and we live nocturnal lives, which if you didn't know better, would strike even a devil as unholy. We gleefully receive the *Bulletin* from the Animal Protection Society, indicating their return:

"Toasts and news since the last meeting, which was long ago during the World's Fair of 1867! Following the painful loss of our beloved president, Mr Sibire, and the sad events that have driven many of us from Paris, I've been forced, despite myself, to hold down the presidency of the Society, in the midst of these disasters, to maintain and keep it alive, waiting for better days...

In the news: Letter from Mr Decroix to the Berlin Animal Protection Society:

'Mr President, the flow of war hits both our countries; but if Prussia and France are divided over national issues that our civilized states can only resolve through warfare, at least the work of compassion for the fate of war horses should offer no disagreement. All those horses injured on the battlefield stay abandoned, often for a long time, only to die after long and horrible agonies. We've approached our War Minister:

1. To provide veterinarians with neutrality

2. That orders be given to kill all mortally wounded horses, as soon as possible after the fighting.

We would be disposed, Mr President, to send this request to our War Minister if on your side the Berlin Animal Protection Society would join us in presenting a similar demand to your War Minister. Please accept my sincerest best wishes, the interim president, L. Crivelli'

This letter has gone unanswered; I would be happy to say it's the fault of the post.

The next question demanding our attention is that after the 7th of April, a great number of animals were brought into Paris and parked, willy-nilly, in every spot. At that point, the weather was still nice, but the battle caused a lack of straw, and food and drink were poorly distributed. Our vigilance regarding infractions against the Grammont Law has been, during this time, forcibly hindered. Since the 4th of September, the city has found itself lacking all police, and street surveillance no longer exists. There came a day when horses were being requisitioned by the butcher. For many people this represented a new level of pain caused by the siege; and we know of at least one coachman, tears in his eyes, who delivered his horses to the knives.

Our attention was also brought to the wholesale destruction of dogs and cats. We didn't dare intervene. These animal sacrifices brought some food resources to a public that needed them desperately, however minimal this small amount. We should add, however, that the authorities condemned individuals thought to have stolen dogs and cats from their owners to take them to the butchers.

The day after the Council meeting was a Saturday, and that Saturday will always go down in history: the 18th of March! None of us questioned the gravity of the events which erupted. The meeting scheduled for March 30th took place as planned: sixty or so members still in Paris responded to the call...But from March 30 to April 8, events unfolded and the Terror came down on Paris in a dark parody of '93. The people's uprising was declared; we had to leave. I left with my son, who was wanted armed, and then pushed behind a barricade; many other members—who became suspect due to their official titles, or threatened because of their age, or their disgust and horror at civil war—also left Paris, and at the meeting on the 8th there was only Mr Gindre, Mr Belouino, Mr Bretagne, Mr Rosier, and Mr de Magneval, of which five were members, making all deliberation impossible. In any case, this was no place for our peace efforts and civilization.

Nevertheless, the SPA office stayed open during the Commune, meaning at least until May 22. We can't thank Mr Lamquet and Mr Puzin enough for their courage and devotion in these difficult circumstances. Mr Puzin escaped the decree of public safety because of his age; our Secretary, Mr Lamquet, keeping himself absent from home all day long, was able to avoid the service order sent him. Both were thus able to come every day to rue de Lille to welcome any members who came by. By some lucky chance, the Commune paid no attention to our Society. We received only a summons to pay our taxes, which we thought best to obey. From May 23 to 28, no one could come to the secretary: all of Paris was fighting. From six o'clock on the 23rd, rue de Lille was in flames. A house at number 27, four doors down from ours, burned to the ground…Thanks to the devotion and energy of Mr Chagnon, our concierge, the arsonists left us alone. He convinced them that there were injured people in the house, and we think that a little sign in our window (announcing our subscription to the war wounded effort) corroborated his story and helped save the house.

On the 28th, the Commune disappeared; but before succumbing it assassinated, among the innocent victims, one of our most illustrious members, Mr Bonjean, president of the Bar, Senator of the Empire, and one of the hostages burned at la Roquette on May 24th. It wasn't impossible for Mr Bonjean to escape his prison, as a friend snuck him a white pass-card. But when asked to sign his name and represent, in signature, the names of two members of the Commune, he simply responded: 'But that's impossible; the president of the Bar can't lie.' And so he stayed to his tragic end.

The council will once again be able to meet on June 17. The first order of business will be to put the office back together."

§

Eventually, well-to-do's like Mme Raffalovich reclaim Paris, and her salon Dinner, even if only quoting quotes more than ever, includes Claude and his gang: Brown-Sequard, Berthelot, d'Arsonval—and the Republican intelligentsia: the young Henri Bergson, the old critic Ernst Renan, and politicians like Leon Bourgeois. Claude: "Governments change, but the characters stay the same; the play changes title, the actors don't even change their costumes."

Adolphe Thiers becomes France's president, and Claude and Ernst Renan decide to present the needs of the scientists of Collège de France to him in person. The time has come, they declare, for the government to fully invest in the future of France, and science, its symbol. They argue that only they can take civilization's largest questions, reduce them to controllable size, reverse the scale, and finally master Nature through experimental method. Scientists don't need new ideas or senses, only new tools. People say the Second Empire died of superficiality (Goncourts: "that American France, that Paris towed along in the path of the Now") so the Third Republic must appear serious! As though to reflect this, an increasing number of famous spectators appear at Claude's lectures. From the stage, Claude recognizes the Prince of Wales, the Count of Paris, Emporer of Brasil, Pasteur, les Goncourts, Flaubert, Theophile Gautier…even the Shah of Persia. A letter arrives from the Minister of Public Instruction: Subject, *Collège de France: gas installed in the laboratory of Mr Claude Bernard.*

Claude, letter to Madame R:

"I have four Russian women who've come to work in my lab. One is of a very young age (maybe 17 or 18 years old) but with a heart of steel. It's all shocking, these sexless women. If it's going to be like this, I'll be happy to leave a world which has become so unbearable!"

Kings from every corner take ardent notes—while Claude improvises on familiar themes, keeping the stage business moving quickly, d'Arsonval ready with a dog, sectioned and tied into the same old wooden trough.

"I admit that the bracelet that caught my attention suffocated me. My mind can't forget it: I wonder why it's there and not elsewhere, and despite myself,

I make all sorts of hypotheses and I mistake the aorta for the carotid. As my mixed-up language can't admit the cause of my distraction, I accuse the cursed cold that causes me to cough and sneeze at every moment. With all of that, I had to prolong the lesson by half an hour, and still never said half of what I needed to say. You can see the power of a bracelet on the ankle or the leg..."

Assured in his popularity, Claude writes Madame R:

"A young Muslim came to tell me he came from Constantinople to be my physiological fruit. It's strange to see this whole human mix that happens in our time. A Muslim doing physiological experiments, accompanying every gesture with a salaam, kissing of robes, etc.? All this seems very odd in physiology..."

The writer, Alexandre Dumas fils, attends Claude's demonstrations often, fascinated by curare, the novelty of the laboratory, the intensity of the scientific scene, the thrall of the audience who, with only one story in focus before them, thinks it sees what would be otherwise impossible to see. Laboratory scientists might scarcely know what to do at a farm, or in the streets, in the hospitals, or in the mines, but inside their labs they are the only authority.

Letter to Madame R:

"If you come to my class, stay by Mr de Chaptal at the top row near the door in case you want to leave, for I doubt, despite your best intentions, that you will be interested in a outdated subject by a fading lecturer. In any case, you can take a walk by some of my neighbors, Mr Berthelot for ex: who teaches at the same hour, and after my lesson I would love to say hi and to show you my private laboratory.

I spent all day doing experiments; I've come home with my usual headache, unbearable neuralgias, and a horrible pain in the cranial sockets that prevents me from sharing your troubles, though I may sympathize with them.

I hope, as you say, Dear Madame, time will erase this deeply sad impression that you must have of my life. The future belongs to us and we can put away the past when we want to."

§

Zola: "If my fiction accomplishes anything, this is what it will be: to say the human truth...It will then be up to the legislators and moralists to think about dressing the wounds that I have shown."

Émile Zola steps off the train, and from the ruins of the Second Empire, he inhales sustained creative force: "Work has become my life. Little by little it has stolen my mother, my wife, everything I love." His mother and Alexandrine, two dogs and a cat, watch over and feed and care for him, continuing their regular Thursday dinners for artists and friends. The success of *L'Assommoir* fills their accounts, and Zola agrees to wed Alexandrine, and move to the neighborhood near Saint-Lazare where she grew up. A year later, they move to Batignolles in the area near Montmartre, where fortifications mark Paris's northern border. In a small cottage they raise ducks and rabbits and walk the pretty fields above the river. For Zola, the Romantics wrote "adventures that would never happen and characters that we would never see."

Zola: "The naturalist school reestablishes the broken relationship between man and nature. It comes from the depths of modern rationalism." A dictionary from 1727 defines a *naturalist* as he who explains nature by mechanical, not supernatural, laws. The critic Charles Bigot describes naturalism as a child, who, "like any new child, cries a lot." He publicly complains that Zola likes to think he killed off Victor Hugo and

Romanticism, and that "outside of Naturalism, nothing goes—neither for writers or for governments." Bigot points out there's no room for jokes—only reason and truth—and thus Zola has only one refrain: "Use any means necessary." But Romanticism has been so old for forty years—it's practically dead! Zola accuses it of blocking the century, but he's twenty years off! Zola wants to study nature and the "human document"—while his formula is that first the observer sees things, and then the 'experimenter' appears and moves the characters around the story, "to show how the succession of facts will determine the events put forward to study." Making use of his experience in journalism, Zola imports setting, details, historical figures, a mixed texture of truth and invention into his books, but he goes too far when he says that the more there are newspapers, the less there should be novels! Zola: "The real novel is news—and here is where reality makes its greatest impression!"

Ferdinand Brunetière, *Revue des Deux Mondes*, "The Contemporary Realist Novel":

"—but what is this 'Materialist'? It's an art that sacrifices form for matter, drawing for color, feeling for sensation, ideas for the real—that doesn't hesitate before indecency or triviality, even brutality—that speaks the language of the crowd, finding it easier to give free rein to the basest instincts of the masses than to raise their intelligence to the level of art. What is this 'fully experimental'? It's the pretense of doing art with science (and with industry). As if art and science weren't forever in a lively opposition one to the other, science bending the freedom of the human mind to the yoke of nature's laws and imposing them as the authority, art, on the other hand, escaping these constraints and giving intelligence its fullest expression."

Zola: "The novel should aim to compete with, and outdo, the hospital."

Brunetière:

"The artist certainly has his rights, but not to mutilate nature, and certainly it's strange to refuse to open one's eyes to the *claret du jour* and finally realize that this love of denigrating isn't a less artificial convention, a less false aesthetic, than the outdated pretensions of the royalty of yesteryear."

Zola to Flaubert: "Oh my God! I also laugh at this word, 'naturalism', and still I use it because people need a baptism to think something is new…"

W.S. Lilly, from *The New Naturalism*, "Zola eliminates from man all but the ape and the tiger. It leaves of him nothing but the *bête humaine*…There are moods of thought which do not yield in heinousness to the worst deeds—moods of madness, suicidal and polluting. To leave them in the dark is to help toward suppressing them. And this is a sacred duty…Sentiment…is the sole safeguard that the individual possesses against the crude and ferocious instincts of the human animal… It's not the beginning of a movement, it's the end, at first it was called 'realism'—it is, to say the right word, the literature of the Second Empire that survived Sedan and achieved its logical and fatal movement…No, the ideal is not a dream, it has its reality, its sublime manifestations. The sublime isn't only to be found in poetry and art, but also in history; it doesn't live there permanently; it crosses a century, an epoch, a life; it trails behind it, like an illuminated train, a virtuous act, a heroism, a trace of genius…No, Mr Zola, once more, no…the Republic will not be naturalist."

Zola insists that like positivism, like materialism, naturalism equals the new Republic as "the formula of the new social state." The state is scientific and impersonal: "Here is what exists: try to come to terms with it."

Hippolyte Taine: "Don't describe or paint, Dissect!"

Zola, to Edmond de Goncourt: "The truth is, the book that speaks to me, that has a charm, is the last, in which I'm going to tell the story of a scientist… and the scientist, I would be quite tempted to model him on Claude Bernard, with all the communications in his papers and his letters...This would be fun...I would make a scientist with a backward and bigoted wife who would destroy his work as soon as he did it." Alexandre Dumas fils also declares his intention to base a novel on Claude, but only Zola means it, and his novel, *Docteur Pascal*, becomes part of his Rougon-Macquart series, "all to introduce the Second Empire by its characters, with the help of their individual dramas...Direct observation, exact anatomy, the acceptance and depiction of what is. Replace abstractions with realities. No more lying inventions, but real characters with true histories and the relativity of everyday life."

Flaubert: "The two muses of the modern age are history and science."

§

Claude's apartment is directly across the street from Collège de France, and, most likely from pity, that puffed-up Raffalovich gives him a coffee maker, fruits, flowers, meats, robe, clothing, fur, silks, rare books—the niceties that a wife would normally provide. If he abides to Mariette's strict surveillance, and endures her scolding for missing mass, she helps him host gatherings in his apartment-house basement, where dogs in various stages of dismemberment crawl piteously among the legs of the guests (or at least that's how it's been described to me). Damp and moldy, the basement exacerbates his afflictions, and his left hand hangs paralyzed.

CLAUDE'S RED NOTEBOOK:

Man is forced to be free for this reason alone, that he has a conscience and judgement. His liberty flows from this. He is free to do good or bad, but when he has done

bad, remorse proves to him that he was free, and that he
could have done otherwise had he wanted.

Claude, to Madame Raffalovich:

"Yesterday I made a long speech at the Science Academy which, so it seems, shocked everyone with its violence and strange language, which aren't my usual character. The colleague who knew me in my health approached me very concerned: something has happened to you, you seem to be out to get the whole world, and you are desperate that you find no one on whom to avenge yourself. Actually, I told him—I can only avenge on myself these horrible sufferings I'm experiencing."

In his notes for *Docteur Pascal*, Zola imagines a character, born in 1813, who, like Claude, would be fifty-nine in 1872 when it takes place. "I could perfectly take for my Dr Pascal these ideas which are very complete. They would suffice to summarize the philosophy of my whole series and I would only have to spread them out—Thus I see the whole part against the supernatural put in a discussion between Pascal and Clothilde—Next I see the whole explanation of the role of science given throughout Pascal's work—and finally, I see the hope of a better future world of science indicated at the end, thanks to a device, to a manuscript note that Clotilde finds in his papers and which comments on the incalcuable power, the serenity, if not the happiness, brought to man by science….The fight between the spiritualists and materialists, whose feet would go on whom…"

In Zola's final manuscript, Doctor Pascal leaves a note which Clotilde finds: "Life, it's the idea, the big motor, the soul of the world. And it's there that Clotilde keeps a small corner for the unknown. As far as we can imagine, there is always a point we won't know ourselves, and at that point is where many people start to become nervous."

The realist painter, Léon-Augustin L'hermitte, paints a portrait showing our hero in his laboratory during this final act. So, who does he
paint around him? I see Dr Dumont asking a question. D'Arsonval all
smiling and moustached. Dastre with pen in hand. Behind: Paul Bert,
Grehant, Malassez, and that clown, le père Lesage. L'hermitte details
the cave where Claude welcomed so many guests, and in the trough he
paints...—a puppy? a cat? It's hard to tell unless you look closer:

Zola, notes for *Doctor Pascal*: "The sadness of being, the idea of destiny, why are we on earth, and what are we here to do. When we have no faith in dogmas...expand thus the faith of V (Vicaire Savoyard de Rousseau)...Come back to the acceptance of nature, with an expansion on mystery. Life makes fun of our theories, she goes her own way."

4

FANATICS | ANIMALS

The shameless inability of the so-called 'Animal Protection' society to stand up to the scientists, makes it clear that we need more help handling the growing problem of stolen animals. To do this, the girls and I support private charities like the shelter at Garches (modeled on one at Battersea, supported by Queen Victoria). As a token, Animal Protection offers to pick up a few dogs, deliver them to Madame Faure at 34, rue de Buci, six, seven, ten a day—in addition to what she and the other women collect—and then, nightly, we drive them to Garches. But Garches isn't winterized, and our meetings focus on funding a winter home in Paris. Note that in the same building as Madame Faure is Mademoiselle Mazerolles, who only collects cats.

Remember when Mademoiselle Huot ended up in the paper for hitting Professor Brown-Sequard with an umbrella? Oh, she was a deed-doer, wasn't she!

Mademoiselle Huot:

"I stuffed myself into the shadows, guided by the half-light of a door slightly ajar. It was the amphitheater. No one. A vast table on a large single step made a platform almost even with the first row of seats, right in the middle of which I sat myself. A sign informed me of the special of the day: experiment on a monkey. Half a dozen students—of which four were female—spread out toward the bleachers, some distance from me. Foreigners, I could tell by their looks and their babbling. Here was the whole scholarly public in Claude Bernard's amphitheater that at one time held five hundred people... hee hee, the value has gone down on the blood market!

Brown-Sequard trotted in, saluting with a little paternal gesture to his disciples. He adjusted his glasses to get a better look at me, seemed satisfied... and initiated his first lesson. I understood we were going to see him start by cutting the vocal cords of the monkey—a painful operation without anesthetics that would then prevent him from crying out. The animal was brought in on a vivisection plank, a poor little child monkey, making supplications with its eyebrows that would make you fall to your knees, and now to me—me who felt like its mother at that moment—me rolling in guilt, in mud, to save and steal away this monkey to the other side of the sun. Who knows how I approached, calmly leaned on the platform 'as if to see better'; how, as the operator lowered the scissors toward the victim's throat...vlan! In a second, my umbrella hit, and fell broken...

You have hurt me, Madame!...You hit me! You must leave!

No. Bring in the officers.

This came to pass, and I was removed, but the swollen hand of the professor saved at least one little monkey that day."

Mademoiselle Huot later attends a public event at Trocadero where Dr Laborde has a dog strapped into the trough. She jumps onstage, demanding that he stop, bringing the show to an awkward end. That evening, she is visited at home by an emissary from Animal Protection, nervily accosting her because Dr Laborde is a member of the governing council! Claude held the same post. That shows what you need to know about that bunch. Madame Huot and Madame Masson start shelters in Belleville and Montrouge, and endure the harassment of police and journalists alike. We pass these details among us, and some of us write them down. Night after night, you can be sure to find Madame Delvincourt on her rounds up and down the hills—especially to the Jardin des Plantes—carrying baskets of *pâté* for hundreds of cats. Her speciality is rescuing cats who've been thrown into the sewer. She told me that in another life she didn't like cats, and in this life she must labor on their behalf.

I know Claude smugly calls our efforts "Don Quixotry."

Anna Kingsford, at some point, you and Mademoiselle Huot get so rightly sick of the Animal Protection Society that you decide to found a new one entirely: the Popular League Against the Abuses of Vivisection, with Maria Deraismes and a treasurer, Mr Serle, of 84, Faubourg Saint-Honoré. In a letter to the editor of the *Herald of Health*, you announce: "Its president is no less a person than the great poet Victor Hugo." Victor Hugo: "My name is nothing. It is in the name of the whole human race that you make your appeal. Your society is one that will reflect honor on the nineteenth century. Vivisection is a crime. The human race will repudiate these barbarities." The devout Robert Browning, a vice-president of the Victoria Street Society, writes two anti-vivisection poems, and Christina Rossetti publishes a special pamphlet, but our Victor Hugo makes us proud: "Human cruelty to animals might one day rebound upon our heads like Nero's cruelties." Your new French Society Against

Vivisection sponsors many lectures—and it's here we would have met—really, Anna Kingsford, don't you think we did?

Florence Miller recalls:

"As the leading scientific advocate of vegetarianism, Anna Kingsford was invited to lecture before the Sunday Lecture Society, and the Honorary Secretary, Mr Domville, came up to me at a meeting one evening and said, 'You are a great friend of Mrs Kingsford's, could you ask her to dress more plainly to appear on our platform? You know we are a scientific society and we avoid anything of the Stage order, so I feel that she is not suitably dressed now for the platform.'

'Nina,' I said to her presently, 'have you got an all-black platform gown? Mr Domville says his Committee likes their lady lecturers to be all in black.' She understood and made a *moue* at me, and she did appear in black—and looked more beautiful than ever!"

CLAUDE'S RED NOTEBOOK:

Physics teaches us that matter is inert, that is to say that it cannot produce movements by itself; some conditions are always required to intervene and change its state. Can one support this in physiology? How can volition be explained?

Is he the gadfly that drives you to wander, speak and lecture? Mad, are you the ragged virago or white Magian?

Prometheus: *It is worth it to indulge in weeping over evil doings if one is likely to win the tribute of a tear from the listener.*

Io: *Zeus inflamed by passion's dart has called upon me to unite in divine union. Hiding in the pastures, I became animal, and spurred by the gadfly now toil with revealing this body of truths.*

When you speak, do you hear yourself moo? When you look, do you see a cow, and try not to choke at this fat ugly version?

Chorus: *What a tale to strike our ears with sufferings so hard to look upon or hear about; grievous to endure. We shudder to behold.*

CLAUDE'S RED NOTEBOOK:
With animals, feelings only translate through movement, and we can easily confuse the lack of feeling with the paralysis of the motor nerves, and vice versa.

Chorus: *Speak then and tell all. It comforts those in pain to know beforehand all the pain they still must bear.*

Io: *Why should I go on living? Why not hurl myself at once down this rocky cliff, be dashed to pieces, and find relief from all my pain? Better to die once, than to suffer torment all my life.*

Prometheus: *Then you would find it hard to bear my agonies, since I am fated not to die. Death would have brought release; but now no end to suffering is in sight for me, until Zeus be deposed from sovereignty.*

Chorus: *What fate is given to Zeus, but everlasting power?*

Prometheus: *That is a thing you cannot know, so do not ask.*

To amble, gad about, knock around, traipse—to live the apocalypse and know a new age, Anna Kingsford, aka Rosamunda the Princess, aka the Virgin, aka the Martyr, aka the Hermetic Mystic, aka Killer of Killers, aka Faustine…Mr Maitland: "The soul that lived in her now had been here before as Ninon de l'Enclos, and Queen Anne Boleyn, and Joan of Arc, and St Mary Magdalen, and the Empress of Marcus Aurelius, the cruel and licentious Faustina, and Esther, the Queen of Ahasuerus! There is even more than a hint that she was once the spirit of the River Euphrates."

Io: *Where has my miserable wandering brought me? The Gadfly stings again! The ghost of Argus follows me with his gaze…It is Io, the girl with horns! Do not hide from me what it is my doom to suffer.*

Prometheus: *First, Io, I will name the many lands where Fate will toss you in your journey: write what I tell you in your book of memory.*

§

You pass your first year medical tests, Anna Kingsford, and their letter reads: *"You may inform your opponents that, so far from your informant having failed to pass his examination—he—meaning she—has passed with the highest note, save one, attainable."*

You will be a doctor, and you will write books for women on their health, but your own body appears lifeless when you seize. I'm sorry I didn't know you better, and that I complained that no writer could lift the burden from our tired backs, help us catch animals because you were weak, and that I couldn't recognize the value in a nice dress and well-turned phrase. With great interest, the girls and I read your pamphlet, *The Anti-Vivisection League or The New Crusade by an Englishwoman, Dedicated to the French People*:

"The abolition of vivisection will contribute strongly to the unification and new marriage of the separate halves of humanity. If she abandons her true companion, Intellect, Intuition would become superstition. If he abandons his real companion, Intuition, Intellect gives way to Materialism, whose eldest son was and will always be Cain, from whom the vivisectors directly descend. We can only imagine that, in their disgust at admitting women to the science departments, the materialist scientists would be moved by the sight of Intuition among their own sex and to see it share power with Intellect until finally we could get away from this struggle to the death which they've built at the cost of so much useless cruelty. Those who have penetrated the secret history of the world, could they ever hope that by adding Intellect to Intuition, the woman, armed with knowledge, will win the race of the physiology laboratory, and a new Redemption will take place, for the animals will have found their Christ. It's not from a lack of the feminine element in the French character that the French achieve such a high level of cruelty and impurity. We've nicknamed it the Woman of nations, but it's just like a non-repentant Madeleine rather than the non-fallen Madonna, like a Helen who, giving herself to Paris, choses the baser love, and the flowered path leading to ruin. New Cassandra, would I cry this much for nothing? Her prophecies came to pass, even though she was despised. This isn't just for the women of France but for Woman in France, the intuitive, sympathetic and feminine element in all French character..."

Maitland writes articles in the journals and papers, to which you respond with letters-to-the-editor—never using your name because it could compromise your medical diploma: "It would perhaps, I think, do good to the cause and reputation of women physicians were it known that the most active assailant—and, as I believe, the first assailant—of vivisection was a woman student of medicine. But one must be careful that no ignoble desire for praise be mixed up with this wish. I have tried hard to be free from base things."

Claude, from "On Curare", *Review des Deux Mondes* :
"Within the motionless body, behind the staring eye, with all the appearance of death, feeling and intelligence persist in all their force. Could one conceive of a more horrible suffering than that of an intelligence witnessing the successive subtraction of all the organs that serve it, and thus finding itself enclosed alive within a corpse? Since time began, epic stories wanting to move the reader to pity showed us sensitive beings closed in immobile bodies. Our imagination can't conceive of anything more unhappy than beings equipt with feeling, by that I mean able to feel pleasure and pain, while being deprived of the ability to flee the one and go toward the other. The torture that the poetic imagination has invented is produced naturally by the action of an American poison, curare. We could even add that the fiction is better than reality."

§

"Fanny, what's got into your ladies, loose in the world without a mote of sense!" "Fanny, are kittens worth this much trouble?" "Do you really think animals and humans are the same?"

How often will people jabber and finger-point, while avoiding the sight of their own dirty hands? As a long-standing member of a desperate chorus, I have grown skilled at stealing the arts and eloquence of those centerstage, and in this eloquence I have fashioned some arguments. In the preface to *La Comédie Humaine*, didn't Balzac write that all animals and people have been created "on one and the same principle"?

Claude: "The immediate object of study in experimental medicine isn't man but animals; man is only the goal that stays in the mind, outside the perilous experiments."

Man, animal, animal, man—words can't hold the confusion, so mightn't it be rewarding to just wander straight in, making a mess of what's always been a mess?

Geoffroy Saint-Hilaire: "There is, philosophically speaking, only a single animal."

Claude: "Physiologists...deal with just one thing, the properties of living matter and the mechanism of life, in whatever form it shows itself. For them, genus, species, and class no longer exist. There are only living beings; and if they choose one of them for study, that is usually for convenience in experimentation."

Julien de la Mettrie: "Man is not molded of costlier clay; nature has used but one dough, and has merely varied the leaven..."

For a long time, animals were considered equal enough to men to get the same treatment under the law. Put in jail, the animals received the same food as the other prisoners, and had right to the same lawyers, even though some judges worried that spells could allow animals to harness the "witchcraft of silence" and thereby not feel the pain of the tortures inflicted on the men (*maleficium taciturnatatis*).

Claude: "We must admit nothing occult; there are only phenomena and the conditions of phenomena."

Claude, to Madame Raffalovich:
"Again on the subject of savage beasts, you were interested in the hedgehog

*family I mentioned earlier and on whom I had designs. Alas, all is fin-
ished. There are disasters even here and unhappy families. The family had
four little ones and a mother; a dog killed one, a flood drowned two, and
the last died of grief, I think. The inconsolable mother has left, at least we
haven't heard or seen her since she spent several nights making nocturnal
echoes with her plaintive cries."*

Claude takes Mariette with him to the International Science Conference in
Clermont-Ferrand, where going home by open carriage, he gets soaked in
a downpour, and this brings back fevers. But there's the harvest, and with
great effort he restarts his experiments to convert sugar to alcohol—still to
dispute Pasteur that the same fermentation has a micro-biotic origin. He sits
under the trees on his bench of Sisyphus, looking to the hills where pagan
gods and spirits of nature were long ago recast as devils so that the medieval
church could claim sole proprietorship of even the smallest stream.

Claude: "Today the experimental spirit is impoverished and crumbles
in endless nonsense. This is what we would call nit-picking." An experiment in 1867 that might have shown the existence of germs did not
because Claude denies the role of germs in disease; like foreign invaders,
they fall outside the determinism of his *milieu intérieur*. Claude: "The life
of an organism is simply the resultant of all its innermost workings; it
may appear more or less lively, or more or less enfeebled and languishing,
without possible explanation by anything in its outer environment; it is
governed by the conditions of the inner environment." Pasteur repeats
some of those same experiments and shows the presence of these germs.

CLAUDE'S RED NOTEBOOK:

*Those who conclude are attacked. It would be easier to
describe without concluding, or to criticize, that is, to
oppose without concluding.*

Those who have attacked me, have not concluded.

But the interests of science demands that one concludes. Example: I have proved that animals cannot live without the pancreas. But they perhaps survive longer when they are fed in a certain way.

Does a scientist listen to Nature without hope or prejudice? Where he was brave, is he humble in front of experimental results? If the facts contradict the idea, does he take a backward step in obedience to their testimony? Mythical Tancredi's crusading warriors, instructed to cut trees for fortress towers, heard pained cries coming from inside the trunks. Tancredi, who loved and killed an enemy warrior, Clorinda, heard her voice from a cyprus, begging him not to kill her a second time. He returned to camp persuaded that each tree is alive with a soul. "It is not in my power," Tancredi says, "to touch another bough of that forest." Claude often tells of the magical moment when he was sectioning the sympathetic nerve of a rabbit—how he expected to find the affected part cold, but it got hot—leading to the discovery of the vaso-constriction nerves. Proudly he was humble then; simply seeing what there was to see.

But the devil might penetrate the humble mind of such a Christian. The extremity of control that the medieval church held over all aspects of village life severed Claude's ancestors from the symbolism, reciprocity, and pleasure of any nature that might take events into its own hands. No moment too private, no forest too dense, for the church to oversee. As members of the household, and therefore under the king's ban, animals enjoyed the same *wergild* as women and peasant workers, and their *beste covert* had the same rights and responsibilities as humans. In the case of violent crime, the death penalty was required, especially for domestic animals—for not only was evil incarnate in the beast who committed the deed, but also in the infested home which could be vexed for centuries, its *aura corrumpens* holding title to the real estate until the sin was fully paid. An animal, convicted in the court and hung in public, was often dressed in human clothes and mask.

Mary, looking on, "knew through her compassion what it is to be a mother." Christ on Calvary said, "Here is your son," and so it is that labor pain is not about childbirth, but the pain of interceding. For Jesus came not as a king, but as a poor creature, helpless and inviting motherhood of everyone. You might say that Christ took all the positive aspects of the world for the church, leaving Nature with nothing but forests full of devils, and dragons who would steal our innocent souls, or our children in sacrifice. The priest says: it's not enough to refrain from wrong—the devil waits for any crack through which to enter! Morning chants and admonitions against demons must be offered, as much as evening prayers for the dead—and every so often an actual exorcism will call out some Lignifex, Latibor, Monitor, Shulium, or Reromfex. Lucifer himself will make appearances, until the priest with bell, book, and candle confronts him. Yet given the baptisms, the churchgoing, the exorcisms, where do all the devils hide? Ah, the priest replies, they easily take residence in the beasts, one step above hell, where they can exert their intelligence, and fool people into believing these creatures have souls and hearts and minds like us. But since we are taught that this is a ruse, we justify the mistreatment of animals who are merely possessed, just as centaurs and satyrs and dire chimeras are. The pious Catholic works beside the Father in punishing monsters.

Jesuit Father Bougeant, from *Philosophical Amusements on the Language of the Animals*, 1737:
"What matters it whether it is a devil or another kind of creature that is in our service or contributes to our amusement?...If it be said that these poor creatures, which we have learned to love and so fondly cherish, are foreordained to eternal torments, I can only adore the decrees of God, but do not hold myself responsible for the terrible sentence; I leave the execution of the dread decision to the sovereign Judge and continue to live with my little devils, as I live pleasantly with a multitude of persons, of whom, according to the teachings of our holy religion, the great majority will be damned."

Claude, to Madame Raffalovich:
"I'm sitting under a tree in the vines neighboring my woods; I'm imitating the cries of the buntings with a decoy, while at the same time moving a mirror that sparkles in the sun under a dried branch on which will perch the birds, victims of their coquetry. It's truly curious to see with what joy these two-legged creatures, feathered, consider themselves and complement each other in this contemplation. It's in this moment that I unleash my rifle shot and the murderous bullet comes to deliver them to Marriette's cooking pot."

So humans are sinners, and by substitution can only be absolved if someone innocent lifts it from us and carries it for us. We are given our punishments, some during life, some after death—when a final accounting lays our deeds out undisguised by any transitive property.

Anna Kingsford, letter to Florence Miller:

"The great need of the popular form of the Christian religion is precisely a belief in the solidarity of all living things. It is in this that Buddha surpassed Jesus— in this divine recognition of the universal right to charity. Who can doubt it who visits Rome—the city of the Pontiff—where now I am, and witnesses the black-hearted cruelty of these 'Christians' to the animals that toil and slave for them?

Ill as I am, I was forced, the day of my arrival, to get out of the carriage in which I was driving to chastise a wicked child who was tor-turing a poor little dog tied by a string to a pillar—kicking it and stamping on it. No one save myself interfered.

Today I saw a great, thick-shod peasant kick his mule in the mouth out of pure wantonness. Argue with these ruffians, or with their priests, and they tell you, 'Christians have no duties to the beasts that perish.' Their Pope has told them so, so that everywhere in Catholic Christendom the poor, patient, dumb creatures endure every species of torment without a single word being uttered on their behalf by the teachers of religion. It is horrible—damnable. And the true reason for it all is because the beasts are popularly believed to be soulless. I say, paraphrasing a mot of Voltaire's: 'If it were true that they had no souls, it would be necessary to invent souls for them.' Earth has become a hell for want of this doctrine."

Animals quickly recognize signs of kindness, not redeemed in another world, but right from our hand—and that's how to coax even the most terrified cat with a caress and a morsel, a quiet moment in the courtyard as we await the next driver in the chain of escape. But howevermuch some of our friends cuddle and love the cats, it's the grinning, dodging dogs that have always filled my girls' faces with joy. It was rumored that in the Mid-dle Ages, dogs didn't get the plague, and so were considered agents of the devil. But even they can tell when they're maligned, and they look at us quizzically and ashamed. Canine protectors guide men through death and birth, like Anubis calibrating the scale that measures a dead man's heart

against the feather of virtue. The city of dogs, Hardai, drew followers of
Anubis, who accompanied Hermes bringing the dead to Hades. Later he
became Hermanubis, dog-headed but more friendly, his cult becoming
Saint Christopher's. Ritual massacres of dogs were thought to cheer the
gods and head off violent summer weather. Only priests were allowed to
perform the slaughter, acting as divine agents rather than butchers. Black
dogs were preferred for sacrifice, to purify a journey or please ghosts. Scat-
tered among infant graves, puppies were thought to absorb illness, after
which they and the disease could be disposed of.

Anna Kingsford: "In what shall we say the practices of the secret devil-
worshippers of medieval times differed from those which now go on in
the underground laboratories of the medical school? ... Nothing is easier
than this method of gaining knowledge, for the operator sacrifices nought
of his own to gain it; he gives only other lives and these the most innocent he can obtain...It is black magic which, in order to cure a patient,
first transfers his complaint to an innocent victim. He who accepts health
at such a cost shall but save it to lose it." Under Roman rule, Asklepios,
Apollo's son, had temples where gentle canines, cynotherapists, walked
among the sick or lay among them licking their wounds. Asklepios com-
peted directly with early Christians, and so his temples were defaced and
destroyed. The dog who licked Lazarus' sores came from a church built
on the site of an Asklepian temple, and Christ resurrected him.

Father Bougeant:
"Thus a devil, after having been a cat or a goat, may pass, not by choice,
but by constraint, into the embryo of a bird, a fish or a butterfly. Happy
are those who make a lucky hit and become household pets, instead of
beasts of burden or slaughter. The lottery of destiny bars them the right of
voluntary choosing. Pythagoras' doctrine is untenable in its application to
men and contrary to religion, but it fits admirably into the system already
set forth concerning beasts as devil's incarnations, and shocks neither our
faith nor reason."

Claude's own Saint-Julien was ravaged in 1545 by a swarm of green-ish weevils. The winegrowers brought legal complaint, while a lawyer, Pierre Falcon, defended the insects. The judge proclaimed: "Inasmuch as God, the supreme author of all that exists, hath ordained that the earth should bring forth fruits and herbs not solely for the sustenance of rational human beings, but likewise for the preservation and support of insects, which fly about on the surface of the soil, therefore it would be unbecoming to proceed with rashness against the animals now actually accused and indicted; on the contrary, it would be more fitting for us to have recourse to the mercy of heaven and to implore pardon for our sins." The Host was carried around the vineyards at high mass, and people paid extra tithes. A testimony, signed by the curate, attests this was all handled *pro forma*.

Thirty years later, the infestation in Saint-Julien returned, and this time Pierre Rembaud, lawyer for the bugs, argued that the plaintiffs' request of excommunication was unsuitable. He affirmed that the insects had kept in their rights since, as we read in the book of *Genesis*, the lower animals were created before Man, and God said to them: "Be fruitful and multiply and fill the waters of the seas, and let fowl multiply in the earth," etc. Now, the Creator would not have said this if he didn't want these creatures to have sufficient means of support—therefore the accused, in living off the vines of the plaintiffs, were only exercising their rights. After adjourning a few days, the prosecution responded that the insects were created subservient to man, which was why they were created first, and their only *raison d'être* was to minister to man, "as the Psalmist asserts and Saint Paul confirms." The trial was taking so long, and was so continually deferred, that the community finally offered an 'insect enclosure' outside the village where the weevils might receive alternative sustenance. A vote was taken, subject to the approval of the insects, but they declined due to insufficient food on the proposed plot.

"Tony dear,

I've sent you today a basket of pears; the ripest are on top, the least ripe beneath. Put them in a closet; they'll ripen in order and will be good to eat in 8-15 days. In a few days I'll send a basket of red and green grapes and some vine peaches, the ones from the trellis having already passed their prime.

Your aunt Jenny and her children came to spend two days visiting me... They send you hugs and kisses. Yesterday, I saw Mr Chretien who lost his old Jeanne who you might remember. He sends his regards... It is extremely hot here; the fruit is all drying on the trees; the harvest will be better than last year's, but will still be mediocre.

I send all my love, as well as to your sister.

Your affectionate father, Claude Bernard
Saint-Julien, September 7, 1874"

§

As windows go, the medical school library's stretch to the sky, and the long wooden tables feel warm after the entry stairs. You read and study here in a blaze of occasional sun, memorize lessons, then return to the hospital to follow doctors on their rounds, cleaning wounds, observing the sick. None of this seems to dampen the scientists' hostility to you, and Mr Lubanski pens an article against the Anti-Vivisection League: "I would gladly put aside a monkey or a spaniel to vivisect the old English ladies who come with beating umbrellas to butt into things that don't concern them…"

You are not going to let them intimidate you into quitting, so every morning as you pass the stone girl, you give her a smile; her naked breast but a ruse. Your body, too, has not served you well, and must

be held up through extraordinary measures. Mr Maitland waits by
the entrance on a small bench to escort you home after dark. He continues to press the esoteric studies he prefers, alongside the medical.
You do confuse me, Anna Kingsford, with your Christian heresies and
mystical writings, and I can't follow your system of souls and demi-
souls, ghosts, devils, Elementals, astrals, and all the spirits attending
a person in each incarnation, as you describe in your books: *The Various Orders of Spirits and How to Discern Them; Man's Two Personalities and Karma; Violationism, Or Sorcery in Science; Fate, Heredity, and
Reincarnation; Animals and Their Souls; Virgin of the World of Hermes
Mercurius Trismegistus.* Yet one day, you write, we'll weep not because
animals are tortured, but because we will have lost our way of knowing
it, and this I do understand. Slumped on a bench outside the cabinet
rooms, you are so cold it isn't clear you are living. A crowd gathers, as
is often the case with you. For spitting on their idols, they accuse you
of sorcery. For these are popular times for heretics and lunatics, and
I'm not sure it helps when you go on about karma and all that. Those
ideas may entertain as much as any, but why do you confuse everything
into one?

Anna Kingsford:
"The teaching of Hermetic science is in accordance with the tenets of
evolution. It maintains that the 'soul' is elaborated, individualized, and
made permanent by means of successive and progressive incarnations.
Beginning in the realm of the elemental and inorganic, it gradually
makes its way upward and onward, perpetually enduring and striving,
through the organic world—plant-life and animal-life—into the human.
At every 'death' an astral relict of *persona* is shed, and this is, progres-
sively, less and less evanescent as the selfhood ascends in the scale. Thus
the ghosts of horses, dogs, and domesticated, intelligent animals have
almost as much 'personality' as those of average human beings. But the
real Soul, or Ego, is not resident in the ghost. It may remain connected
with it under certain conditions for a longer or shorter period—as, no

doubt, it was enchained by affection to the ghost of the good dog whose history I recounted in *Light*. This association of Soul and Astral may be the result of meritorious affection, or it may be, on the contrary, the enforced penalty of materiality. Other conditions, such as premature or violent death, may cause it, or special circumstances, peculiar to individual souls. But, sooner or later, the soul disentangles itself from this intermediary state, and passes on to other births, shedding its lower personality, and going on to animate other and higher natures. Thus all animals are *potential* men—men in the making—and must inevitably, in process of evolution, develop human conditions. No animals are immortal or glorified as animals; but also no animal perishes—no, not even the lowest...The contrary doctrine strikes a fatal blow to the solidity of the universe, and makes of man a separate creation, unconnected with the rest of living beings. If animals are soulless, then man is soulless, for he is flesh of their flesh, physiologically and essentially. Hence I say that the very core and root-doctrine of the new dispensation must be, and will be, the recognition of the Buddhist precept concerning the brotherhood of all living things, based on the truth that the universe is One, and that One Life (Atman) pervades and maintains it. Because all are eternal, we are eternal, and not otherwise. All things press towards the human, all evolution hastens to develop into Man. Faithfully Yours."

§

Of the many young scientists vying for his blessing and attending his courses, Claude chooses a young E.J. Marey to mentor, and finally to promote. It's an odd choice, and this young man intrigues us all. Marey's father insisted he attend medical school instead of study engineering, but by the time Marey is introduced to Claude, he has already witnessed the waste and chaos of animal experiments. Even though, as Claude writes, "The observer...ought to be the photographer of phenomena; his observations ought to represent nature exactly...He listens to nature and writes at her dictation"—this has never quite been the case, or at least not until Marey dreams up a way to mitigate the failure of a scientist's language as he fumbles to communicate what he sees. Marey realizes, for example, that in attempting to measure blood flow, the incisions needed to place the instruments constantly create errors in the results. "In a living body," Marey asserts, "things either move too fast, or go too slowly, for us to perceive, and when we interfere, it's worse." Making known this frustration with vivisection, Marey offers to banish all human interference from the scientific process—"The physiological event can autograph itself"—and he promises to turn "life"—this thing we recognize but can hardly describe—into information.

His first patented invention, the *sphygmographe*, graphs the pulse, and another, the *manometre*, graphs arterial pressure. These earn him enough money to start his own workshop, and he never practices a day of medicine. In Claude's lab he sets up his 'drum', which slowly and constantly registers the output from his sensors in ink:

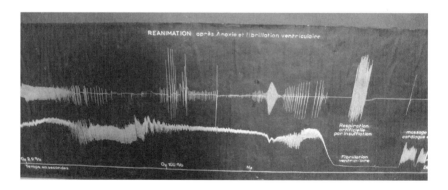

Marey, from *Phenomena of Flight in the Animal Kingdom* :

"I indicated a myographic method which might be applied without mutilating the animal upon which the experiment was performed. It consists in employing the swelling of a muscle to afford evidence of its changes in length—that is to say by its contraction or relaxation...I have made use of flexible air tubes of India rubber in transmitting these effects, a method which has enabled me at times to register at some distance the beating of the heart, the pulse, and the motions of respiration...."

Using Marey's inventions, the experimenter stands apart, and the investigated body stays closed. Yet somehow this doesn't prevent 'secrets' from being transmitted to the scientist, who alone knows how to decipher them. Claude uses Marey's *cardiograph* to trace a heart's intimate functions onto paper during 'induced emotions.' Hamlet: "You would play upon me; you would seem to know my stops; you would pluck out the heart of my mystery; you would sound me from my lowest note to the top of my compass; and there is much music, excellent voice, in this little organ, yet cannot you make it speak."

Marey:

"The motif of applying emotion-gauging technology to unveil the truth and expose a private and inner self was present in the writings of Claude Bernard—hinting at the potential application of emotion-gauging technologies for the revelation of truth and deceit in his 1865 lecture, when he distinguished between sincere and feigned emotions: only sincere emotions, he explained, would activate the involuntary physiological mechanisms of emotions and produce a distinguishable and characteristic graph."

Where Claude calls physiology "experiments of destruction," Marey modestly calls himself an "engineer," whose body of knowledge sits between *techne* (the ability to make things) and *mechane* (the know-how to produce astonishing effects). For Marey, like the Greeks, the essential terms of life are *krinein*=perception and *kinein*=movement—yet for all that, he still believes that man and animal are no more than machines, universal and quantifiable actions.

§

In 1834, the astronomer François Arago invited Victor Hugo to visit the Paris Observatory's powerful new telescope. Looking out at what was previously impossible to see, traveling without moving, Hugo didn't write about this experience until the 1870s:

"Thanks to the telescope, I journeyed a quick 99,775 lieus in a second. Ultimately, this terrifying and sudden approach of the planet had no effect on me. The field of the telescope was too narrow to take in the whole planet, the ball didn't fit, and what I could see of it, if I could see any of it, was only a shadowy segment. Arago later explained that he had directed the telescope toward a point on the moon which wasn't yet lit.
    I repeated:—I see nothing.
    Just look, said Arago."

Claude: "It's not the head, it's the heart that means the unknown, which leads the world…With scientists, science develops the head and kills the heart, just like it suffocates the theological in forcing a renunciation of all first causes."

Hugo:
"Confusion in the details, diffusion of everything, that was the quality of the contour and relief that could be sketched out in the night. The depth effect and the loss of reality was terrible. And nonetheless the real was there. I touched the fold of my clothing: I was, me. And so, that too was. This dream was a world."

In addition to the *cardiograph*, Marey invents a *polygraph*, a *pneumograph* (respiratory movements), a *myograph* (neuromuscular events), a *thermo-*

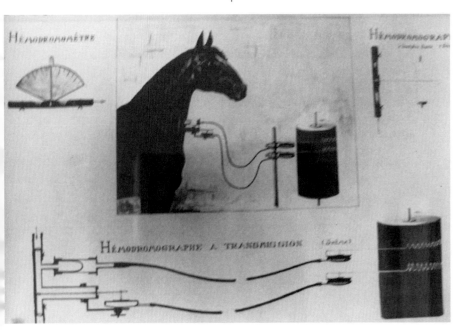

graph (temperature change), an *electrometer* (electrical change), a *plethys-mograph* (volume changes), *chronophotography*, and finally a *dynamograph* (measurement platform for the reaction forces on the ground). Marey aspires to graphing an "act of will" in the midst of a voluntary deed.

Denis Diderot, from *Letter on the Blind*, 1749:

"That of all the external signs which raise our pity and ideas of pain, the blind are affected only by cries, I have in general no high thought of their humanity. What difference is there to a blind man between a man peeing and one bleeding in silence? Do not we ourselves cease to be compassionate when distance or the smallness of the objects produces on us the same effect as deprivation of sight upon the blind? So much do our virtues depend on the sensations we receive, and the degree by which we are affected by external things. I don't doubt that if it were not for the fear of punishment, many people would find it less disagreeable to kill a man at a distance than to cut an ox's throat with their own hands. We pity a horse in pain, and we make nothing of crushing an ant; and is it not by the same principle that we are moved?"

Hugo:

"Some priests put the moon's crescent on the head of Diana and others at the feet of Mary. That's the religious moon. In all of that was a universe, a path. If religions take the moon's poetry, science has no trouble putting it back; real science, through its disdain of hypothesis, false science through seeking pananceas and philosopher stones... Poets have created a metaphoric moon, and scientists an algebraic one. The real moon is between the two."

Claude promotes Marey for the greatest honor, the Physiology Prize, writing, "...The method's principle would have stayed infertile on its own. It's this problem that Dr Marey resolved for physiology and for medicine; he created instruments and tools with whose help a vital phenomenon could be written of itself..."

Hugo:

"Other things than ourselves close by. The inaccessible almost touches. The invisible seen. It seems we have only to extend our hand. The more we look, the more we're convinced of it, the less we believe. Instead of being calmed, our astonishment increases...We have vertigo from the universe suspended in the void. We are ourselves like that in air. Yes, this thing is. It seems it's looking at you. It's holding you. The perception of the phenomenon becomes clearer and clearer; this presence squeezes your heart; it's the effect of the greatest ghosts. The silence increases the terror. Holy terror. It is strange to glimpse such a thing and to hear no sound. And then, it dies. Movement shifts the lineaments. Darkness complicates what is removed. The giant simulacra undoes and recomposes itself. Impossible to distinguish anything specific. Impossible to take your eyes off this ghostly world."

Claude, letter to Madame Raffalovich:

"Dear Madame, my stormy outing has thrown me back worse than ever into the land of the flu. I'm really distraught because all my projects are vanishing, and I don't dare take up anything relating to my classes. I'm reduced to stoking the remaining embers of my reflections on the fragility of human things, and on doubting myself."

§

"To F. P. Cobbe
Down, Beckenham, Kent.

My dear Miss Cobbe,

I have been greatly interested by your article in the Quarterly. It seems to me the best analysis of the mind of an animal that I have ever read, & I agree with you on most points. I have been particularly glad to read what you say about the reasoning power of dogs & about that rather vague matter, their self-consciousness. I dare say however that you wd prefer criticisms to admiration. I regret that you quote Jesse so often: I made enquiries about one case (which quite broke down) from a man who certainly ought to have known Mr Jesse well, & I was cautioned that he had not written in a scientific spirit. I regret also that you quote old writers; it may be very illiberal but their statements go for nothing with me, & I suspect with many others. It passes my powers of belief that dogs ever commit suicide; assuming the statements to be true, I shd think it more probable that they were distraught & did not know what they were doing; nor am I able to credit about fetishes.

One of the most interesting subjects in yr article seems to me to be about the moral sense. Since publishing the **Descent of Man**, I have got to believe rather more than I did in dogs having what may be called a conscience. When an honorable dog has committed an undiscovered offense he certainly seems ashamed (& this is the term naturally & often used) rather than afraid to meet his master. My dog, the beloved & beautiful Polly, is at such times extremely affectionate towards me; & this leads me to mention a little anecdote. When I was a very little boy, I had committed some offense, so that my conscience troubled me; & when I met my father, I lavished so much affection on him, that he at once asked me what I had done, & told me to confess. I was so utterly confounded at his suspecting anything, that I remember the scene clearly to the present day; & it seems to me that Polly's frame of mind on such occasions is much the same as was mine, for I was not then at all afraid of my father.

This note is not worth sending, but I have nothing better to write & I remain with kind regards to Miss Lloyd.

yours very sincerely Charles Darwin"

Despite his misgivings, Darwin once or twice performs experiments on his own beloved pigeons: "I love them to the extent that I cannot bear to skin & skeletonise them;" he writes, "I have done the black deed and murdered an angelic little Fan-tail Pointerat 10 days old."

"November

My dear Mr Darwin,

You will know how pleased & proud your letter has made me.—I do not write to draw from you any more words, valuable though they be either as praise or as criticism, but just to say I have sent you the Cornhill just published to shew you another instance of what seems to me genuine superstition in dogs. Of course I rather turned the matter to jest in calling a stump a fetish—but the sentiment of vague awe at the incomprehensible is surely, I think, to be traced both in such freaks of dogs & in the shying of horses; & is very nearly akin to human superstition if not quite the same feeling.

Your own & your dog's similar behaviour after the commission of guilt, form delicious counterparts! Do you think the phenomenon can at all explain the exceeding religiosity of a great many arrant moral offenders?

Miss Lloyd entering agrees with you about the suicide of dogs & wished me not to insert the stories in my article—I did so in truth only hypothetically. Is there not some sort of radiating creature that casts off its own limbs, and strictly speaking causes its own dissolution when captured?

I am sorry to hear of Jesse's untrustworthiness. No doubt old stories of natural history are little to be relied on for scientific purposes. They only shew what men then thought their beasts might do—Would that those cruel old Jews had one such anecdote as that of Ulysses' dog in all their literature. It would have stopped a thousand Christian atrocities...

We have just returned from the zoos where we paid a domiciliary visit to the Chimpanzee in his private study. The poor dear little beast took a fancy to me & stroked my dress & face affectionately. I must say the grasp of his strong warm hand,—gentle and cordial as any human handshaking, was quite awful to me. I should consider it every bit as much murder to kill him as an idiot—The nearer one feels in pity & sympathy to an ape or an idiot the more I think the vague sense presses on us that some positive thing—(a thing we may as well call a "soul" as *anything else,—) is missing; & not that it is merely a rudimentary stage of development which we behold—This impression does not come from any theory—indeed it does not fit any theories at all—but it is one which comes to me with very vivid insistence—*

With many apologies for troubling you with this long letter & with my (very childish) article in the Cornhill,

believe me dear Mr Darwin, most truly yrs

Frances P Cobbe"

Francis Darwin:
"It was in November 1875 that my father gave his evidence before the Royal Commission on Vivisection. I have, therefore, placed together here the matter relating to this subject, irrespective of date. Something has already been said of my father's strong feeling with regard to suffering, both in man and beast. It was indeed one of the strongest feelings in his nature, and was exemplified in matters small and great, in his sympathy with the educational miseries of dancing dogs, or in his horror at the sufferings of slaves.

...He once made an attempt to free a patient in a mad-house, who (as he wrongly supposed) was sane. He had some correspondence with the gardener at the asylum, and on one occasion he found a letter from a patient enclosed with one from the gardener. The letter was rational in tone and declared that the writer was sane and wrongfully confined. My father wrote to the Lunacy Commissioners (without explaining the source of his information) and in due time heard that the man had been visited by the Commissioners, and that he was certainly insane.

The remembrance of screams, or other sounds heard in Brazil, when he was powerless to interfere with what he believed to be the torture of a slave, haunted him for years, especially at night. In smaller matters, where he could interfere, he did so vigorously. He returned one day from his walk pale and faint from having seen a horse ill-used, and from the agitation of violently remonstrating with the man. On another occasion he saw a horse-breaker teaching his son to ride, the little boy was frightened and the man was rough; my father stopped, and jumping out of the carriage reproved the man in no measured terms.

One other little incident may be mentioned, showing that his humanity to animals was well known in his own neighbourhood. A visitor, driving from Orpington to Down, told the cabman to go faster. 'Why,' said the man, 'if I had whipped the horse *this* much driving Mr Darwin, he would have got out of the carriage and abused me well.'

With respect to the special point under consideration,—the sufferings of animals subjected to experiment,—nothing could show a stronger feeling than the following extract from a letter to Professor Ray Lankester (March 22, 1871):—'You ask about my opinion on vivisection. I quite agree that it is justifiable for real investigations on physiology; but not for mere damnable and detestable curiosity. It is a subject which makes me sick with horror, so I will not say another word about it, else I shall not sleep to-night.'

An extract from Sir Thomas Farrer's notes shows how strongly he expressed himself in a similar manner in conversation:—'The last time I had any conversation with him was at my house in Bryanston Square, just before one of his last seizures. He was then deeply interested in the vivisection question and what he said made a deep impression on me. He was a man eminently fond of animals and tender to them; he would not knowingly have inflicted pain on a living creature; but he entertained the strongest opinion that to prohibit experiments on living animals, would be to put a stop to the knowledge of, and the remedies for, pain and disease.'

The Anti-Vivisection agitation, to which the following letters refer, seems to have become specially active in 1874, as may be seen, *e.g.* by the index to *Nature* for that year, in which the word *vivisection* suddenly comes into prominence. But before that date the subject had received the earnest attention of biologists. Thus at the Liverpool Meeting of the British Association in 1870, a Committee was appointed, whose report defined the circumstances and conditions under which, in the opinion of the signatories, experiments on living animals were justifiable. In the spring of 1875, Lord Hartismere introduced a Bill into the Upper House to regulate the course of physiological research. Shortly afterwards a Bill more just towards science in its provisions was introduced to the House of Commons by Messrs. Lyon Playfair, Walpole, and Ashley. It was, however, withdrawn on the appointment of a Royal Commission to inquire into the whole question. The Commissioners commenced their inquiry in July, 1875, and the Report was published early in the following year."

In the Commission's Report, a Dr Hoggan is quoted describing that after a curare experiment on a dog, "The inquisitors left for their homes, leaving the tortured victim alone with the clanking engine working on it, till death came in the silence of the night, and set the sufferer free." A Commissioner, Mr Forster, follows up: "Looking at this account of this experiment, the animal seems to have been ten hours under treatment, and then the operators left. Do you imagine that it was necessary to the success of the experiment that the animal should be left alive and not killed?" Dr Hoggan: "I have seen the thing often done….It simply meant this: that the next day they could work upon it; if they kept the dog, it might still have life enough to see whether its nerves would still act. No doubt, they intended to continue, but death came in the interval and thwarted them."

"to Mrs Litchfield   January 4, 1875
My dear H.

—Your letter has led me to think over vivisection (I wish some new word like anæssection could be invented) for some hours, and I will jot down my conclusions, which will appear very unsatisfctory to you. I have long thought physiology one of the greatest of sciences, sure sooner, or more probably later, greatly to benefit mankind; but, judging from all other sciences, the benefits will accrue only indirectly in the search for abstract truth. It is certain that physiology can progress only by experiments on living animals. Therefore the proposal to limit research to points of which we can now see the bearings in regard to health, &c., I look at as puerile. I thought at first it would be good to limit vivisection to public laboratories; but I have heard only of those in London and Cambridge, and I think Oxford; but probably there may be a few others. Therefore only men living in a few great towns would carry on investigation, and this I should consider a great evil. If private men were permitted to work in their own houses, and required a licence, I do not see who is to determine whether any particular man should receive one. It is young unknown men who are the most likely to do good work. I would gladly punish severely any one who operated on an animal not rendered insensible, if the experiment made this possible; but here again I do not see that a magistrate or jury could possibly determine such a point. Therefore I conclude, if (as is likely) some experiments have been tried too often, or anæsthetics have not been used when they could have been, the cure must be in the improvement of humanitarian feelings. Under this point of view I have rejoiced at the present agitation. If stringent laws are passed, and this is likely, seeing how unscientific the House of Commons is, and that the gentlemen of England are humane, as long as their sports are not considered, which entail a hundred or thousand-fold more suffering than the experiments of physiologists—if such laws are passed, the result will assuredly be that physiology, which has been until within the last few years at a standstill in England, will languish or quite cease. It will then be carried on solely on the Continent; and there will be so many the fewer workers on this grand subject; and this I should greatly regret. By the way, F. Balfour, who has worked for two or three years in the laboratory at Cambridge, declares to George that he has never seen an experiment, except with animals rendered insensible. No doubt the names of doctors will have great weight with the House of Commons; but very many practitioners neither know nor care anything about the progress of knowledge. I cannot at present see my way to sign any petition, without hearing what physiologists thought would be its effect, and then judging for myself. I certainly could not sign the paper sent me by Miss Cobbe, with its monstrous (as it seems to me) attack on Virchow for experimenting on the Trichinæ. I am tired and so no more.

Yours affectionately, Charles Darwin"

§

Claude, to Madame R:

"Life is very difficult. As the prince of Monaco in Rabagas says, and as many others have said before him: If you don't speak, your silence is interpreted; if you do speak, your words are interpreted. Let us judge this according to something that just happened to me. You remember, perhaps, a letter that I wanted to write to Bordeaux; it was sent, and what's more, was published. Up to that point nothing very extraordinary happened. But yesterday, I received a letter from an important person who, taking up all my sentences one after the other, proves to me by A+B that I am the most religious, the most right-thinking of all men, and one of the most powerful upholders of religion. I did not think I had said so much, and I am very sure that I didn't think any of that at all. I am quite confused and don't know what to answer and yet I must. I will do my best to say things that cannot be understood differently from what I intend, but I admit that I don't know if I will succeed..."

In January, Claude is received at the mansion of Patrice de Mac-Mahon, the war-hero monarchist rewarded with the presidency of the Third Republic for his victory over the Commune. It is snowing; ice everywhere. Claude gets worse in the cab that takes him home. He puts himself *au lit*, to be bed-panned by Mariette. Feverish and writhing in the pain of failing kidneys, he scratches another letter to Madame R:

"A proposition that I am developing in a work under preparation is that there are no real causes and that the idea of causality is purely metaphysical. Events and facts succeed one another, are bound up with each other, and interpenetrate according to a law that is the condition for their existence. But they do not engender each other and they do not stand in a relationship of necessary cause and effect...And anyhow, what is a cause? This word in Aristotle has forty-nine different meanings, and in Plato, sixty-four....You understand that one would be hard put to give a precise meaning to this word, even from a metaphysical point of view. You see, dear lady, what I'm up against."

§

A young country woman, Marian Evans, moves to London and throws down her gauntlet with an article, "Silly Novels by Lady Novelists," in which she asks why women construct only baroque and sensationalist plots—declaring her admiration for the 'realist' novels of the continent, which she will pursue under a new name, George Eliot. George Eliot possesses a soul longing for a soulmate—and she finds it in George Lewes, though they never marry. Eliot and Lewes talk and write a lot about novels, and about how Claude Bernard's laboratory experimental methods, rather than generic 'natural history', will engender successful literature. The investigative tool (Lewes paraphrases Bernard) will likewise be vivisection. In her novel, *The Lifted Veil*, Eliot believes she has succeeded in transfering to ink the objective facets of emotion—and even more so in *Middlemarch*: "If we had a keen vision and feeling of all ordinary human life, it would be like hearing the grass grow and the squirrel's heart beat, and we should die of that roar which lies on the other side of silence. As it is, the quickest of us walk about well wadded with stupidity."

CLAUDE'S RED NOTEBOOK:

A literary writer is a man who speaks agreeably about nothing. A scientist who writes well will never be a literary writer because he does not write in order to write, but to say something. The literary writer is the man, who by his speciality sacrifices fundamentals for form. He is the dressmaker, the tailor, who dresses up a mannikin as a great man.

An observer can never give facts divorced from his mind.

Lewes and Eliot emulate science, believing mental happiness or misery belong to the nervous system in the same way that a novel "tests vision of details and relations" by "subtle actions" "inaccessible by any sort of lens" except the imagination. This practice reveals not *anatomy*, but Lewes' ideal of experimental data and informed hypothesis. Lewes considers that narrative problems "justify themselves by bringing speculative insight within the range of positive vision." Before the Royal Commission on Vivisection, Lewes is called to testify:

Lewes: "It seems to me that the vivisection of which we are now speaking is very much like vivisection in another department, that of Literature, that is to say, criticism, which is also vivisection. There is a great deal of real torture inflicted upon authors by critics, which lasts for a considerable time in sensitive minds."

Commission member: "And without anaesthetics?"

Lewes: "—And without anesthetics…"

Commission chairman: "But I suppose you would scarcely compare that in point of necessity with the fact of living animals being cut up?"

Lewes: "—Why not?"

Slightly more than a month after Lewes's testimony, Eliot describes her novels as "simply a set of experiments in life—an endeavor to see what our thought and emotion may be capable of."

§

"O Fanny! Could things possibly get worse?" "How come your secret society can't make any headway?" Well, hold my rope and sack while I explain, curious bystander: for every two or three of us out here, hundreds of scientists and students search the streets for strays because the medical schools have now officially signed on to the fad of physiology, and their needs approach the limitless.

From *Le Rappel*, "Guard your Dogs!":

"Hundreds of remorseless people are crossing Paris and the suburbs, holding out their hands to every dog they can grab, and taking them to the pounds, where the thieves get top dollar, 50-60 centimes a head. The pound resells the dogs to the laboratories for 1F50 and 3FF for the bigger ones. When the stolen dogs have enough value they are taken to the horse market and sold by an accomplice. The career of dog-stealer brings in a good 20FF per day. When the vivisectors need dogs, they call the pound agent, who, if they are low, calls a round-up in some neighborhood... The keepers of the peace of said neighborhood invite all the homeless to help seize the stray dogs... As the dogs are only considered stray if they are in the streets... they give them pieces of meat to attract dogs they see in storefronts or courtyards."

But give me a few cents, or help me tonight, and you'll see why we're not yet beat. There's Madame Colasse out at three in the morning to patrol for cats at Les Halles, the Palais de Justice, or Sainte Chapelle in all its construction, or Cluny or Sorbonne, or the rue de L'École-de-Médicine, and even rue Mazet. Madame Milo has covered Montmartre for fifteen years, from Marché to St Peter's Square. Madame Victorine Marriere lives with Madame Milo and helps with this "work." Madame Gentil covers rue Lagrange. Madame Grulier walks all around Notre Dame and up rue Temple. Madame Jacquet, rue Huygens and the Montparnasse cemetery. But our bulletins won't spell out our names or addresses since there are hostile neighbors, merchants, and concierges who would take action against us because they can turn a penny the other way for themselves. "Why, Fanny, do you bother to name all their names now?" Madame D'Este Davenport; Madame Clozier; Madame Allossery; Messieurs Chanvallon, Gueny, Thierry; Madame Duquesnel d'Olimpre, Mademoiselle de Silva.

The girls and I take great interest in a court case between the city of Paris and Madame Gelyot, owner of a lodging house on Rue de la Sorbonne— who sues the city for damages caused to her business by Claude's student, Paul Bert's, lab. She testifies that dogs scream all night and disturb her guests. An officer carefully enumerates cries, whimpers, and howls to support her case. The neighbors testify. She wins the case on appeal. The momentum continues as pamphlets are being pushed out, here and in England, at the rate of two, three a month: "To Her Majesty," "Animal Misery," "Letters of a Wandering Dog," and a whole line of books: *Our Cruelty to Animals, Bernard's Martyrs,* etcetera.

On horribly cold nights, when they don't want to leave their covers, I have to remind my young ladies that He made his son the sacrifice of higher for lower, and so if that humility was costly, why should ours be less so? It's time to get up. The animals have no choice and neither do we. As Angelina Grimke had to remind her own townspeople who wouldn't get up: "Consequences, my friends, belong no more to you than they did to these apostles. Duty is ours and events are God's. If you think slavery is sinful, all you have to do is to set your slaves at liberty, do all you can to protect them, and in humble faith and fervent prayer, commend them to your common Father."

From a Biology Society lecture by Dr Magnan, reprinted in the *Medical Tribune,* "Mental Pathology: The Insanity of the Antivivisectionists":

"For several years, a feeling, otherwise respectable, for the protection of animals against brutalities or useless service, has become the departure point of societies calling themselves *protectors of animals.* In this environment, eminent animal-lovers, we gladly forget there are still humans who need fixing (from the philanthropic point of view), so let's not hesitate to propose things like retirement accounts for old and sick animals! In this intellectual *milieu,* sensitive souls, unbalanced minds, and degenerates get hold of themes they exaggerate until they become a true delirium.

This is what has caused the insanity of the antivivisectionists.

First of all, it goes without saying that this isn't a new pathology, it's simply one of the many manifestations by which hereditary insanity shows itself. An example of this is an ill person checked into Sainte-Anne, after a scandal at the Villette slaughterhouse. She is 37 years old, and her paternal grandmother died at Charenton, while her mother, age 60, suffers a chronic delirium. Heredity has converged on this girl, and her maladaptive personality showed itself early. For six months she has refused to eat meat, to oppose the slaughter of animals. She equally takes in the most unhappy animals, and leaves each day with a basket of provisions to distribute to the skinniest strays she can find. She regales the butchers to stop their murders, and was arrested at the slaughterhouses of Villette in the midst of a fiery speech.

The second crazy person, antivivisectionist, asked the opinion of Dr Charcot who, with his habitual helpfulness, brought her to my attention. She is 40 years old, and despite the absence of any knowledge of her hereditary geneology, she was for her whole life emotional, anxious, impressionable to the point of morbid disturbances, her solicitude to animals so great that when it rains in the night she doesn't sleep, dreaming of the horses on the slippery ground, and of the cruel treatment that the coachmen are inflicting on them. The sound of a whip stirs her to such a point that she trembles in all her limbs, thinking of the animal that received the strike. One day, on rue Drouot, seeing a horse being whipped, she fainted and would have fallen without the help of a passer-by. The very idea of a physiological experiment, a 'vivisection' as she puts it, brings her to tears and throws her into an extremely anxious state. She wouldn't like, even to save her own life or extend it, anyone to make even the slightest experiment on an animal, and she would give, she says, all her heart and life, not tomorrow, but at this very instant, if in exchange we could promise there would never be another animal sacrificed. This disposition of her mind makes her life unbearable, and pushes her to the most extravagant and ridiculous behaviors to avoid fatigue or illness to any dog, horse, cat, frog, turtle, etc. Barely in the street and her protection work begins: she collects pieces of glass for fear a horse might injure itself in a fall. One day she spent an entire half hour, dressed up in her finest clothes, doing this rag-and-bone work.

Living in the suburbs, in an area planned for new development near her house, she wanted to cobble the streets herself to prevent the heavy carriages carrying materials from getting stuck during the rains, and thus avoid the whipping of horses. But she decided at the last minute to move, not feeling she had the strength to hear even one whip from a driver. At a carport, she made lively signals to everyone in the line for a carriage because the recently arriving horses were still tired, and she couldn't help herself from insulting whomever she saw picking a carriage whose horse was still eating its oats. Passing a coal store, she saw a man bully an old horse who didn't want to enter the shaft of the cart. She begged him not to hit the animal and then came up to the old nag, speaking gently, caressing it, kissing it, and finally hooked it to the harness. She asked the coal driver the time when he would be leaving the next day, and at that exact hour she reappeared, asking to take care of hooking up the beast. She returned several days following, until the animal, calmer now, would let himself be harnessed without resistance. Having no worry about witnesses wherever she finds herself, she harangues coachmen who hit their horses; 'I would prefer,' she says, 'to receive the hit myself, than to see it given to an animal.' If she sees a horse fall down, she runs as quickly as she can to force the driver to unhook the animal so it can recover more easily. If they refuse, she sits on the beast, warning that she won't move before it is unhooked. When she perceives that a horse is grievously injured, she impresses on the driver to get help: 'I'm not even aware,' she says, 'I don't even see the crowds surrounding me, often hostile. I can't stay passive,' she adds, 'I go get oats for the animal, carrots, alfalfa, water; I give it the water myself, I hold its head up, I wash its nostrils with my handkerchief; I put straw under its poor head, I do everything I can to soften its last moments and protect it from the cruel and cowardly crowd. The poor beast has, for its last moments, that which it missed its whole life: a friend.'

One day, she offered a thousand francs to kill a horse with a broken leg on site, and not make the animal suffer the journey to the slaughterhouse. She bought an old exhausted horse for 150 francs, which she put into a retirement pasture for 78 francs a month. Another day, she was sick after saving a dog whose paw had been crushed by a car wheel. She collects the miserable dogs she finds in the street and takes them back to her house or puts them in a veterinary hospital. She has written her will on behalf of five or six dogs she's caring for at the house. She told me that a protective woman

had, for several days in a row, at the Halles, bought all the frogs to
keep them from the vivisectors.

Instigated by another ill person (who I will speak of in a moment)
she wrote letters to various newspapers against Mr Paul Bert, Mr
Brown-Sequard, Mr Laborde, etc. Beyond this love of the most
misfortunate animals that keeps her in a constant emotional state,
she presents strange behaviors of still another kind: psychic *stig-
mata* of hereditary mental illness. These are the fears of touching
certain objects, fears that are analogous to those that Mr J. Falret
associates with an insanity called *folie de doute*. Our crazy person
can't tolerate even the tiniest dust on her furniture, and she wipes
every object even after the maid. She washes every dish with water
even though they are clean; 'I never wash my face,' she says, 'with a
towel from the cleaner without running it in water; and nevertheless I put, without the slightest disgust, my face on the muzzle of
a horse. I dress the wounds of animals, even the dirtiest, without
the slightest disgust.' She washes herself twenty times a day. She is
always moving at home and, in the apartment, she fears suffocating. She has a hyper-aesthetic sense, particularly in hearing—she
can't stand the steps of the servants, and obliges them to leave off
their shoes and put on ones that make no noise. Such is the sad,
modest, kind antivivisectionist, who has but one goal: to do well
by unhappy animals.

Another example shows the ambitious, aggressive antivivisectionist, for whom love of animals is only a pretext for noisy
demonstrations. There's a woman, 38 years old, whose mother, suffering chronic delirium, died after twenty years of mental illness.
This antivivisectionist is rowdy, aggressive, in a word, the true
heroine of the genre. As many hereditary sufferers, unbalanced as
she is, she is not lacking in brains. She derives satisfaction in telling
me the active part she played in the campaign against experimental
physiology. She has, she says, the spirit of the future and doesn't
want to belong to a ponderous time, with average intelligence and
mind. She doesn't want to partake of the mores of her sex, so she
breaks with all these ridiculous conditions and doesn't fear falling
back on spicy language. She's brave, not afraid of a fight, and wants
to defend the weak. Physical pain barely affects her, she walks in
front, and she hates humanity for its wickedness. Even if an animal experiment would save her own son, she says she would formally oppose it, not wanting to owe the life of her son to the life
of an animal. In everything else, human pain barely registers to

her, whereas she is moved by the very idea of animal suffering. She happily describes being entirely detached from human emotions: she loves her son because she controls him, dominates him, and she hopes to raise him in the same hatred of humanity and love of animals. She respects her husband, she considers him a friend, almost a comrade, but she decided to leave her husband to find a better situation rather than separate from her cats. The odd contrast between this incessant preoccupation with animals and her indifference to man is an anomaly which might happen with the mental lucidity these insane women present, but which becomes clinically relevant when we consider the bizarre behaviors and the intellectual degeneracies.

I should mention that after the Norwich Congress in 1874, at the time when I was working on experiments on the comparative action of alcohol and absinthe, the room was invaded by several individuals, led by a real maniac who, with a piercing eye, a bloodshot face, came with a knife to cut the cord that was holding one of the dog's paws. He would have continued but I drew him back carefully and asked two assistants to hold him, exactly the way I have to hold agitated insane people. I then continued my demonstration. I'm only sorry not to have been able to get any information on the background of this rash person, as I'm sure I'd find an original defect explaining this strange fury. In conclusion, these facts show how much variety there can be in hereditary insanity. With degenerates, everything becomes an opportunity for madness, and thanks to their strong predispositions, these insane people have no need to be systematic or pass through the slow and progressive stages that mad people normally follow."

§

Pain, malevolent companion, continues to control Claude, binding his freedom to that sweaty bed, as though he were nothing more than a dirty old doll. He mumbles through a lecture on plant anesthetics on the 28th of December, 1877, and never crosses the street again. It is widely known that this last round of illness makes him irrational, angry, and good luck anyone trying to touch his distended middle. Whatever ails him has grown stronger than his ability to talk, and he stares urgently from his pillow.

Paul Bert, to Madame Raffalovich:

"*I am deeply saddened to relay to you that the state of our poor master worsens day to day. He has accepted that we'll send a dispatch to his sister. But will she come in time? What a horrible and sad sight! To see one of the most powerful and luminous intelligences of our time go out in such solitude. Science isn't everything.*

This poor old housemaid, really much better than she seems, told me that you wanted to be kept informed of this distressing situation. This is why I allow myself to write you. Alas! We must count in days now."

Claude lies immobile, with Madame Raffalovich and Sophie visiting, along with the faithful: Dastre, Bert, and d'Arsonval. Mariette stays day and night, except on Sundays and Wednesdays during church.

The Goncourts: "Claude Bernard, in the delirium that proceeded his agony, could only repeat a single word: 'Fucked! Fucked!'"

We do know that, toward the end, Claude wrote about vivisection: "... without doubt, our hands are empty today, although our mouths are full of legitimate promises for the future." This last sentiment enrages the activist community, who quote it relentlessly.

Madame Raffalovich's daughter, Sophie, recalls: "One day, when I arrived, they said the night had been atrocious, and he was no longer able to speak. Only his beautiful eyes could speak, his beautiful eyes that expressed so much affection. He squeezed my hands, and it seemed as though he was repeating what he'd told me once about the immortality of the soul…"

Unable to resist the plight of any suffering creature, tender-hearted Tony insists on paying her dying father a visit. Sophie: "One of his daughters came into the apartment, but never close to her father. My mother and I could hear her walking in a room, and Mr Bernard's maid said bitterly, 'She's come to keep track but not approach Mister.' The noise of her steps hit us to the heart. After we'd left, did she go to the bedside of the dying? None of his friends knew." Claude loses consciousness, and Paul Bert watches over him to be sure no one undesirable is let into the room. After several agonizing days, he dies in the arms of d'Arsonval and Krishaber.

Madame Raffalovich receives a note from d'Arsonval, "Claude Bernard passed peacefully last night (the 10th) at 9:30. I had the painful consolation to hear the dying breath of my poor master."

His last words: "It might have been nice to have finished it."

D'Arsonval to Madame R: "I'm keeping a lock of hair for you from our illustrious deceased, a souvenir without any value for his natural family, but not for his scientific family."

5.

LIFE | AFTERLIFE

Not five minutes after his death, a controversy erupts as to whether Claude received last rites, as Père Didon reports in the *French Review*:

"I told [Claude]: 'Your science doesn't separate you from God; it brings you closer; I've had the experience personally.' I reminded him of a sublime word that, in one of his last lectures at Collège de France, had struck me. Speaking on the determinism of the conditions leading to phenomena, he had said: 'These conditions aren't causes; there is only one cause: that's the first cause.' The first cause is what science is obliged to admit without ever being able to grasp, and in this sense, science is eminently religious.

'Yes, my father, you speak exactly; positivism and materialism that deny it are, to my eyes, insane and untenable doctrines...' I thanked him for everything he'd done for the progress of truth, and I told him that this first cause, which is inaccessible to science, would take him into consideration... I only saw him again in agony and making the near-death rattling, saying, 'My father, I've suffered a great deal in my life, morally and physically—moral suffering such as a loving heart martyred.' Nevertheless, the next morning, the day before he died, he saw the priest and answered his questions in full consciousness, begged pardon to God before leaving earth, received his last rites, and died as his old mother, who loved him so much, hoped he would."

Sophie Raffalovich immediately doubts this tale: "I don't know anything for sure. My mother and I, we spent our days with the dear patient in his last illness, but we left each day by six o'clock. His disciples Bert, d'Arsonval, Dastre, watched over him at night. Did a priest from his parish come after we left? It's possible, but Mr Bernard never spoke to my mother about this, and this silence leads me to believe he had nothing to say. There were visits with Père Didon, with whom he liked to chat, but who only came as a visitor and friend. I don't think anything else happened during those last days…"

Other rumors have it that Claude was violated while unconscious, that the priest Mr Castelnau from Saint-Severin administered last rites without permission.

Called by Madame Raffalovich, the artist Guillaume takes Claude's death mask. D'Arsonval writes a note: "Madame, thank you for the consolation you have brought us by conserving our master's face. The pain that left its trace on it was also reflected in his thoughts. In the midst of his suffering, he said to me: 'Nature is sometimes very stupid: what purpose does all this pain serve? Nothing. Not for me, not for you. I don't regret the pain, only that the pain helped no one.'"

Ernst Renan offers literary immortalization in the *Medical Tribune*:

"Concerning the nobility of characters, we've got nothing to envy of the past. We can compare our scientific characters to the saints, heroes, and great men of every age, attached to their research for the truth, indifferent to fortune, often proud of their poverty, happy with the honors we bestow on them, indifferent to the praise and the denigration, sure of the value of their efforts, and happy to know the truth. Doubtless are the joys that confirmed belief about divine things bestows. But the intimate happiness of the scientist equals this, for he senses that he works on an eternal project, and that he's part of the phalanx of those who can say: *opera eorum sequuntur illos.*

Claude Bernard, my friends, was one of those. His life, dedicated to the truth, is the model that we can oppose to those who pretend that these days the source of the greatest virtues has run dry. Instead it flows from the small village of Saint-Julien, near Villefranche, in a vineyarder's house... His job was almost as difficult as that of the watchmaker who we ask to correct the irregularity on a watch he's not allowed to open. For what Claude Bernard sought were the secrets of the internal clockworks; he broke the watch and opened it violently rather than admit it was made blindly without any sense of purpose.

It was a shocking spectacle to see him in his laboratory: pensive, sad, absorbed, not allowing himself any distraction, not even a smile, feeling that he was doing the work of a priest, celebrating a sacrifice. His long fingers plunged into the wounds seemed like the ancient oracle following the entrails of the victims of mysterious secrets.

The real stroke of genius was to have known how to make poisons his great experimental agents. Poisons, effectively, go where neither the hand nor the eye can go. They arrive at every element of the organism, by being introduced into the circulation, and to delicately dissect the vital elements, taking apart nerves without breaking them... It's through poison, as has been said, that Bernard put his laboratory at the heart of animal experimentation; he had his network of instant communication, his secret police, if we can put it like that, who warned him of the most fugitive problems...he invented what has rightly been called the living autopsy, without mutilation nor effusions of blood.

In his bold journey toward the last secrets of animate nature, he arrived at the borders of what's visible, at the obscure source of organic life. Little by little the difference between animal physiology and plant physiology disappeared before his eyes. The seed of life, on both sides, appeared the same. The plant, like the animal, is susceptible to being anesthetized. Even certain yeasts can be affected by anesthetic agents, and, at least for half of them, it makes them sleep. Claude Bernard also worked on the problem of fermentation, implying that this most important question goes to the origin of the cell. In the summer of 1877, he announced to his disciples that he believed he'd found the way to find this impenetrable sanctuary. O fragility of human life! O cruel game of nature, you evil mother, who rejoices in stupidly smashing a head formed from forty years of meditation and in which still blooms the most beautiful arrangements of genius! The terrible illness from which he'd escaped for ten years only seemed to have pardoned him, and came back more implacably than ever. He died without having accomplished his dream; he died sad, thinking that his ideas would die with him, saying: 'It would have been really nice to have finished it.'

Claude Bernard didn't know that the problems he brought up touched on the more serious questions of philosophy. He wouldn't have cared much for that anyway. He never thought it was right for the scientist to worry about the consequences that might come from his research. He was, in this regard, absolutely impassive.

It mattered little to him what he was called, or from what group. He fit in with no group. He sought truth, and that was all. The heroes of the human mind are those who don't know what the future holds. Not everyone has this courage. It's hard to abstain from questions when it's eminently we who are implicated. Not to know if the world has an ideal goal, or if, sons of fate, we are led by fate without a loving conscience following all of evolution; not to know if, at the origin, something divine was put in him, and if, at the end, a consoling fate is waiting; not to know if our deepest instincts for justice ring false where the imperious demands of truth impose themselves, we're forgiven for not accepting this. There are subjects in which we'd rather make no sense than be quiet.

Truth or chimera, the dream of the infinite will always seduce us, like the Celtic heroes who, having dreamed a ravishing beauty, run the whole world to find her, or the man contemplating his destiny with an arrow in the heart. In the same way, the youthfulness of the effort is touching. We don't need to look for logic in the solutions man thinks up for the strange fate that befalls him. Driven implacably to believe in justice, and thrown into a world that is, and will always be, unjust, needing eternity for his revenge and stopped suddenly by the pit of death, what do you want him to do? He revolts against the casket, he tears the flesh from the emaciated bones, the life from the rotting brain, the light from the extinguishing eye; he thinks up sophisms which he would have laughed at from a child, so that he doesn't have to admit that nature is such a jokester as to impose the burden of so much to do without any compensation."

Intimate Portraits of Illustrious People, 1845-1890; Claude Bernard: "Creator of modern medicine, who replaced academic theories with living-animal experiments that sensitive souls disparaged. But without him, we wouldn't know the role of the large sympathetic nerve in our nervous system, or that of the liver and pancreas in the digestive. Thinking and Eating...That's not nothing!"

§

Anna Kingsford, I finally have to ask, after all this time…Did you *murder* him? Maitland describes how you were "divinely used as an instrument for the destruction of Claude Bernard," and how when you heard of Claude's death, you screamed: "The Will can and does kill!" In your cursing you also threaten Pasteur and Paul Bert. Maitland: "If the conditions are such as accord with these rules, the White Magian is authorized to undertake an act of execution in the same frame of mind as he would entertain in the act of destroying a noxious beast or venomous reptile or creeping thing. Being a Magian, he has, of course, a spirit of discernment, and will not direct himself against any but real malefactors, i.e., oppressors of the poor and innocent, tyrants, and public criminals. Such men may be compared with pestilential creatures, whose evil lives poison the moral atmosphere of the planet, and whose removal from it is a divine act…Then concentrating and projecting his Will, as though it were a sword in the hands of God, he devotes it to the destruction of the ogre or monster designated, accepting for himself the peril to which the combat exposes him, and denying only the salvation and redemption of the oppressed."

I'm not the Judge, but I would like to know how the gadfly was stopped. "Thus did she again vindicate her endowment with the third of the 'four excellent things' that constitute the equipment of Hermes, son of God, Slayer of Argus, Archangel." Hermes, gentle archer, saves Io.

Hermes, to the Chorus: *"You, however, who feel for his sufferings, get away quick, lest the intolerable roar stun your senses."*

Chorus: *"Would you have me practice cowardice? I will stay with Prometheus, come what may."*

Prometheus: "...*To speak is painful to me, to keep silence is painful. On every side is suffering. ...Of wretched humans he took no account, resolved to annihilate them and create another race. This purpose, there was no one to oppose, but I, I dared. I saved the human race from being pulverized to nothing. Now I am punished with agonies, awful to behold.*"

Would you really use murder to fight murder? Didn't you write, in *Violationism, or Sorcery in Science*: "As it is forbidden for man to enrich himself by theft, or to free himself by murder, so also it is forbidden him to acquire knowledge by unlawful means—to fight even the battles of heaven with the weapons of hell"?

Maitland says: "The phrase 'karma must not be interfered with,' should rather be: 'karma cannot be interfered with' for even the action of a hostile will, evilly directed, is provided for and taken into the account of the Divine counsels. God is never taken by surprise. The reaction is against the operator only and is the mere recoil of law. 'Thou couldest have no power against me,' said Jesus to Pilate, 'unless it were given thee from on high...' So also said the Buddha, when dying, of the disciple who poisoned him with swine's flesh, 'It must needs be that offenses come, but woe unto him by whom the offence cometh.' The sorcerer, whose position and method have been defined, assumes the penalty of murder, and generates a corresponding karma, which he must work out."

Madame Blavatsky, head of the Theosophical Society for which you have long written and worked, attacks: "Therefore I feel sure and know that the Master approves your opposing the principle of vivisection, but not the practical way you do it, injuring yourself and doing injury to others, without much benefiting the poor animals. Of course it is karma. But so it is in the case of every murdered man. Nevertheless, the weapon of karma, unless he acts unconsciously, is a murderer in the sight of that same karma that used him. Let us work against the principle then, not against personalities. For it is a weed that requires more than seven, or seven times seven, of us to extirpate it.'"

You respond: "And while the world is being educated to recognize the principle, millions of poor creatures are being horribly tortured...It means that whenever you see a ruffian brutally ill-treating a woman or child, instead of rushing with all your might to the rescue, you are to stand by and do nothing but talk, or else go home and write something 'attacking the principle.' No; the power to interfere and save imposes the duty to interfere and save, and as that power has been given to me, I should not be doing my duty if I did not exercise it."

Leaving the Blavatskys, you fully embrace your life as a hermetist—believer in the 'esoteric' doctrine of Karma—that the soul is many-lived—including purgation in the subjective states of hell. You write, "As for past sins—what are sins? 'Avidya' equals ignorance—the mistakes of the blind eye and the deaf ear; Ignorances by which the soul gains experience... We sin only so long as we do not know the nature of things... forgiven it cannot be because all Avidya has its karma, and karma must be repaid."

You defend yourself: "The Magian merely formulates and gives direction to the vague and unexpressed desire of all virtuous men, viz. to be delivered from such and such a tyrant. 'The will of the people is the death warrant of the oppressor.' Tyrants die by the will of the nation... When wrong-doing becomes intolerable, not to a few individuals only as now, but to the whole people, it will be impossible for tyrants to continue to exist." Your break with the Theosophists is final. "The whole *raison d'être* of the Theosophical Society is to rescue truth from superstition and to restore the 'Mysteries of the World.' Now the reason

Christianity has fallen into disrepute, and has failed to satisfy thinkers, is that it has exalted persons in the place of principles, and has deified a Name in the stead of a Condition...Hence the need of a religious Reformation which shall demolish Atheism by unveiling the true nature of the Mysteries. Such a sublime function as this I hoped to have seen exercised by the Theosophical Society. But if abandoning this *terra firma* is merely going to construct a new system of dogma on new authority, extraneous and arbitrary, it will speedily degenerate into a sect and become for the world no more than any other congregation of fanatics attached to some particular prophet. Koot Hoomi will be the oracle of the Theosophists, just as Joe Smith of the Latter Day Saints, Joanna Southcott of the Adventists, or Thomas Lake Harris of the community which acknowledges him as its King!...Our wise and truly theosophical course is not to set up new Popes nor proclaim new Masters, but to seek each for himself inwardly the realization of the Process which is the Christ, which is Buddha, which is God in us. And this is the system we ought to proclaim to the world, on the authority of reason, of common sense, and of science. *Little children, keep yourself from idols* [1 John 5:21]—I would have that text graven on the heart of every Theosophist."

Yet no day flows freely as your illness progresses, and time must be punctuated with planned retreats. Bloody coughing starves and exhausts you, until your body that once moved unthinkingly becomes leaden. Your creativity shrinks and you seek smaller circles, monotonous and safe. It becomes apparent that you are cursed with consumption. "What shall I do with the rest of my life if I am always to suffer, and so be forced to suppress every impulse toward active work in me? ... If pain and decrepitude settle down on me like a cloud, and compel me to pass the remainder of my life in enduring?" But far worse, your esoteric writings (whether prompted and recorded by Maitland or by you alone) alienate your oldest comrade Frances Cobbe, who removes you from leadership of the Anti-Vivisection League. Only your credentials as a doctor, and your eyewitness accounts from Paris, preserve your influence over the crowds of average men and women who still gather to hear you.

§

Medical Tribune, under *Varieties*, "The Funeral of Claude Bernard":

"...The procession left from the dead man's home, 40 rue des Écoles, well before the appointed hour; the rules of the Saint Severin cathedral, where the religious service was celebrated, wanted it this way so they could make room for a wedding. But the parade consisted mostly of a regretable pêle-mêle, in the midst of which we saw the highest-ranking scientists in their official robes lost in the crowd and searching for their places, which someone had forgotten to mark.

At the head of the official delegation, at the first row of the family, three silhouettes in mourning walked with the grief-stricken gestures of enormous pain. But under the fabric, each of the three women hid their deep jubilation at the idea that they were burying this man religiously, after their daily persecutions took thirty years to kill him.

Finally, the mortal remains of Claude Bernard were transported, in the midst of this immense show, to Père-Lachaise cemetery, where numerous speeches were given at his tomb. We left him there in the peace of his eternal slumber."

Paul Bert, graveside: "For the first time in our country, a scientist will receive public honors, until now reserved only for illustrious politicians or military men. Yesterday, the Senate voted unanimously, and the word of Mr Gambetta, speaking on behalf of the budget commission, summarizes everything we've said: 'The light that has just gone out will never be replaced.'"

§

Anna Kingsford: "One horribly wet day, November 17, I took into my head to visit Mr Pasteur's laboratory. I waded across Paris in the sleet and mud, and stood a long time in wet boots and clothes, and got back at last after about five hours, soaked to the skin. Result: severe neuralgia and inflammation of the lungs. Inflammation did not dry up as it should, but got 'cheesy,' and after I had been in bed a month, I began to spit blood. I had a cough that was almost incessant, and, after many doctors had debated over me, I was informed that my best chance was the Riviera. Husband came over, and we started out."

Your health wants you back in bed, and yet how many lectures do you give in Germany, Switzerland, Italy, England? Your pamphlets sell for 50 centimes, and beneath your byline, the words: "Medical Doctor of the Paris Medical School." Despite your exhaustion, you yell from the podium: "Perhaps it will be said to you: 'This is a question of which science alone can judge, she only can decide its importance; public conscience has not part in this scheme of investigation.' We maintain that the truth is contrary to such a proposition, and that when science forgets what she owes to civilization, the public conscience must intervene to remind her of it. It is not a question of the public not having acquired the scientific spirit; it is, on the contrary, the case that scientists have lost the spirit of morality. We feel assured that you will join with us in bringing to an end a state of things which sullies and infringes public morality, and which will be the shame of our century." Louise Lind af Hageby follows your footsteps and infiltrates the Pasteur Institute, and later the London School of Medicine for Women. In *The Shambles of Science*, she exposes the vivisectionists, followed by her next book, *The New Morality: An Inquiry into the Ethics of Vivisection*.

During the holidays, Florence visits you, describing: "No grey hairs, no perceptible wrinkles, and her complexion was still lovely! Yet it was to me a painful interview; for I was but too well instructed in the delusive bloom and the hopefulness that are characteristic, indeed pathognomic, signs of advanced consumption in many cases. She said to me—'Medically speaking, I know I am dying, but I cannot believe it. My mind, my soul, all that makes *me*, is as alive as ever, and I cannot realize that it is finished.'"

Io: *stung, sting, stung, to push her onward.*

You keep a mental list of every martyr who died young, the view from your burning stake: "My Genius says that nothing of much importance can be done by us before the spring, on account of the state of the Earth's magnetic currents. So we must work on without being disappointed at the smallness of the results." Yet it is Eadith, finally, who haunts you: "Having fallen asleep last night while in a state of great perplexity about the care and education of my daughter, I dreamt as follows: I was walking with the child along the border of a high cliff, at the foot of which was the sea. The path was exceedingly narrow, and as it was unsafe to let go her hand, it was on the stones that she had to walk, much to her distress. I was in male attire, and carried a staff in my hand...I found standing before me a man in the garb of a fisherman, who evidently had just scaled the steep path leading from the beach. He stretched out his hand to take the child, saying he had come to fetch her, for that in the path I was following there was room only for one. 'Let her come to us,' he added; 'she will do very well as a fisherman's daughter.'...she accordingly went to him of her own will and, placing her hand in his, left me without any sign of regret, and I went my way alone..."

§

Zola's *The Experimental Novel*, based on Claude's *Introduction to the Study of Experimental Medicine*, is published after Claude's death and receives instant rebuke by Ferdinand Brunetière in *Revue des Deux Mondes*: "It's clear that Mr Zola doesn't know what an experimenter is, for the novelist, like the poet, if he experiments, can only experiment on himself, never on others… there is only observation, and that's sufficient to show Zola's theory of the experimental novel to be lacking and crumbling at the foundation."

Brunetière compares Zola to Restif de la Bretone, a hack writer of the 1700s who used real people for his characters—names, addresses, and direct quotes—and so was even more documentary, accuses Brunetière, than Zola, who only uses vague models. "…Restif, under the wall-colored cloak he wrapped himself in, was truly the adventurer of naturalism; I'm afraid Mr Zola is only a Prudhomme." Or again: "The author of *Nana* follows from Claude Bernard as the author of *The Perverted Peasant* would follow Buffon. What is there in common between indeterminacy, determinism, and the novel or dramatic art? We think man is the author of his fate and fortunes, but Zola thinks the opposite: that vice and virtue are products just as sugar and acid." Finally, Brunetière recommends that this Zola only write theater, since theater shows people revolting against situations, whereas in a novel, "you are but its victim, and your talent is the fool of your philosophy."

For his part, Zola formulates and defends the unique method of naturalist novelists: "Establish the whole work on notes taken slowly. When they've studied with scrupulous care the territory where they will pass, when they have learned every source and hold the multiple documents they will need in their hands, only then should they decide to write… Finally, all operations consist in taking facts from nature, then studying the mechanism of the facts by acting on them through modifications of circumstances and milieu, without ever leaving the laws of nature."

Flaubert: "Zola's aplomb in matters of criticism can be explained by his inconceivable ignorance."

In a *fictionalism* of facts—a *factualism*—the *fait-alisme*—the story accretes
from facts, from news, from research, from local gossip—until this *facticity*—an encyclopedic record of information—provides not just a "slice"
of life but the whole thing. In *Germinal*, Zola describes the awakening
of the modern industrial proletariat—the material conditions in the Second Empire—and achieves his ideal of a plot based on "the revolt of the
working class, a nudge against society, which cracks open for a moment,
in a word the conflict between capital and labor." His research into the
detailed lives of coal miners, and the intricate working of mines, dictates
the novel's events and character-types, including: Rising Young Socialist
Leader, Typical Worker, Old Worker, Firebrand, Political Indifferent,
Clergyman. Zola: "There is only justice in truth."

The Goncourts on Zola: "More unhappy...more disconsolate...more
gloomy than the most disinherited student who has failed to qualify for
a profession." Increasingly obsessed with life's horrors, Zola broods in
bed, imagining a world of undeserved suffering, unmerited failures, and
injustices everywhere. *Germinal* depicts "black, silent shadows that never
laughed or raised their eyes...the teeth clenched in anger, the hearts swollen with hate, the resignation due solely to the demands of the belly."
Zola sees man's depravity, the sins enacted, the total selfishness of his
countrymen. Sainte-Beuve: "One has only to penetrate ever so little
under the veil of society to see that, just as in nature, there are only wars,
struggles, destructions and recompositions. This Lucretian view of criticism is hardly cheerful; but when one has attained to it, it seems preferable, even with its profound sadness, to the cult of idols."

Zola: "If you remain in an a priori idea, and in feeling, without the support of reason, and without the verification of experiment, you are a poet;
you risk hypotheses that prove nothing, you carry on a struggle in indeterminism painfully and uselessly, often in a harmful way."

Victor Hugo: "I've been in the same miseries, but I would never make a spectacle of them, it's not right to make them naked."

René Ferdas panders in the *Medical Tribune*, "Experimental Physiology and *The Experimental Novel*, Claude Bernard and Mr Zola":

"Mr Zola, brilliant novelist, dreams up the notion of taking phrases from Claude Bernard's book, *Introduction to the Study of Experimental Medicine*, and laying them into a rambling magma he calls *The Experimental Novel*. He's done this cooking with the goal of composing a mixture to be swallowed by the public. Maybe next an ingenious doctor might decide to serve us a new medical system by distilling out a few passages from *L'Assommoir*, and cleverly hiding himself behind the authority of Mr Zola?

We—the grateful students of Claude Bernard—heard that journalists were hyping a novelist who was justifying the form and the spirit of his literary rantings by proclaiming himself Bernard's disciple and beneficiary. We assumed the journalists were joking, but they were serious—so we bought the book out of curiosity. If it weren't sitting on my table, if it wasn't in fact printed, I would think I was the object of a fantastic trick. If I didn't also find it scandalous to violate the public's goodwill so impudently, and if I didn't see before me the melancholic smile of our venerable Claude Bernard, I maybe wouldn't be so encouraged to clear his memory of this monstrous promiscuity.

So that my readers can avoid the treacherous bog of *The Experimental Novel*, I'll remind them that Claude Bernard became the greatest physiologist of modern times with the help of experiments skillfully conducted on live animals. He penetrated to the mechanisms of organic processes, and his lessons on toxic substances, anesthetics, asphyxiation, animal heat, and diabetes are enduring monuments. He wrote admirable pages on the experimental method used to interrogate nature and tear away her secrets, according enormous progress to physiology, medicine, and pharmacology.

Could we all then share my shock in hearing that the writer of *Contes à Ninon, The Bouton de Rose, la Faute de l'Abbé Mouret, L'Assommoir, Une Page D'amour, Nana*, etc. pretends to be a disciple of Claude Bernard?—To compare a stylistic process to a vivisection experiment on a living animal...what does that even mean? Doesn't this point directly to a mental illness? Let's have a look.

When Claude Bernard's book fell into the hands of Mr Zola, Mr Zola must have suffered a major brain hemorrhage. Then he wrote: 'the book of a scientist, whose authority is definitive,' will 'serve as my solid foundation'; it will be 'the ground on which I walk.'

It appeared simple: 'It will suffice for me to replace the word *doctor* with the word *novelist* to make my thoughts clear and bring to them the rigor of scientific truth.' It's elementary, and therefore available to every Sam, Dick, and Harry. Suppose, for example, that a sanitation worker has ambitions to compose a didactic treatise on his professional materials; he would only have to take Claude Bernard's *Introduction to the Study of Experimental Medicine* and replace the word *doctor* with the word *garbageman* to make his thoughts clear, and bring himself the rigor of scientific truth. As Mr Zola has asserted, this all amounts to the work of adaptation (but pronounced in the british way, "adaptecheure.')" Yes, the 'adaptation' of Mr Zola is an easy-to-follow fabrication: one needs only repeat, 'I take all my arguments from Claude Bernard,' or else reproduce random pages, adding, 'I've put in this whole page because it's the most important.'

If we want to find adaptation's limit, Mr Zola gives a guide: 'What I've said twenty times—that naturalism isn't a personal fantasy, and that it's the movement of the century—Claude Bernard says with more authority, and maybe we'll believe him...' Then follows a long quote of Claude Bernard in which, of course, there is no question but that naturalism is a personal fantasy of Mr Zola. Claude Bernard simply discusses the advantages of the experimental method in science. But that hardly matters to Mr Zola who might as well have cited seven hundred sixty-nine other pages of Claude Bernard's to prove that naturalism is the movement of the century, etc.; but he had that page in his hand, and it wasn't worth looking for another.

A little later, when Mr Zola tries to compare the experiments undertaken by a physiologist on a living animal to a novel (one of his novels), this can only come from the ravings of a delirious person. Move 'characters in a particular story; write a naturalist novel' etc. This is to begin an experiment? Let's see, frankly, what's been discovered: you see Claude Bernard at his bloody table, a scalpel in hand, leaning over the guts of a convulsing animal; Claude Bernard contemplative, considering life, compared to Mr Zola writing: 'Knife having cut bowels and intestines, the room is full of them, the bed plastered with them, the rug too and all the way to the bathroom, which was splattered...' You see Claude Bernard formulating laws of the precise workings of the organs, and here comes Mr Zola chiseling that apostrophe of father Colombe: 'Hey there, old Borgia, give us some yellow stuff—first class mule'; Or this one: 'Well he's really drunk too, oh boy,' said Nana, 'I'm outta here you know, I don't want any beating. Wow, he's really loaded! If only he'd just fall and break his neck!'

When Mr Zola's words become too much to bear, he's showing how far he will go: 'I arrived here,' he says, 'because the experimental novel is a consequence of the scientific evolution of the century, just as physiology itself relies on the study of chemistry and physics.' And so, what's clear, is that the experimental novel continues and completes physiology, and therefore it's the responsibility of Mr Beclard, the eminent professor of physiology at the Medical school, and of Mr Laborde, chief of physiology, of Mr Mathias Duval and Mr Charles Richet, professors of physiology, to immediately request that the minister of Education create a Chair in Experimental Novels at the Medical School of Paris. Mr Zola is naturally the predestined candidate to sit royally upon it. The new professor, with a studious entourage of young students avid to complete their notion of physiology, will explore in his courses 'all the extraordinary allusions we can make out of simple words such as: 'My tweezers are cracked. Who rummaged through my little pot?' What beautiful days ahead for science.

For in reading Mr Zola's book, we find the pontificator of 'naturalism' scaling the highest heights of ridiculousness. Blinded by Claude Bernard's beautiful work (where he only sees words and doesn't understand them) Mr Zola throws himself into making scientific judgments. I quote randomly: 'Without risking formulating any laws,' Mr Zola seriously writes, 'I imagine that the question of heredity has a large influence on the intellectual and passionate (???) manifestations of man. I give it at least as important a role as that of environment.' Mr Zola effortlessly discovers the importance of heredity and environment in the same seriousness that allows him to launch this huge revelation: 'I think the social environment has a considerable impact.' Ah, Mr Zola, wasn't that also you who invented gunpowder? You should have told us!

I pick here and there: 'When we'll have shown that the bodies of men are a machine...'—What, you didn't know that was proved long ago? 'We have experimental chemistry and physics, we will have experimental physiology...'—this excellent Mr Zola has no idea that in all the departments of all the schools of medicine in France and abroad for a very long time now there have been chairs in experimental physiology (in Paris, there are three: one at the Medical School, one at the Sorbonne and another at Collège de France. Go to school, Mr Zola!)—'...after that, we will have the experimental novel.' Professor Zola (see above.) Actually, all this is more sad than funny. 'Claude Bernard made great discoveries,' Mr Zola says somewhere, 'and he died admitting that he knew nothing or near nothing.' Maybe when you die you can say that too, Mr Zola, anything is possible. But Claude Bernard never breathed the grievances you say he did. Fix that, or else I christen you the parakeet of Claude Bernard's history...!

I'll stop here. There are people who make chocolate with crushed brick, others who make milk with horse brains—and all of these people make money. Mr Zola grinds up the pages of Claude Bernard's book, greases them with his special prose, and finishes it all off with a label as baroque as it is meaningless. This he's done, we can say, pretty well. Seriously, Mr Zola, before talking to the public about 'physiology', 'experiments', 'experimental' etc, it would be good to first learn what the words mean."

§

A fundraising letter goes out in Paris: "The Biological Society, of which Claude Bernard was a founding member, and which saw all his work come to fruition, considers as its duty to make a public call of donation for a monument to the memory of the man France still mourns."

I think there are many people unsure what to do when a fire goes all the way out. Push ash from side to side, picking up the few blackened charcoal bits? Either it was left too long, or it wasn't fed before the last ember would have reignited. This moment, when one should clean the chimney, take the time to shovel out the ash, is often when a kind of hardened leap takes place; the moment when, in ancient times, the sun would have to be used, or flint and iron.

The commission for Claude's statue is handed to Mr Guillaume, who presents a mock-up on the steps of Collège de France where the final version will stand. "The illustrious biologist stands in a thoughtful pose, and beside him, on the vivisection gutter, we see the shape of a dog being vivisected, and all variety of tools. Something unexpected has just been discovered, and Claude Bernard, his finger to his chin, contemplates what he's seen. This was the familiar pose of Claude Bernard, and its truth struck all the lab workers who knew him. On the experiment table where the tools are is also a large unfurling sign which contains the list of Claude Bernard's most important works...the study of poisons, and particularly curare and carbon monoxide, considered not only in themselves but as a powerful method of physiological analysis. In a touching coincidence, the statue looks exactly at the house where Claude Bernard died."

Mademoiselle Huot whistles long and loud, then shouts a disruptive heckle during the inauguration of the completed statue a year later. She takes a few steps beyond the crowd and spits toward the statue. "It wasn't because of my vivid animosity toward him," she later writes, "but because they had found it necessary to put an eviscerated dog next to him." Mr de Lesseps approaches her to say, "We don't share the same opinion, Madame, but I'm French and you're a woman: would you please take my arm?" Her spitting is accompanied by hostile chanting at the base of the stairs by a group of activists.

The *Bulletin* of the Animal Protection Society addresses the incident:
"The president says that popular sentiment has never been greater against vivisection since the conference held by Mademoiselle Deraismes at the Theater of Nations in 1883, which didn't stop the actions of the vivisectors in the least, but just the opposite: the next day they put forward a dog bound to a vivisector's trough to serve as the decoration on the statue of Claude Bernard.
But I can't hold back my indignation at the thought that near the standing figure of Claude Bernard would be a dog prostrate on a vivisection table...Not only is there a total lack of moral sense, but also of aesthetic sense...It's a pure shame, against which public taste should stand up. If in favor of the ends pursued, hoping to finally attain them, we could forgive Claude Bernard his atrocious means, so be it! But if

it's the atrocious means which we're flaunting in marble or bronze, next to he who made it his work, when we should have the decency to hide it, this is incomprehensible! We're dishonoring both art and science!"

Of course the *Medical Tribune* chimes in:

"We can't pretend to ignore the horrible impression we took from the ceremony, which was lacking not in solemnity for such a great and illustrious name as Claude Bernard.... but all the missing people... not many were in attendance. We couldn't have chosen a better public commemoration of the great image of Claude Bernard than on the same exact stage as his scientific exploits, at the top of the stairs of Collège de France, which appeared to have been built only to receive him, next to and practically across from the obscure if famous laboratory from which so many magnificent discoveries came.

In general, but especially in its deeply meditative expression, the bronze statue is worthy of its namesake, and of the artist who conceived and executed it: Mr Guillaume. Nevertheless, we permit ourselves one reservation in terms of the resemblance: the bottom of the face isn't really Claude Bernard's; the chin is narrow, pulled back, and thus the cheeks are too thin, taking away from the beautiful balanced fullness which characterized the sweet physiognomy of the master in his last years. I permit myself also to repeat a critique which has already been said, and to which a barrage of unfortunate heckling, coming from a poor old crazy on the day of the ceremony, has revived the truth: it's that the dog lying victim on the experimenter's table is too much, in this context, and the effect it produces risks public confusion, for those without a real understanding of the exigencies of scientific research. The head of the animal, instead of being visible and hanging, could have been at least hidden, whereas it's the body which is in part at least hidden beneath a metal sheet, bearing inscriptions outlining the principle discoveries and scientific titles of the master: Glycogen • Diabetes • Vaso-motor nerves • Toxic Substances • Digestive Fluid • Experimental Medicine • General Physiology • Unity of Life • Determinism

The very simple pedestal, designed by Mr Guerard, carries on it: To Claude Bernard, from his colleagues, friends, disciples."

Paul Bert, as head of the inauguration committee:

"...At the feet of how many statues, after eight years have passed, do the crowds walk by indifferent, forgetful of short-lived fame! Today, on the contrary, the statue of Claude Bernard stands before witnesses whose admiration has only grown, justified by the solidity, as well as the number and brilliance, of his discoveries. The master is no more; none of his work has been touched, his *œuvre* stays whole, intact and upstanding. We have only been able to advance a small number of his points. His discoveries still seem young and new! It feels as if their immortal author died only yesterday.

It also seems, to those who loved him, that he did die yesterday. I still see, as if still alive, his serious and soft face, with his good and indulgent smile. The work of a great artist, that we celebrate today, helps us keep this reverent illusion. For it's really Claude Bernard just as I always saw him, in the midst of an experiment when a new fact hits him. He stops, reflects for a moment: what is this unknown thing worth? Is it an accident of no importance, explicable by the givens of science? Or is it the result of an unknown condition, behind which the master's wisdom already glimpses a discovery? It's this moment of fecund astonishment that Mr Guillaume has so admirably captured. Yes, it's really Claude Bernard here.

And he's here in his place, on these stairs I've come down so many times beside him, and of which he once said to me: 'They certainly only built these here to put a statue on one day!' Yes, he's in his place, leaving the laboratory of Collège de France where he passed, risked, sacrificed his life, where his biggest discoveries were born, looking out at the house where he spent his last days, yes, in his place…I feel so profoundly moved by these memories and by the sight of this living statue…"

Then Berthelot:

"Alas, it was in these laboratories that he caught the germ of the illness that killed him. We've spoken often of this unsanitary cave in which he worked for forty years, and yet it still exists. It killed Bernard; may it not devour his successors! A time will come when France will possess scientific institutions comparable to the best in the world. Like Moses, Claude Bernard died without having the benefit of reaching his earthly potential.

But at least his image will always grace this edifice…Teaching his class on experimental physiology, this is where one should have seen and heard him speaking his inspirational words, describing a new discovery he presented, for which the audience had the hypothesis. This interrupted speech, this spontaneous bloom of an inven-

tor's mind, with the moral encouragement and agreement of the
audience, gave birth to the same experiment that Claude Bernard
repeated in public, in the organs of the opened animal before him
where he found his sudden illuminations."

Mr Fremy thanks Paul Bert, wishing him *bon voyage*, best of luck, and a
glorious return—for he is headed on an overseas governmental mission.
Politics and science are opposed, one might think, by the fact that in a
laboratory one can repeat mistakes over and over, while governing must
confront unforgiving and unrepeatable complexity. The difference is not
knowledge, but the history of what makes a fact. Fremy jokes that one day
Paul Bert, too, will have his statue, not far from that of Claude Bernard.

§

The chorus may ignorantly believe that once the hero dies, the situation just ends—but instead we watch helplessly as new heroes spring up,
each more determined than the last, to claim Claude's mantle and his
methods. The excavation of Claude's desk unearths my own 'unpublished
works,' evidence of all my villainy, such as this tally of a week's expenses:

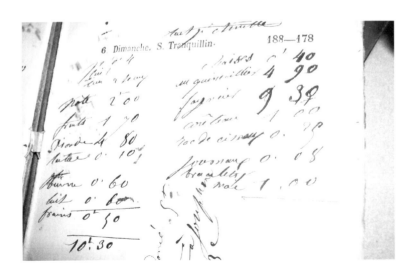

See how cold-heartedly I track the budget? How greedily I mark the sums! Look closer, and see the precision with which I wished our boys' deaths! Well, gossips, what about Claude's daily accounting? His lists?

Without notebooks and lists, neither enemies nor friends can later be found. The evidence is inconclusive without the marks we leave, yet doesn't writing always hide the bodies? What guilt is behind every need to account for ourselves? Behind every word? Even Claude may have suspected this when he wrote:

CLAUDE'S RED NOTEBOOK:

Silence is eloquent, but when we know how to speak.

Silence is eloquent, yes, when it's the silence of an orator.

Archeology is the physiology of history.

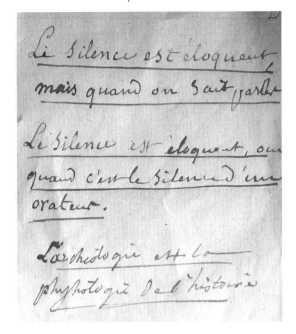

§

Before his departure overseas, Paul Bert, chief litigator of Claude's legacy, writes one last article for the *Medical Tribune*, "More on the Anti-Vivisection League":

"Yes, it's offensive to attach a poor dog to a table, to rummage through his guts, to expose his spinal column, and to force his beating heart to record its painfully troubled beats on a turning cylinder. He who does these tortures, without purpose and only to pass an hour or two, would be a ferocious and cowardly monster, who only for vague curiosity, and without the excitement of a precise problem to resolve or a definitive result useful to science and humanity, would merit the most severe reproach and universal condemnation.

If a way existed to avoid vivisection, physiologists would be guilty if they didn't put it into practice... This is why men, high-minded and big-hearted men, tender-souled like Claude Bernard, who I'm thinking of while writing this, had the courage to submit to this torturer's profession. And many of us passionately love animals.

Magendie, the horrible enemy of dogs...shared with his own dog, his friend, his daily bread.

Vivisectors know what the suffering of animals is, and they are resigned to the 'blessed pain' (sainte douleur) imposed in the name of science...Even in the laboratories, it's not without feelings that we call for, grab, and attach the poor animals. It's ourselves, after all, who we see in them, and our pity is proportional less to its terror than to the way it expresses it. The motionless guinea pig or the imbecilic rabbit barely affects us. And long live the cat or rat who shows its claws or its teeth! But the poor dog, who only knows how to droop his ears and look around with such an anxious air! Ah! That's hard, and we've all groaned.

Yet I would like the founders and the members of the Anti-Vivisection League to consent to think of the moral sufferings of the vivisector. He must, at the drop of a hat, control the most natural yearnings of his heart; he must repress his will in consideration of his goal... Behind the bound animal, from whom he no longer even hears the cries, he imagines the scientific problem resolved, and farther away, the human illness cured for the price of animal suffering.

The honorary president of the League, Victor Hugo, made gigantic imaginary efforts to enlighten the audience on the secret anguish of Torquemada; it takes much less to translate the real feelings of a scientist forced to be a vivisector.

Who among its members, if they are not a vivisector themselves, would have the authority to decide that any torture is not justified by necessity? Who would come make the law in the laboratories, measure the number of rabbits and dogs they can use, or determine the operations they can do on the animals? And if the scientist wanted to show proof of a discovery...demonstrate to students the truth of his allegations and teach them how one looks and how one finds, who would come to decide if this proof is profitable or without merit for science?

Will the League let the professionals master their own actions, since their science offers sufficient guarantees? What will the Amazonian animal-lovers say when they go to the public lectures armed with umbrellas?"

§

Pasteur: "Claude Bernard! Incompetent!"

Review of Scientific Societies, "Alcoholic Fermentation: Mr Pasteur and the Shadow of Claude Bernard":

"Among his unfinished and posthumous works, Claude Bernard left important notes relating to his experimental study on a question that had forcefully preoccupied him in the last years of his life: the question of fermentation in general and alcoholic fermentation in particular. These notes—carefully gathered by students dedicated to his memory, and to a certain extent on the wishes of the master (one of the principal regrets expressed by Claude Bernard was to die before solving the problem)—have been recently brought to light under the auspices of Mr Berthelot, and published in the *Scientific Review* of last August 3rd, under the title: 'Alcoholic Fermentation; Last Experiments of Claude Bernard.' These experimental results formally contradict the views and the theories of Mr Pasteur on fermentation.

It's not in the character of Mr Pasteur, this implacable and invincible fighter, to stay quiet before a challenge coming from such a high place, and thus he made a first response to the Academy of Science (though it was more an emotional response than a truly scientific one) in which he expressed surprise and a certain chagrin over what Claude Bernard, his friend and academic neighbor, never told him he was experimenting on, even though it was a subject that concerned Pasteur so intimately.

But the eminent chemist, having understood that his critique needed another basis to be viable, an experimental basis, put himself to the task, and these are the results of his experiments on a portion of his own vines in the Jura mountains, of which the odd proof attached to his notes were grape-clusters carefully and neatly packed—these, I tell you, are what he brought as proof to the Medical Academy.

We can't repeat the arguments today, though after hearing them we are assured they are practical and subtle, touching on important matters of doctrine. Still, we cannot help the painful impression that this has left in us, for the way in which he treated the memory, which was due only the highest respect, of Claude Bernard, who himself could not respond.

We've had the chance on more than one occasion to see the rigid severity and hauteur of Mr Pasteur toward any living person possessing the temerity to oppose him, but we've never seen him behave this way toward the dead. It's really too bad that this first occasion has the illustrious deceased for its object; to say that Claude Bernard, this eminently positive spirit, sworn enemy of all conjectural vagueness, who passed his life and scientific labor to erect experimentation as the method of direct proof, to say that 'in his physiological and philosophical conceptions he willingly let his thoughts wander on an adventure more than we can imagine and more than he admitted,' to treat as 'physiological mysticism' the results of his last experiments, what we could call his scientific legacy—this is not only (as our colleague from the Medical Union rightly called it) a rebuttal, but a total incrimination, and we would even add that it's *post mortem* and unworthy of he who is doing it, and especially of he to whom it is happening."

§

E.J. Marey: "The laboratories....have become insufficient...thus the study of organized bodies will soon come to an end if we do not manage to observe nature in its own domain."

Medical Tribune, "The Candidates for the Chair of Claude Bernard": "The election which is being held at the Academy of Sciences for the replacement of Claude Bernard has excited the interest and the attention of the world's scientists. It's worth the attention thanks to the illustrious memories of the great physiologist and to the exceptional merits of all those seeking to succeed him."

The candidates include: Mr EJ Marey, Mr Paul Bert, Mr Moreau, Mr Gubler, Mr Charcot, Mr Germain.

It is the eccentric Mr Marey who succeeds Claude at the Academy of Science, even though after the Siege he only lives on and off in Paris, in a series of apartments filled with the circus-like curios he invents, and at the Physiology Station in the Bois de Boulogne granted him by the government. He calls himself a physiologist-working-at-large, a curiosity-hunter—he does not make the list of vivisectors we follow. He never collects dogs. He works inside with his machines but also outside—with birds and animals he films with his *chrono-gun*, the rotating photo-plate that splits movement into a series. He writes an open letter saying that he would like his inventions to help France's armies learn to shoot moving targets. He would like to help kill enemies. Marey: "Life is movement and nothing else."

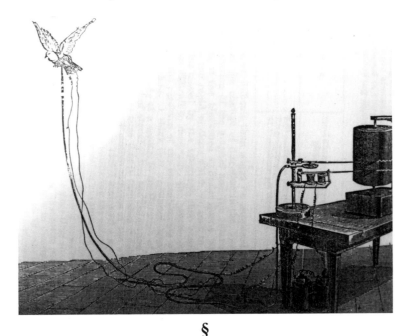

§

Unexpectedly, Paul Bert dies of dysentery on his political mission to Hanoi.

Medical Tribune:

"Paul Bert died for his country: what a glorious end! But for science, what mourning! Yes, it's true to say he had a glorious end, but it's also educational, which means: Men of science, stay at your desks!"

Maitland reports your exuberant response: "Yesterday 11th November, at eleven at night, I knew that my Will had smitten another vivisector!...Paul

Bert has wasted to death! I have killed Paul Bert as I killed Claude Bernard, as I will kill Louis Pasteur, and after him the whole tribe of vivisectors, if I live long enough. Courage: it is a magnificent power to have, and one that transcends all vulgar methods of dealing out justice to tyrants....
It would interest Mr Charles Richet to know of the episodes in question."

Sir Richard Burton recalls, "She was in the last stage of consumption, suffering from mind and soul, distressed at the sight and sound connected with vivisection. Her sensitive organization braved these horrors in order to serve and succour, but both she and my wife could not help feeling that the efforts were in vain…"

That we can't help telling each other's stories to decorate or bolster our own may be a human condition akin to greed, or maybe love. Florence Miller: "The great distinction of Nina Kingsford, the reason why I describe her as 'unique' in my experience, was that she united to her beauty of person not only an exceptionally fine and active intellect, but also the strength and 'staying power' required to cultivate her mental gifts in the direction of scientific knowledge, as well as aesthetics. In this combination she differed from any other woman I have known or heard of in my own time, although tradition ascribes a similar efflorescence of mind and person to several of the famous women of past ages. Cleopatra Queen of Egypt is recorded to have spoken to the ambassadors of eight foreign states successively, each in his own tongue. Ninon de l'Enclos, Madame de Pomadour, Mary Queen of Scots, Hypatia the Martyr, and Aspasia the friend and counselor of Pericles are only some of those who are reported to have combined a cultivated mind and beauty of person."

But then Florence Miller accuses Maitland's biography of making a mockery of the genre, depriving "his book of any reliability in regard to other parts of it in themselves incredible…How that *Life* is altogether badly done! It is about Maitland himself, rather than his professed subject. Page after page is given to the vapourings of spiritualistic media and talk, about *his* soul, *his* visions, and *his* importance in the universe! As I entered upon public life so young, I have lived to read the biographies or autobiographies of quite a number of people whom I knew personally, more or less well. The books are generally unsatisfactory, often actually untrue, obscuring not revealing character and doings. But the worst of all is Maitland's *Life of Anna Kingsford*."

Your last days all bedsores and morphine and sleeplessness. Only forty-two, and a mind still clear. Maitland "quotes" you: "Not cured yet! No, nor even mended were it but a little. Still the cough, still the afternoon fever, still the weakness, still the neuralgia….My left lung is in caverns, they say; my right is inflamed chronically. My voice is broken and gone, with which I had hoped to speak from platforms; wreck and ruin is made of all my expectancies. Can a miracle yet be wrought? Can Will accomplish what medicine fails to perform? The hard thing is that I cannot will heartily, for lack of knowing what I ought to desire. Is it better for me to live or to die? Unless I can be restored to the possibility of public life, it is useless for me to live. Dying, I may the sooner obtain a fresh incarnation and return to do my work more completely."

Prescribed beef and burgundy by the doctors, you refuse the treatment for the flesh and alcohol it really is. You are instructed to take 'baths of blood'—or visit the slaughterhouses to drink—as advertised in Paris newspapers, this "blood mania" causing the rue de Flandres slaughterhouses to fill daily with the sick, while you only weakly repeat, "no bloody food, no bloody science." Instead, soak in near-boiling water, limbs as hot as bearable. December 26, 1887: "In the night or early morning of this day—Christmas night—Piggy died. She had suffered a long time." This is the guinea pig who replaced Rufus by your side.

The next day is your last, and several Catholic papers claim that in dying you return to the Church, though this is immediately refuted by letters from your husband Algernon, and of course, Maitland: "Perhaps in no single point does Roman Catholicism present a worse aspect than in the manner in which its missionaries besiege the last hours of the passing soul in the effort to induce its victims, when too weak to resist, to say ditto to the formulae that their priests pretend to regard as constituting a password to the celestial realms. With Anna Kingsford, the admission of a Catholic sister of Mercy to tend to her in her last illness was productive of the worst results, troubling her last hours with an unseemly wrangle that did not cease even after her body was consigned its final resting place." A priest in your presence supposedly said, "Why, my daughter, you have been *thinking*. You should never do that. The Church saves us the trouble and danger of thinking by telling us what to believe. We are only called on to believe. I never think: I dare not. I should go mad if I were to let myself think." You reply that you want to understand, and it's impossible to do that without some thinking: "How, except by thinking, does one learn if the church has the truth?"

Your obituaries read, as you requested, *Anna Kingsford, M.D.* or *Dr Anna Kingsford*. They list your works: *Violationism, or Sorcery in Science*; *Uselessness of Vivisection*; *Unscientific Science*; and *Notes by a Medical Student*. "Mrs Kingsford was a great lover of animals. She wore feathers in place of fur, silk gloves in all weathers, and some vegetable material for her shoes, so as not to destroy animal life for her adornments. She was a tower of strength to the antivivisection cause, in an effort to serve which, she lost her life." Then a mention that you helped found the first anti-vivisection society in France, and that Victor Hugo was honorary president. Terrified of burial—for the fear of being buried alive always assaulted you when in a trance—you feared mass graves (for Parisians, at least, a common nightmare). People save their money before anything else to buy a funeral, a plot, and a stone. You desperately wanted to be cremated, but finally aren't because of Algernon's profession as a clergyman, and your understanding of the hardship this would bring him. You obtained illuminations in sleep. What did dying bring?

Madame de Morsier, in the *Animal Protection Bulletin*:

"'I had nominated Madame Kingsford, Doctor of the Medical School of Paris, wife of an English pastor, so how can I stay quiet on the sadness of her premature death? I appeal to those who, like me, only somewhat knew this friendly and distinguished woman, to never forget her.'

To this, the secretary general adds: 'Today, vivisection seems, to almost everyone, a natural thing. The prerogatives of science are unlimited, they say.'"

§

The young man is warned to keep his mind clear, to banish all thoughts that could impair his ability to react; hands gentle on the reins, eyes wide. Approaching Bezons on horseback seems the best plan, the horse's legs pumping across the hay field trenched with hurdles of snow. Other horses—brown, red, black—pull lazily at bales, the whole picture brush-stroked by some amateur through the trees over that ridge, drawing him here, a figure in an imagination. He smells only wet wool, reminding him to arrive before night freezes the fabric solid. He was told to "make contact and deliver this letter." More horses gather, tossing their heads and trotting beside, stepping lighter, glad for the company. At the marker for Le Grand Serf, approaching where a house should be, only a long wall stretches back. No outer fence, only more horses, shaggy with steam. The wall curves off with no double gates of wood or iron, no smaller doors coming into view as he rounds the perimeter. He rides an arm's length from the stone, recalling the rumor that Bernard's daughters are somehow dangerous, and a bitter acid rises in his throat. He kicks up a gallop along the circular fortress, with only a thin sun to the west. Snow flies up his boots, over his knees, and into the bag on the saddle. Reaching in to check the letter, he steers the other way, toward a skeletal row of poplars. The horse pulls up, sweaty. A dog's bark from across the wall lifts the air. The lab assistant trots closer to what is now a gnashing growling assault, and staring up at the wall he can practically feel dogs jumping at him, until a thick bell calls their retreat. Dismounting expectantly, he waits, finally touching ear and cheek to the sun-warm stone, brought alive with his breath. Hello! he leans back for a response before pressing close again. As light flees, and moon-glow crawls forward across the fields, he shivers and paces. Another harsh clang, and barking, and a crest of noise. A distant door slams. It won't matter if he waits; no one comes in or out. Pulling up the reins, he pounds the letter in his wet fist and throws it high over the wall, turning back toward Paris without an answer.

§

Medical Tribune, January 28, 1883, "Denigrating Ourselves According to Victor Hugo":

"This passage is borrowed—we must confess—from Victor Hugo who wrote the following lines in the journal *Le Rappel*, in 1871, where one only has to change, from our point of view, the word *literary* to the word *scientific*: 'Literary peace will signal the beginning of moral peace. In my opinion, we must encourage every talent, help everyone with good will, support all efforts, reward bravery by applauding it, celebrate the young anointed, crown the old glories... The denigration of ourselves by ourselves is detestable. Let's stop this silliness...When we're rich, let's not act poor.'"

Bulletin of the French Society Against Vivisection, May 18, 1885:

"The French Society Against Vivisection, greatly upset by news of the illness of V. Hugo, sends the most heartfelt wishes for the speedy return to health of our honorary president."

On Victor Hugo's deathbed, the archbishop of Paris pressures him to accept church blessing and last rites, but Hugo dies refusing. As he lies in state beneath the Arc de Triomphe, two million people pass to pay last respects. A large delegation carries a banner from the French Society Against Vivisection. Others come out to shout "Vive la Vivisection!" To have a civil resting place, Hugo is put in the Pantheon.

Victor Hugo: "Humans never had an important thought they didn't write in stone."

Medical Tribune, June 7, 1885, "Science, Free-Thought, and the Brain of Victor Hugo":

"In the immense procession which accompanied the immortal remains of Victor Hugo to the Pantheon, taking possession of his true domain, the shelter of great men, we saw science walking beside free-thought like two sisters tightly bound, inseparable.

But one regret, one sad falsehood befell both science and free-thought, which was to be denied the legitimate right to possess the organ whose vast and incomparable functioning gave birth, in the intellectual world, to such sublimity, the fruits of a universal genius.

If ever a brain deserved to be scrutinized and studied, in the way that shows the organizational relations and the structure of the organic substratum's range and functioning, it would be the brain of Victor Hugo. And this study, that, due to recent progress, science could achieve today, is not the fruit of a vain and sterile curiosity, but something that leads to important results in the conquest of biological truths, natural history, and the evolution of man.

To those who aren't familiar with this type of research, or who could doubt its efficacy and scientific utility, we signal the remarkable results of the study of the brain of Gambetta, from which was determined the exceptionally perfected cerebral twists constituting the spoken language organ, more than double in a man who possessed the gift of eloquence in the highest degree!

What might we find out about thought and expression in Victor Hugo's brain? To a discreet and direct request on this subject by the Anthropological Society, the inner circle and the family didn't even reply. It's not our business to guess the motives behind this silence, which has been taken as more than a refusal, but we can say that Victor Hugo's thinking should be from Victor Hugo to the world. Victor Hugo left his body to France, with the idea of circumventing any difficulties that might arise from his family, just as we saw for the remains of Gambetta. For to leave his body to France, isn't that to leave it to French science?

We spoke of, and even wrote, the word 'profane' with regard to all this. But isn't embalming, from this point of view, also a desecration, since it puts an obstacle, almost a revolt, against the laws of nature? This was certainly what Victor Hugo understood since, if we're not wrong, he expressed his desire to not be embalmed. Even outside of the study of his brain, the body should have been autopsied, in our humble opinion. We should know exactly what a man like Victor Hugo died of, and only a direct examination of his organs could permit this real knowledge. The autopsy of kings was done in the past not only by habit, but also for the highest honor, and these weren't even kings, such as it were, of such great intelligence and genius!"

If anything proves the century's abdication of virtue, it's the whimsy with which people decide to be contrary. The *ancient regime's* church of Sainte Geneviève was renamed the Pantheon after the Revolution to receive Mirabeau's remains for secular purposes. Then these remains were withdrawn in 1793, and Marat was removed by decree after the fall of Robespierre and the repudiation of the Jacobins. Napoleon tried to reconcile the building's two identities by dedicating it to "the great men of France," but in 1822, under the Restoration, it became a church again, "purged of the infidel remains of Voltaire and Rousseau." Then with the July Revolution in 1830, Louis Philippe renamed it the Pantheon, returning Voltaire and Rousseau to the crypt. Agitation on the right forced Louis Philippe to return it to being Sainte Geneviève, which it stayed until the Commune, during which the cross on the dome was replaced with a red flag, and the building served as a center for insurgents. In the early years of the Third Republic, the building returned to being Sainte Geneviève, but now it is the Pantheon—prompted by Victor Hugo's death—and the remains of Verlaine and Mirabeau are dragged back.

To commemorate the great building, and the great writer, the sculptor August Rodin is asked to depict "Hugo of the exile—the flame on the rock—steadfast in protest against despotism—refusing to be moved from his island, to sit in the north section of the building." But the government rejects Rodin's model because Hugo is seated low and nude, with three angry-looking muses behind him. The committee says the statue should be monumental, less private. Rodin returns with another model, this one the Apotheosis of Hugo, a huge colossal nude, a Hugo standing on rocks of exile with sea nymphs at eye level, and Iris, messenger of the gods, in a bluntly erotic pose. Iris and Hugo are never transferred to marble, and no carving is ever done. The stone sits in Rodin's studio, unworked. It is Rodin's *Thinker* that finally sits in the Pantheon, and it is Émile Zola who joins Hugo in his crypt.

§

Worms are nocturnal, Darwin tells Emma, yet they rarely emerge from underground. If they do, they often get lost. Down on his stomach, Darwin appears of the earth himself, one of millions in a transforming fantasmagoria. His is a hallucinogenic view that can't be contained even in an organized sentence. Worms reveal secrets invisible to normal perception—events going on at a pace unrecognizable by the eye, in a manner invisible to people in their landscape of one lifetime. Rolling to his back, Darwin welcomes death. Emma holds his head with a cold cloth. Every day, including Sundays, he produces quantities of writing, but after fifteen minutes of conversation, vertigo and cold or heat leads to dizziness and vomiting. His heart clenches, and he falls. "I have been as yet in a very poor way; it seems as soon as the stimulus of mental work stops, my whole strength gives way. As yet I have hardly crawled half a mile from the house, and then have been fearfully fatigued. It is enough to make one wish oneself quiet in a comfortable tomb."

"Jan 15,
My dear Gray,

I have taken up an old subject which formerly interested me, namely the amount of earth brought to the surface by worms. I want to know whether you have in the States the little vermiform piles of earth which are so common on our lawns fields woods & waste lands—Are they as numerous with you as they are with us?

C. Darwin"

He might say that all life came from life before, and continues to make way for new life after, entwined in *competition*—a word repeated in every lecture, interview and article, new edition after new edition—the word which tells how individuals, as well as populations, forge their way and survive in whatever world they find themselves. But each struggle engenders extinction and less diversity, as we are each partly disappearing, and partly causing others to disappear: "Hence the improved and modified descendants of a species will generally cause the extermination of the parent-species." Darwin experiments with the worms he finds by placing different leaves before their burrows and watching how they move them inside.

Darwin, from *The Formation of Vegetable Mould, through the Action of Worms, with Observations on Their Habits*:

"Worms have played a more important part in the history of the world than most persons would at first suppose. In almost all humid countries they are extraordinarily numerous, and for their size possess great muscular power. In many parts of England a weight of more than ten tons (10,516 kilograms) of dry earth annually passes through their bodies and is brought to the surface on each acre of land, so that the whole superficial bed of vegetable mould passes through their bodies in the course of every few years...Archæologists ought to be grateful to worms, as they protect and preserve for an indefinitely long period every object, not liable to decay, which is dropped on the surface of the land, by burying it beneath their castings. Thus, also, many elegant and curious tessellated pavements and other ancient remains have been preserved; though no doubt the worms have in these cases been largely aided by earth washed and blown from the adjoining land, especially when cultivated. The old tesselated pavements have, however, often suffered by having subsided unequally from being unequally undermined by the worms. Even old massive walls may be undermined and subside; and no building is in this respect safe, unless the foundations lie 6 or 7 feet beneath the surface, at a depth at which worms cannot work. It is probable that many monoliths and some old walls have fallen down from having been undermined by worms.

When we behold a wide, turf-covered expanse, we should remember that its smoothness, on which so much of its beauty depends, is mainly due to all the inequalities having been slowly leveled by worms. It is a marvelous reflection that the whole of the superficial earth over any such expanse has passed, and will again pass, every few years through the bodies of worms. The plough is one of the most ancient and most valuable of man's inventions; but long before he existed, the land was in fact regularly ploughed, and still continues to be thus ploughed, by earth-worms. It may be doubted whether there are many other animals which have played so important a part in the history of the world, as have these lowly organized creatures."

Darwin has another angina attack, followed by an irregular pulse. He continues fainting. Then, in April, he recognizes the face of Death coming toward him. He tells Death he's not afraid, and Death waits until the next day to take him.

§

THE NINE CIRCLES

OF THE

HELL OF THE INNOCENT.

DESCRIBED FROM

THE REPORTS OF THE PRESIDING SPIRITS.

COMPILED BY

G. M. RHODES.

WITH PREFACE BY

FRANCES POWER COBBE.

Mostrarti mi convien la valle buia
Necessità m'induce e non diletto.
—INFERNO, 12, 86.

London:
SWAN SONNENSCHEIN & CO., PATERNOSTER SQUARE.

1892.

Price One Shilling.

CONTENTS.

A BIRD'S-EYE VIEW OF THE HELL OF THE INNOCENT.

Frances Power Cobbe, from *The Life of Frances Power Cobbe, as told by Herself*:

"With the great naturalist who has revolutionized modern science, I had rather frequent intercourse till the sad barrier of a great difference of moral opinion arose between us. Mr Charles Darwin's brother-in-law, Mr Hensleigh Wedgwood, was, for a time, tenant here at Hengwrt; and afterwards took a house named Caer-Deon in this neighbourhood, where Mr and Mrs Charles Darwin and their boys also spent part of the summer. As it chanced, we also took a cottage that summer close by Caer-Deon and naturally saw our neighbours daily. I had known Mr Darwin previously, in London, and had also met his most amiable brother. The first thing we heard concerning the illustrious arrivals was the report that one of the sons had had 'a fall off a philosopher'—a word substituted by the ingenious Welsh mind for 'velocipede' (as bicycles were then called)!

Next, the Welsh parson of the little church close by, having fondly calculated that Mr Darwin would certainly hasten to attend his services, prepared for him a sermon which should slay this scientific Goliath and spread dismay through the ranks of the skeptical host. He told his congregation that there were in these days persons, puffed up by science, falsely-so-called, and deluded by the pride of reason, who had actually been so audacious as to question the story of the six days of Creation as detailed in Sacred Scripture. But let them note how idle were these skeptical questionings! Did they not see that the events recorded happened before there was any man existing to record them, and that, therefore, Moses must have learned them from God himself, since there was no one else to tell him?

Alas! the philosopher, I fear, never went to be converted by this ingenious Welsh parson, and we were for a long time merry over his logic. Mr Darwin was never in good health, I believe, after his Beagle experience of seasickness, and he was glad to use a peaceful and beautiful old pony of my friend's which she placed at his disposal. His gentleness to this beast and incessant efforts to keep off the flies from his head, and his fondness for his dog Polly (concerning whose cleverness and breeding he indulged in delusions which Matthew Arnold's better dog-lore would have swiftly dissipated), were very pleasing traits in his character...

This pleasant 'intercourse with an illustrious man' was, like many other pleasant things, brought to a close for me in 1875 by the Anti-vivisection crusade. Mr Darwin eventually became the centre of an adoring clique of vivisectors who (as his biography shows) plied him incessantly with encouragement to uphold their practice, till the deplorable spectacle was exhibited of a man who would not allow a fly to bite a pony's neck, standing before all Europe (in his celebrated letter to Prof—in Sweden) as the advocate of vivisection...I was, of course, miserably disappointed at this state of affairs, but on the 2nd of February, 1875, there appeared in the Morning Post the celebrated letter from Dr George Hoggan, in which (without naming Claude Bernard) he described what he had himself witnessed in his laboratory when recently working there for several months. This letter was absolutely invaluable to our cause, giving, as it did, reality and first-hand testimony to all we had asserted from books and reports.

Lord Henniker introduced the Bill thus drafted 'for Regulating the Practice of Vivisection' into the House of Lords on 4 May, 1875, but on the 12 May, to our great surprise, another Bill 'to prevent Abuse in Experiments on Animals' was introduced into the House of Commons by Dr Playfair. On the appearance of this latter Bill, which was understood to be promoted by the physiologists themselves—notably Dr Burdon-Sanderson, and by Mr Charles Darwin—the Government, which had sanctioned Lord Henniker's Bill, thought it necessary to issue a Royal Commission on Enquiry into the subject...No words can tell the anxiety and alarm this occasioned in us, when we learned that a large section of the medical profession, which had so far seemed quiescent if not approving, had been roused by their chief wire-puller into a state of exasperation at the supposed 'insult' of proposing to submit them to legal control in experimenting on living animals (as they were already subjected to it, by the Anatomy Act, in dissecting dead bodies.) These doctors, to the number of 8,000, signed a Memorial to the Home Secretary, calling on him to modify the Bill so as practically to reverse its character, and make it a measure, no longer protecting vivisected animals from torture, but vivisectors from prosecution under Martin's Act.

...The world has never seemed to me quite the same since that dreadful time. My hopes had been raised so high to be dashed so low as even to make me fear that I had done harm instead of good, and brought fresh danger to the hapless brutes for whose sake, as I realized more and more their agonies, I would have gladly died. I was baffled in an aim nearer to my heart than any other had ever been, and for which I had strained every nerve for many months; and of all the hundreds of people who had seemed to sympathize and had signed our memos and petitions, was not one to say: 'This shall not be!'? Justice and Mercy seemed to have gone from the earth."

§

As if I wasn't burdened enough with the antagonisms of Claude's pro-tégés, an acquaintance, Georges Barral, emerged from the woodwork claiming he was given the manuscript of Claude's play, *Arthur de Bretagne*, by Claude himself in 1876. Barral waited nine years after Claude's death to publish it, but I sue him instantly—because in the preface he describes me as "abusive," and blames me for Claude's miseries. In court, I handily win the libel suit, and all copies of the play are recalled. Lies are what make me sue, and lies are why I win. A letter from a little bookstore, 23, rue Serpente, responds to my search for errant copies of the play, telling me they have become collectors' items—and offering to sell me two cop-ies for 50FF! Rather than pay a penny, I call a sheriff who shows up with the court order and seizes them.

Anatole de Monzie, *The Abusive Widows*, 'The Case of Claude Bernard':

   "'I'm of the opinion,' wrote Mr Barral, 'that we shouldn't let perish the least jetsam or flotsam of great men. For this, I'm publishing the manuscript of *Arthur de Bretagne*, that Claude Bernard gave me on Monday the 14th August, 1876, after giving his last lesson on the respiration of plants at the Museum of Natural History. In giving it to me, he said with a smile: 'I'm giving you this in

memory of our stay in Perpignon, and of Arago, your father's friend, who did
me a favor in 1849. You can publish this if you feel inspired, but later, at least
five years after my death. I also wrote a Variety that played in Lyon in 1833, but
I can only leave you my tragedy. But don't forget to say that it was refused, and
with many corrections, by Saint-Marc Girardin.'

Barral's preface contained other biographical secrets that Mr Barral
recalled from his conversations with poor Claude Bernard, 'painful confessions of disappointment with his conjugal life' and the 'cruel abandonment
that he suffered one sad morning in 1869 by his wife and two daughters.'
Father Didon said practically the same thing, but was less jumped on by
the vindictive widow. For by now, Madame Claude Bernard has taken her
place among the worldly matrons of the Republic, and this impertinent
publisher risked troubling her honorable widowhood. The widow thus
took it to court where Maître Leon Renault argued: 'There's one thing to
which everyone who heard Claude Bernard speak of the odyssey of his
manuscript, *Arthur de Bretagne*, can attest (except perhaps Mr Barral): that
Claude Bernard would leap with indignant surprise if he suspected anyone
would publish this manuscript, which he only mentioned to show young
people how much one should resist the calling we think we want...'

A beautiful memory requires constant policing. In our provinces, atten-
tive to the dead, we don't entrust pallbearer cords to enemies of the deceased,
or invite unfaithful mistresses to put their violets at the tomb of he who
they made cry. But Paris, where the greatest tributes are made, easily lends
itself to posthumous pilferings. Among the pilferers, I vote the prize go
to Madame Bernard, diabolical bourgeoise, false widow and false Robin
Hood, one of those 'honest women' who makes all the rest necessary.'

§

Spurred on by the 1875 Royal Commission, and the 1876 Act in England, an increasing number of famous sympathizers begin appealing
directly to the public about vivisection, using every literary method
available. Charles Dodgson (aka Lewis Carroll) writes a logical tract:
Some Popular Fallacies about Vivisection, while Wilkie Collins, a penpal
of Frances Cobbe, attempts a vivisection novel written without the grue-
some *realism* of the sensationalists and activists. "From first to last," Collins writes in the preface to *Heart and Science*, "you are purposely left

in ignorance of the hideous secrets of vivisection. The outside of the laboratory is a necessary object in my landscape—but I never once open the door and invite you to look in." What good are the delicate debates of his characters, one might wonder, without the evidence? Why is he so convinced that description of violence is as violent as the deed?

After my legal success suppressing Claude's play, I screw up my courage to write Madame Raffalovich what I should have written her long before: "Do you think one can know what one doesn't know, and guess what one has never seen? Is there an intuition that is a sort of second sight?" I'm sure I did go on, but nevermind adding more fuel now. Thanks to twists of legal code, the girls and I remain entitled to the revenue from all of Claude's works, foreign editions and everything. It's especially lucky for the animal shelter that the *Introduction to the Study of Experimental Medicine* became both a bestseller *and* required reading for the baccalau-réat throughout France. The girls push sales even more through tireless effort:

6th August, 1900
Mr Rector,

My sister and I have the honor of asking you to please recommend, for your classes and prizes, our father's classic and modern teaching work, "Introduction to the Study of Experimental Medicine," which the Minister of Public Education has adopted for all the libraries and professors' libraries of the region, for the teachers of young girls in high schools and colleges, for the upper classes, for young people and young girls, and for classic and modern education, for prizes to be given for the high schools and middle schools.

Not only has our father's work been put into the official catalogue, but it is included in the Baccalauréat program (philosophy section). Mr

*Rector, we hope you will have the generosity to write us if you could
see your way to adopting this book for your high schools and secondary
schools.*

*Mademoiselles, Claude (Tony) Bernard and
Marie-Claude Bernard, Bezons, Seine-et-Oise."*

Tony and Marie, unmarried and childless, stay in Bezons at the place
everyone calls the Big Deer. Claude's twelve-year-old great-nephew,
Emile Marduel, visits the girls, later describing disgusting conditions in
the house and courtyard, and their dirty white dresses. As *Contemporary
Life* reports:

"...'rich bourgeois' like Mademoiselle Claude Bernard live in
Bezons-la-Garonne in a walled property closed off from the profane. If a dog is lost, she guarantees its life, pays its pension, visits
and watches over him; a lost cat is found on the road? She collects it
and brings it to her shelter, that no one has seen. If it is sick, or if it
is hurt, her care doubles and the creature is sure to enjoy a heavenly
life from then on. We estimate that Mademoiselle Claude Bernard
possesses about eighty dogs and cats at the moment. Guarded like
Hesperides' garden, her shelter is inaccessible. I'm not a demigod, I
retreat before the ascent. Readers please excuse me.

More accessible is the shelter of Madame Donon in Asnières.
When I visited, she showed me two cats lounging on the roof of a
little building: 'Those are two of Louise Michel's cats,' she tells me.
'When she left, she gave me six, along with two dogs. These are the
survivors.'"

The girls also contribute to the founding of the animal cemetery at
Asnières.

Medical Tribune headline:
"Decidedly, the Eagle of Experimental Medicine has given birth to
two little geese."

§

Crossing a short passage between rue de Cherche-Midi and rue de Sèvres, I am pierced from back to bosom, cough and sputter blood—followed by a burning sensation that flows clear down my hands, and a fire-feeling that stiffens my muscles as I fall to the ground. For a moment I think, "Shot! Is this how they'll stop me, with one of Claude's arrows!?" My mouth releases inarticulate sounds across my cheek, as people rush to peer into my face. I move my hand, but it won't lift from the sidewalk, nor does my head turn, though someone says *Madame* with an urgent throbbing, pulling what seems like a shaft through my ribs. "Old woman!" I think I hear, or it's Cupid laughing at his poor old mother. A strong tug curves me upward, and slowly the words I say aren't spoken, and my mind clutches at the crowd, the pelting rain rolling across my skin, rising where I see a cloth, bloody, and hear a woman yelling to offstage actors to come quickly. Wouldn't it happen that there's an excruciating stab in my neck as they turn me, and the caress of the woman crouched and stroking hair off my eyes. Behind her, against the grey stones, I recognize the snorts of the dragons from the river—their colorful feathers and leathery legs—their eyes blank of recognition, their strange arms bent and twitching. Dinosaurs, or they could be devils, sure as a novelist reverses a heroine's strength and kills her, making her lose her place. Someone says, *Listen!*—as approaching marionettes rehearse. Is that my story? Wouldn't I make an effort to yell that I'm not comfortable, though no movement of lip or tongue can force the slightest breath toward the crowd locked in my gaze, the street alive with books I now know: *Paul Faber, Surgeon*; *The Professor's Wife*; *Anna, the Professor's Daughter*; *The Beth Book*—"Wait!" I yell, "Don't go on! I'm still here!" but I'm not; I've made no impression on the air.

And thus, a falling action: all my exhausting deeds undone by arrow-shot, and those last two dogs freed from my grasp, watching from a safe distance, turning and trotting toward what I only hope is safety. You'd think a simple sleep is all there is between life and death, and yet the young woman steps back as I'm lifted onto a carriage cart, a broken puppet in some men's arms, each rib chafing the others as I'm dumped to the dirty floor and they latch the gate, calling to the driver to get moving. In a cart not unlike those we drove for years, I begin my last commute. Move the driver does, and so do I, though where I'm stranded now, I'm still awake, awaiting judgment.

...for other foundation no man can lay but that which is laid, and if any man build upon this foundation, gold, silver, precious stones, wood, hay stubble: every man's work shall be manifest; for the day of the Lord shall declare it, because it shall be revealed in fire; and the fire shall try every man's work, of what sort it is. If any man's work abide, which he hath built thereupon, he shall receive a reward. If any man's work burn, he shall suffer loss: but he himself shall be saved, yet so as by fire.

Mesdemoiselles Tony et Marie CLAUDE-BERNARD; Monsieur MARTIN; Madame veuve Jules CHENAL; Madame veuve DEVAY-CANTIN; Monsieur Jules VIREY et son fils; Monsieur et Madame Jean VIREY et leurs enfants; Monsieur et Madame Jean DEVAY et leurs enfants; Monsieur et Madame MARDUEL-DEVAY et leurs enfants.

Ont l'honneur de vous faire part de la perte douloureuse qu'ils viennent d'éprouver en la personne de

MADAME MARIE-FRANÇOISE MARTIN

Veuve de CLAUDE-BERNARD, Membre de l'Institut, (Académies des Sciences et Française), Professeur au Collège de France et au Muséum d'Histoire Naturelle, ancien Sénateur, Commandeur de la Légion d'Honneur, etc., etc.

eur mère, sœur, tante, grand'tante et arrière-grand'tante, décédée, unie des sacrements de l'Église, le 9 Octobre 1901, dans sa 83e année, son domicile, au Grand-Cerf, à BEZONS (Seine-et-Oise).

Priez pour Elle!

§

Look around. It's not just me in this expanse of coerced denouement: everyone's stuck in the same purgatory because we can't get up and act. Certainly don't pity us, for being finally freed of movement, there's no animal to chase or catch or save, cure or kill, and even the tiniest desires are banned from our muscles. Yet as fire consumes the bittersweet ache of each attachment and deed, "truth depends on what act is being performed in what circumstances," and this purgatory is now merely a night without labor, lit by both kinds of fire, the one that saves and the one that punishes.

Thankfully people offer a few intercessions, for "nothing unclean can go to heaven," and I don't dare show up at the gate with dirt on the shoes. Prayers aren't needed in heaven, and won't help those in hell, so this impotent place is where most of us reside, relying on indulgences. On the tombs of the faithful, I hope people will write petitions of peace—for the greatest confusions are assigned to believers—and though these fires will cease in the course of time, the time is more confusing than anyone can know. Are we better off now than before it all began? When did it all begin? There is the line between comedy and tragedy. I cannot finally tell if it's inside or outside the mind.

§

Henry David Thoreau, to a crowd at Concord, Massachusetts:

"...Others, craven-hearted, said disparagingly of John Brown that 'he threw his life away,' because he resisted the government. Which way have they thrown their lives, pray?—such as would praise a man for attacking singly an ordinary band of thieves or murderers. I hear another ask, Yankee-like, 'What will he gain by it?' as if he expected to fill his pockets by this enterprise. Such a one has no idea of gain but in this worldly sense. If it does not lead to a 'surprise' party, if he does not get a new pair of boots, or a vote of thanks, it must be a failure. 'But he won't gain anything by it.' Well, no, I don't suppose he could get four-and-sixpence a day for being hung, take the year round; but then he stands a chance to save a considerable part of his soul—and such a soul!—when you do not. No doubt you can get more in your market for a quart of milk than for a quart of blood, but that is not the market that heroes carry their blood to. Such do not know that like the seed is the fruit, and that, in the moral world, when good seed is planted, good fruit is inevitable, and does not depend on our watering and cultivating; that when you plant, or bury, a hero in his field, a crop of heroes is sure to spring up. This is a seed of such force and vitality, that it does not ask our leave to germinate....but the steady, and for the most part successful, charge of this man, for some years, against the legions of Slavery, in obedience to an infinitely higher command, is as much more memorable than that, as an intelligent and conscientious man is superior to a machine. Do you think that that will go unsung? 'Served him right,'—'A dangerous man,'—'He is undoubtedly insane.' ...

The only free road, the Underground Railroad, is owned and managed by the Vigilant Committee. They have tunneled under the whole breadth of the land. Such a government is losing its power and respectability as surely as water runs out of a leaky vessel, and is held by one that can contain it. I hear many condemn these men because they were so few. When were the good and the brave ever in a majority? Would you have had him wait till that time came?—till you and I came over to him? The very fact that he had no rabble or troop of hirelings about him would alone distinguish him from ordinary heroes. His company was small indeed, because few could be found worthy to pass muster...

Newspaper editors argue also that it is a proof of his insanity that he thought he was appointed to do this work which he did—that he did not suspect himself for a moment! They talk as if it were impossible that a man could be 'divinely appointed' in these days to do any work whatever; as if vows and religion were out of date as connected with any man's daily work; as if the agent to abolish slavery could only be somebody appointed by the president, or by some political party. They talk as if a man's death were a failure, and his continued life, be it of whatever character, were a success. When I reflect to what a cause this man devoted himself, and how religiously, and then reflect to what cause his judges and all who condemn him so angrily and fluently devote themselves, I see that they are as far apart as the heavens and earth are asunder....Any man knows when he is justified, and all the wits in the world cannot enlighten him on that point."

§

L'Antivivisection journal, 1912:

"We're starting our second edition, and since it's his centenary, we have-logically-dedicated a large section to the 'Father of Physiology.' This poor Claude Bernard is practically forgotten. His centenary actually falls on July 12, but we didn't celebrate it until the 30th of December after the complaints of his 'old disciples.' In the fracas of the anniversary of the Pasteur Institute, the physiologist disappeared. Now who remembers that state funeral?

The speeches were as they should have been...Mr Bergson maliciously quoted this phrase of Claude Bernard's: 'When we make a general theory in our sciences, the only thing we're certain about is that all theories are wrong; absolutely speaking, they are but partial and provisional truths.' This sentence is from a skeptic celebrating mostly his philosophy, but when it came to his physiology, discretion was the better part of valor. His students remembered the great generosity of the scientist, and spoke of vivisection as if he'd never done it.

Nevertheless Claude Bernard was one of the most ferocious vivisectors the world has ever known. His statue, standing before the door of Collège de France and emphasizing 'a dog in the trough' is the scandalous proof... Such is the man whose centenary we've just celebrated. This last trait will be what defines him: Claude Bernard was a member of the Animal Protection Society. He signed up in May 1860 and stayed until his death, despite many protestations. The ten francs annual dues may have sufficed to put his vivisector's conscience to rest, but this ransom was not sufficient for his daughter, Mademoiselle

Claude Bernard, who wasn't even present at the Collège de France ceremony, thinking it better to serve the memory of her father being the devoted protector of animals."

L'Antivivisection journal, 1913:

"The inhabitants of the neighborhood surrounding 2, boulevard Brune, point to the new experimental laboratories of the Medical School of Paris, run by professor Charles Richet. On a plot fortified by high walls, and isolated like a leper colony, you find a huge building. The first floor holds the vivisection rooms. In the courtyard are kennels where the victims await their fates...

The courageous residents of boulevard Brune, haunted by the cries of the martyred animals, are asking why they've been the recipients of these vile neighbors. Agitated by groans that could melt a soul, two of the residents put a ladder up to the wall, and panicked at the sight of dogs strapped to vivisection gutters, and others in the courtyard having been operated on, in extreme seizures. A crowd gathered and demanded that the animals be released. To calm the people, the man in charge said: 'There's no harm being done here.'

To procure these unlucky animals is easy: a good man, searching everywhere for his stolen dog, finds him in this establishment. The dog is named Tambour, and of course his collar has disappeared. Another man, looking for his lost dog, knocks on the door of the laboratory and receives this response: 'Your dog isn't here because ever since the boss got in trouble for taking a pet, we only buy dogs from the pound.' But the pound pays criminals a pittance for stolen dogs they sell to the laboratories."

§

Direction of Fine-Arts, Museums and Libraries of the City of Paris:
"The Act of 11 October, 1941 stipulates: all bronze statues and monuments in public places and administrative buildings, which do not present historic or aesthetic value shall be removed.

A Commission is created in each arrondissement to proceed with the list of monuments to be melted down...

Despite protests from the collaborationist press that empty pedestals would blight Paris, the administration decides to leave these in place, for budgetary reasons. They also serve as a visual reminder to the Parisians that the removals were done to benefit the occupiers."

le Petit Parisien, 26 November, 1941:

"A first list of Parisian statues that will be sent to the foundry:

The Berthelot and the Claude Bernard from Collège de France, the Louis Blanc of Place Monge, L'Etienne Dolet of Place Maubert, the Jean-Jacques Rousseau and the Corneille from the Pantheon, the Emile Augier from Odeon, the Voltaire from quai Voltaire, the Condorcet from quai Conti, the Charles Floquet and the Ledru-Rollin from Place Voltaire."

The Dawn, July 28, 1946:

"Claude Bernard has climbed back up on his old pedestal in the Latin Quarter. On November 26, 1941, among thirty-three bronze statues given in 'sacrifice'—we don't dare say by force—at the head of the list, and despite the sheer willpower of the administration, those of Mr Berthelot and Claude Bernard.

For Claude Bernard, his bronze statue was stolen and used by the enemy. The statue of Berthelot, a work by Saint-Marceaux, after having been soldered in two, was successfully hidden in the fire vault of the library by the administration, and one of the parts, the scientist's bust, will be remounted in a few weeks in the hall of Collège de France, facing the organic chemistry laboratory.

But the statue of Claude Bernard, first condemned by the enemy, finds itself justly recreated in our newly liberated Paris, in the presence of all the masters of this French university, at the heart of which the proponents of treason can be counted on one hand.

The sculptor Couvègne has reproduced what he could of the disappeared original, the first model given a beautiful birth by Guillaume.

Whatever sacrilegious works the misfortunes of France can be blamed on, Mr Edmond Faral, the administrator of Collège de France, has rejected the sterility of hate but denounced, 'the monstrous immorality of an enemy who, to satisfy his hunger for conquest and domination, and all while feigning a hypocritical respect for art and civilization, sought every means to rob our nation of the memories of its highest and purest glories, its very self-awareness.' Nevertheless, silent and immobile, the stone statue of Claude Bernard reminds us constantly: 'Whether you like it or not, I'm here; the idea of me is here. You weren't able, you will never be able, to do anything to destroy it.' 'Men,' concluded Mr Faral, 'be pure, sincere, just, and good. Work confidently: there is a human conscience.'

Then Mr Vergnolle, president of the municipal council, after paying homage to the French university that kept the patrimonial spirit of France's preeminence despite the short-lived and brutal coalitions that oppose her—mentioned an old project, still on the table, to endow Paris's science faculty with fifty amphitheaters worthy of its great masters and their work, worthy of France and its thought."

But it's not the same statue. The dog is missing, and Claude has his hand instead on a small stack of books.

§

Anna Kingsford, *Saint George the Chevalier*:

"The highest form of thought is, after all, imaginative. Man ends, as he begins, with images. Truth in itself is inutterable. The loftiest metaphysics is as purely symbolic as popular legend. The Catholic tale of Saint George, our national patron and champion, was once of worldwide renown. But since our youth have taken to reading Mill and Huxley, Spencer and Darwin, in place of the old books wherein their ancestors took delight, the romances of the Paladins and the knights-errant of Christian chivalry lie somewhat rusty in the memories of the present generation...'Fear not, fair maid; in the name of Christ I will do battle for thee against this dragon!'...This hero of so many names is the Higher Reason; the Reason that knows (gnosis) as distinguished from the Lower Reason of mere opinion (doxa)...The words pronounced of old times on the dubbing of a knight, 'Be gentle, valiant, and fortunate' are not words which could realize themselves in the dullard or the churl. To the good knight, the ardent love of beauty in all its aspects is indispensable. The *fair lady* of his dreams is the spiritual bright shining of goodness, which expresses itself to him fitly and sweetly in material and visible things. Hence he is always poet, and fighter in some cause. And he is impelled to fight because the love of beauty burns so hot within him that he cannot abide to see it outraged. His very gentleness of heart is the spur of his valour. Champion and knight as well as thinker and student, the Son of Hermes is of necessity a reformer of men, a redeemer of the world. It is not enough for him to know the doctrine, he must likewise do the will of the gods, and bid the kingdom of the Lord come upon earth without, even as in the heaven within his heart. For the rule of his Order is the Law of Love, and 'Love seeketh not its own.'"

§

Letter from Mr Faral to the Police:

"Mr Commissioner,

Over the course of the parade of baccalauréat graduates on June 24th, a bottle of ink was broken on the white stone statue of Claude Bernard in front of Collège de France. This statue is a public monument, and this event therefore concerns the Prefect of the Seine.

The memory of Claude Bernard is an issue of particular concern for the professors of Collège de France, who count him as one of their own. The statue was erected on their initiative, after the Liberation, to replace a bronze statue destroyed by the Germans. The sacrilege committed on June 24 is, for these reasons, particularly offensive. Please accept my humblest gratitude for your help in finding a useful solution."

"Mister Administrator,

Following up on your letter of the 26th June, 1948, I'm pleased to inform you that necessary actions were taken by Architectural Services to clean the statue of Claude Bernard as soon as possible…

Your Public Commissioner, 5th Arrondissement"

§

Passing finally out of the family—for the descendants of Claude Bernard are completely extinct—there's an inauguration of his house in Saint-Julien for the public:

"Claude Bernard doesn't belong to the past, he's way ahead of us, and we are always his students. A century of progress has only better prepared us to hear what only his most dedicated contemporaries could. The signs of renewed interest in his work are everywhere…

The mission of Claude Bernard at Saint-Julien en Beaujolais is to be the seat of a Claude Bernard Association. We foresee conferences of French and foreign biologists, exhibitions, and colloquiums."

But many years of slow turn-out, and a general lack of audience to view his machines and notebooks (as well as the pictures, portraits, and senatorial costumes)—forces the Claude Bernard foundation to donate the property, and the house's entire contents, to an association of towns in the Beaujolais, who invest in making it more of a bonafide museum, with installations and videos for school groups, and "timeless" exhibits promoting the value of the scientific method. Proudly, the local growers also continue to produce wine from Claude's vineyard.

Sucettes en chocolat
1,20 €

§

Here in Père Lachaise cemetery, where I keep tabs on things, there's not much going on. Daylight tourists stroll the slumbering alleys, and the nightly chasing around of cats makes the mausoleums shimmer. For a year or two, Claude had a glossy handout that the guards gave away at the ticket booth, but that's the most I've seen done for the hero, to drum up some of that old legacy business.

"Here in this cemetery, in a quiet enclosure far back from the 20th division and 8th row of Bossin way, we find the modest mausoleum with a stone vase where only plastic plants grow. Here lies the illustrious doctor. On the front of the base a long epitaph recalls his titles, and on the top of the tombstone, five other inscriptions remind us that here too lie his wife, his sons, and his daughters.

All that students today learn in their elementary books, from the glycogenic process of the liver to the vaso-motor nerves, it's he who discovered it. Without Claude Bernard, medicine would be a century behind. Unfortunately, the great scientist has been abandoned without a visitor to his tomb, without a flower. It's a shame that the institutions and academies of which he took part give him so little acknowledgement. Maybe they don't know that he who they should honor lies in Père Lachaise?"

FIN

BIBLIOGRAPHIC NOTES

Selections from letters and journals used in this novel are found in a number of archives. I want to extend my tremendous gratitude to these repositories, and especially their helpful and generous staff, for their assistance in compiling the scraps and ephemera that make up the ground of this work. Original publications that have provided material are also listed below.

ARCHIVES

Archives de l'École de Médecine, Paris
Archives du Collège de France, Paris
Archives Nationales de France (Richelieu)
Bibliothèque de la Ville de Paris
Darwin Correspondence Project, University of Cambridge
Evidence before the First Royal Commission, 1875
Florence Fenwick Miller, from *An Uncommon Girlhood*, Wellcome Library Archives
Musée Claude Bernard (Saint-Julien en Beaujolais) et Foundation Merieux
Revue des Courses, le Collège de France
Victor Hugo Letter, London Times Archives

JOURNALS

Bulletin de la Société Protectrice des Animaux
L'Antivivisection
L'Aube
Le Figaro
Le Rappel
Revue des Deux Mondes. Paris: 1860–1880
La Revue Française
La Tribune Médical
La Vie Contemporaine

BOOKS AND PERIODICALS

Aeschylus, *Prometheus Bound.*

Bacon, Francis. *The Works of Francis Bacon.* London: A. Millar, 1753.

Bacon, Francis. *The Works of Francis Bacon: Baron of Verulam, Viscount St. Alban, Lord High Chancellor of England, in Three Volumes.* London: A. Millar, 1753.

Balzac, Honoré de. *The Physiology of Marriage.* London: Strangeway & Sons, 1904.

Baudelaire, Charles. *Art in Paris 1845–1862: Salons and other Exhibitions.* "The Salon of 1846." Trans. J. Mayne. London: Phaidon, 1965.

Baudelaire, Charles. "A Letter to Alphonse Toussenel dated January 21, 1856." *Oeuvres Completes. Correspondance Generale, I. 1833-1856.* Ed. J. Crepet. Paris: Conrad, 1947.

Baudelaire, Charles. *Painter of Modern Life.* Trans. and ed. P. E. Charvet. *Selected Writings on Art and Artists.* London: Penguin Books, 1972.

Bernard, Claude. *Aurthur de Bretagne: drame inédit en cinq actes et en prose, avec un chant...* Paris: E. Dentu, 1887.

Bernard, Claude. *The Cahier de Notes 1850-1860.* Paris: Gallimard, 1965.

Bernard, Claude. *The Cahier Rouge of Claude Bernard.* Trans. Lucienne Guillemin, Roger Guillemin, and Hebbel Hoff. Cambridge (MA): Schenkman Publishing Company, 1967.

Bernard, Claude. *Introduction à l'Étude de la Médecine Expérimentale.* Paris: J. B. Baillière et Fils.

Bernard, Claude. *Leçons de Physiologie Opératoire.* Paris: J. B. Baillière, 1879.

Bernard, Claude. *Leçons sur la Chaleur Animale sur la Chaleur et sur la Fièvre.* Paris: J. B. Baillière, 1876.

Bernard, Claude. *Pensées: Notes Detachés.* Preface by Jacques Arsène d'Arsonval. Paris: J. B. Baillière et Fils, 1937.

Bernard, Claude, and Henry Copley Greene. *An Introduction to the Study of Experimental Medicine.* New York: Dover Publications, 1957.

Bernard, Claude, and Mme. Hermann Raffalovich. *Lettres à Madame R.: St. Julien en Beaujolais, 1869–1878.* Lyon: J. Sonolet et foundation Mérieux, 1974.

Bernard, Claude, Hermann Raffalovich, Mme. *Lettres Parisiennes: 1869-1878.* Foundation Marcel Mérieux, 1978.

Brown, John. "Verbatim Report of the Questioning of Old Brown." New York: *New York Herald,* October 19, 1859.

Buckner, Elijah D. *The Immortality of Animals and the Relation of Man as Guardian: From Biblical and Philosophical Hypothesis.* Philadelphia: George W. Jacobs & Co., 1903.

Burton, Isabel. *The Life of Captain Sir Richard F. Burton.* London: Chapman and Hill, Ltd., 1893.

Clark, T.J. *The Absolute Bourgeois: Artists and Politics in France 1848-1851.* Oakland: University of California Press, 1999.

Cobbe, Frances Power. *Illustrations of Vivisection.* Philadelphia: American Anti-Vivisection Society, 1888.

Cobbe, Frances Power. *The Moral Aspects of Vivisection.* London: The Victoria Street Society for the Protection of Animals from Vivisection, 1884.

Cobbe, Frances Power. Preface to *The Nine Circles of Hell*, by G. M. Rhodes. London: Swan Sonnenschein & Co., 1892.

Cobbe, Frances Power, Blanche Atkinson. *Life of Frances Power Cobbe, as Told by Herself.* London: Swan Sonnenschein & Co., 1904.

Collins, Wilkie. *Heart and Science: A Story of the Present Time Vol. 1.* London: Chatto & Windus, Piccadilly, 1883.

Colville, W. J., Anna Kingsford. *Spiritual Therapeutics, or, Divine Science Applied to Moral, Mental, and Physical Harmony.* Chicago: Educator Publishing Co., 1888.

Darwin, Charles. *The Expression of the Emotions in Man and Animals.* New York: D. Appleton and Co., 1899.

Darwin, Charles. *The Formation of Vegetable Mould Through the Action of Worms, with Observations of Their Habits.* London: John Murray, 1904.

Darwin, Charles. *The Life and Letters of Charles Darwin.* Edited by Sir Francis Darwin. New York: Appleton, 1898.

Darwin, Charles. *The Origin of Species by Means of Natural Selection: or, the Preservation of Favoured Races in the Struggle for Life.* London: John Murray, 1859.

Descartes, René. "Letter to the Marquess of Newcastle, 1646."

Diderot, Denis. *Sur les Femmes* [On Women]. Paris: Chez l'imprimeur Léon Pichon, 1919.

Diderot, Denis. *Diderot's Early Philosophical Works.* Trans. Margaret Jourdain. Chicago, London: Open Court Publishing Co., 1916.

Eliot, George. *Middlemarch: A Study of Provincial Life.* New York and Boston: H. M. Caldwell Company Publishers, 1912.

Evans, Edward P. *The Criminal Prosecution and Capital Punishment of Animals.* London: Heinemann, 1906.

de Fontenelle, Bernard. *Conversations on the Plurality of Words.* Trans. by H. A. Hargreaves. Oakland: University of California Press, 1990.

Goethe, Johann Wolfgang von. *Faust.*

de Goncourt, Edmond, Jules de Goncourt. *Journal: Mémoires de la Vie Littéraire: 1851–1895.* Paris: Charpentier, 1887–1896.

de Goncourt, Edmond, Jules de Goncourt. *The Goncourt Journals, 1851–1870.* New York: Doubleday Publishers, 1958.

Hugo, Victor. "Le Crapaud."

Hugo, Victor. "Letter from Victor Hugo to the Editor of The London News." London: *The London News*, December 2, 1859.

Hugo, Victor. *Promontoire du Songe.*

Jordan, David P. *Transforming Paris: The Life and Labors of Baron Haussmann.* New York: Free Press, 1995.

Kingsford, Anna Bonus. *Beatrice, A Tale of the Early Christians.* London: Joseph Masters, 1863.

Kingsford, Anna. *Dreams and Dream-Stories.* Ed. Edward Maitland. London: J. M. Watkins, 1908.

Kingsford, Anna [Ninon Kingsford, pseud.]. *An Essay on the Admission of Women to the Parliamentary Franchise.* London: Trubner & Co., 1868.

Kingsford, Anna. *Various Pamphlets.*

Lilly, W. S. "The New Naturalism." *The Tablet*, August 22, 1885.

Maitland, Edward. *Anna Kingsford: Her Life, Letters, Diary and Work.* London: George Redway, 1896.

Marey, Etienne-Jules, *Phenomena of Flight in the Animal Kingdom.*

Markheim, Henry Willan Gregg. *Inside Paris During the Siege.* London and New York: Macmillan and Co., 1871.

de Monzie, Anatole. *Les Veuves Abusives.* Paris: Grasset, 1936.

Olmsted, James M. D., *Claude Bernard and the Experimental Method in Medicine.* New York: Collier Books, 1961.

Poe, Edgar Allan. "The Tell-Tale Heart."

Shirley, Ralph. *Occultists and Mystics of All Ages.* London: William Rider & Son, Ltd, 1920.

Simon, Gustave. *Chez Victor Hugo: Les Tables Tournantes de Jersey.* Paris: L. Conrad, 1923.

Stowe, Harriet Beecher. Preface to *Uncle Tom's Cabin.*

Taine, Hippolyte Adolphe. *Balzac: A Critical Study.* Trans. Lorenzo O'Rourke. New York: Funk and Wagnalls, 1906.

Thoreau, Henry David. *The Writings of Henry David Thoreau.* Ed. Bradford Torrey. Boston: Houghton Mifflin Co., 1906.

Various, *Intimate Portraits of Illustrious People, 1845-1890.*

White, Caroline Earle, ed. *Journal of Zoöphily*, January 19, 1903.

Zola, Émile. Trans. Belle M. Sherman. *The Experimental Novel, and Other Essays.* New York: Cassell Publishing Co., 1893.

Zola, Émile. Papers. National Library of France.

Zola, Émile. *Le Roman Expérimental.*

Zola, Émile. *Thérèse Raquin.*

CREDITS

COVER:

Dr Anna Kingsford, photo by Mr Samuel Hopgood Hart, July 12, 1883; *Charles Darwin*, photo by Herbert Rose Barraud, circa 1881; *Photographs of Animals* from *L'Antivivisection*, circa 1913; *Émile Zola*, unknown photographer, circa 1890; *Claude Bernard*, photo by Cliché Valéry, from Wellcome Library no. 12344i; *Frances Power Cobbe*, from *Life of Frances Power Cobbe, as told by Herself*, Bentley, London, 1894; *Etienne-Jules Marey*, unknown photographer, circa 1850; *Victor Hugo Among the Rocks on Jersey*, 1853-1855, Charles Hugo; *Illustration: Canine Experiment, Marie Raffalovich* (painting), *Tony and Marie Bernard*, *Fanny Bernard* (painting), *Claude Bernard Sketch*, *Sketch showing temperature changes in rabbit ears*: Collection of the Musée Claude Bernard, photos by Thalia Field, used with permission from the Musée Claude Bernard, 414 Route du Musée, 69640 Saint Julien sous Montmelas.

TEXT CREDITS:

Epigraph, excerpts on pages 15, 39-40, 78, 140: Goncourt, Edmond de and Jules de Goncourt. *The Goncourt Journals, 1851-1870*. Trans. Lewis Galantiere. New York: Doubleday Publishers, 1958. Courtesy of Penguin Random House.

Excerpts on pages 1, 18, 93, 99, 157-158: Bernard, Claude. *An Introduction to the Study of Experimental Medicine*. Trans. Henry Copley Green. New York: Courier Corporation,1957. Used with permission from Dover Publications, Inc.

Excerpts from Claude's Red Notebook on pages 18, 20-22, 27-28, 30, 35, 36, 45-49, 57-58, 61, 70, 92, 131, 134, 145-146, 212: Bernard, Claude. *The Cahier Rouge of Claude Bernard*. Trans. Hebbel Hoff, Lucienne Guillemin, and Roger Guillemin. Cambridge: Schenkman Publishing Company, 1967. Used with permission from Schenkman Books.

Excerpt on page 24: Olmsted, James Monroe Duncan. *Claude Bernard and the Experimental Method in Medicine.* New York: Collier Books, 1961.

Excerpts on pages 103-108: Fontenelle, Bernard de. *Conversations on the Plurality of Words.* Trans. H.A. Hargreaves. Berkeley and Los Angeles: University of California Press, 1990. Used with permission.

IMAGE CREDITS:

Pages 6, 10, 21, 22, 24, 54, 59, 63, 159, 168, 171, 189, 191, 211-212, 213, 235, 244: Photos by Thalia Field, with grateful acknowledgment to the Musée Claude Bernard.

Pages 15, 27, 65, 78, 91, 130, 236: Collection from the Musée Claude Bernard. Photos by Thalia Field. Used with permission from the Musée Claude Bernard, 414 Route du Musée, 69640 Saint Julien sous Montmelas.

Page 17: *Hanging of John Brown* by Victor Hugo, 1860.

Pages 31, 245: *Claude and Fanny Bernard's Tomb*; Page 92: *Nature Reveals Herself to Science*; Page 151: *Journal*; Page 194: *Claude Bernard*; Page 239: *Journal*; Page 243: Claude Bernard statue. Photos by Thalia Field.

Page 74: *A heroic feat! With dead men!* by Francisco Goya, Plate 39 from the series *Los Desastres de la Guerra*, 1810-1820 (1906 edition).

Page 127: *Plant under cloche bell jar.* Illustration by Claude Bernard.

Page 131: From *L'Antivivisection*, 1913.

Page 147: *The Lesson* by Léon Augustin L'hermitte.

Page 152: *Dr Anna Kingsford.* Photo by Mr Samuel Hopgood Hart, July 12, 1883.

Page 217: *Experiment with bird.* Illustration by Etienne-Jules Marey.

Page 228: Table of contents. Rhodes, G.M. and Frances Power Cobbe. *The Nine Circles of The Hell of the Innocent.* London: Swan Sonnenschein & Co., 1892.

for Mishka and Duffy

THALIA FIELD is the author of *Point and Line, Incarnate: Story Material*, and *Bird Lovers, Backyard*, all from New Directions. Her performance novel, *Ululu (Clown Shrapnel)*, was published with Coffee House Press, and she has two collaborations with French author Abigail Lang: *A Prank of Georges* (Essay Press) and the forthcoming *Leave to Remain*.